As little Nkima, Tarzan's messenger-monkey, swung through the tree-tops in purposeless search of distraction--for his heart was sad at his master's long absence--he spied a large party of white men and black, encamped in the African jungle. Had Nikima but known it, he held the fate of Europe in his little pink palm--for this encampment was composed of several men, and one woman, who were plotting in the interests of Communism for the day when Moscow should dominate the world. Their immediate reason for this expedition was to obtain the fabled gold from the treasure-vaults of Opar; this would furnish funds for their plan to embroil the world in war--leading, so they hoped, to the establishment of autonomous Soviet states everywhere.

TARZAN
Guard of the Jungle

Edgar Rice Burroughs

FICTION HOUSE PRESS

Fiction House Edition May 2021

NOTE: The break for Chapter XIII The Lion-Man was missing from the magazine text but would have been at the start of a monthly serial part, and many of the other chapters were misnumbered throughout the text. All have been realigned to the correct numbering and Chapter XIII has been reinstated.

First Edition May 2021

isbn 978-1-64720-324-5

www.FictionHousePress.com

TARZAN
GUARD OF THE JUNGLE

CHAPTER I

STORM

I AM no historian, no chronicler of facts, and furthermore, I hold a very definite conviction that there are certain subjects which fiction writers should leave alone, foremost among which are politics and religion. However it seems to me not unethical to pirate an idea occasionally from one or the other, provided that the subject be handled in such a way as to impart a definite impression of fictionizing.

Had the story that I am about to tell you broken in the newspapers of two certain European powers, it might have precipitated another and a more terrible world war. But with that I am not particularly concerned. What interests me is that it is a good story that is particularly well adapted to my requirements through the fact that Tarzan of the Apes was intimately connected with many of its most thrilling episodes.

I am not going to bore you with dry political history, so do not tax your intellect needlessly by attempting to decode such fictitious names as I may use in describing certain people and places which, it seems to me, to the best interest of peace and disarmament, should remain incognito.

Doubtless very few of you saw and still fewer will remember having seen a news-dispatch that appeared inconspicuously in the papers some time since, reporting a rumor that French Colonial troops stationed in Somaliland, on the northeast coast of Africa, had invaded an Italian African colony. Back of that news item is a story of conspiracy, intrigue, adventure and love—a story of scoundrels and of fools, of brave men, of beautiful women, a story of the beasts of the forest and the jungle.

If there were few who saw the newspaper account

"I am To-yat!" he growled. "I kill!" "I am Tarzan,"
replied the man. "I come in peace."

of the invasion of Italian Somaliland upon the northeast coast of Africa, it is equally a fact that none of you saw a harrowing incident that occurred in the interior some time previous to this affair. That it could possibly have any connection whatsoever with European international intrigue, or with the fate of nations, seems not even remotely possible, for it was only a very little monkey fleeing through the tree-tops and screaming in terror. It was little Nkima, and pursuing him was a large, rude monkey—a much larger monkey than little Nkima.

Fortunately for the peace of Europe and the world, the speed of the pursuer was in no sense proportionate to his unpleasant disposition, and so Nkima escaped him, but for long after the larger monkey had given up the chase, the smaller one continued to flee through the tree-tops, screeching at the top of his shrill little voice, for terror and flight were the two major activities of little Nkima.

Perhaps it was fatigue, but more likely it was a ca-

Swinging through the forest, little Nkima held the fate of Europe in his little pink palm, but he did not know it.

terpillar or a bird's nest that eventually terminated Nkima's flight and left him scolding and chattering upon a swaying bough, far above the floor of the jungle.

The world into which little Nkima had been born seemed a very terrible world indeed, and he spent most of his waking hours scolding about it, in which respect he was quite as human as he was simian. It seemed to little Nkima that the world was populated with large, fierce creatures who liked monkey meat. There were Numa the lion, and Sheeta the panther, and Histah the snake—a triumvirate that rendered unsafe his entire world from the loftiest tree-top to the ground. And then there were the great apes and the lesser apes and the baboons and countless species of monkeys, all of which God had made larger than He had made little Nkima, and all of which seemed to harbor a grudge against him.

Take, for example, the rude creature which had just been pursuing him. Little Nkima had done nothing more than throw a stick at him while he was asleep in the crotch of a tree, and just for that he had pursued little Nkima with unquestionable homicidal intent—I use the word without purposing any reflection upon Nkima. It had never occurred to Nkima, as it never seems to occur to some people, that a sense of humor, like beauty, may sometimes be fatal.

BROODING upon the injustices of life, little Nkima was very sad. But there was another and more poignant cause of sadness that depressed his little heart. Many, many moons ago his master had gone away and left him. True, he had been left in a nice, comfortable home with kind people who fed him, but little Nkima missed the great Tarmangani, whose naked shoulder was the one harbor of refuge which he could with perfect impunity hurl insults at the world. For a long time now little Nkima had braved the dangers of the forest and the jungle in search of his beloved Tarzan.

Because hearts are measured by content of love and loyalty, rather than by diameters in inches, the heart of little Nkima was very large—so large that the average human being could hide his own heart and himself, as well, behind it; and for a long time it had been just one great ache in his diminutive breast. But fortunately for the little Manu his mind was so ordered that it might easily be distracted even from a great sorrow. A butterfly or a luscious grub might suddenly claim his attention from the depths of brooding—which was well, since otherwise he might have grieved himself to death.

And now, therefore, as his melancholy thoughts returned to contemplation of his loss, their trend was suddenly altered by the shifting of a jungle breeze which brought to his keen ears a sound not primarily one of the jungle sounds that were a part of his hereditary instincts. It was a discord. And what is it that brings discords into the jungle as well as into every elsewhere that it enters? Man. They were the voices of men, which Nkima heard.

Silently the little monkey glided through the trees in the direction from which the sounds had come; and presently, as the sounds grew louder, there came also that which was the definite, final proof of the identity of the noise-makers, as far as Nkima, or for that matter, any other of the jungle folk might be concerned—the scent spoor.

You have seen a dog, perhaps your own dog, half recognize you by sight, but was he ever entirely satisfied until the evidence of his eyes had been tested and approved by his sensitive nostrils?

And so it was with Nkima. His ears had suggested the presence of man, and now his nostrils definitely assured him that men were near. He did not think of them as men, but as great apes. There were Gomangani, Great Black Apes, negroes, among them. This his nose told him. And there were Tarmangani, also. These, which to Nkima would be Great White Apes, were white men.

Eagerly his nostrils sought for the familiar scent-spoor of his beloved Tarzan, but it was not there that he knew even before he came within sight of the strangers.

The camp upon which Nkima presently looked down from a near-by tree was well established. It had evidently been there for a matter of days and might be expected to remain still longer. It was no overnight affair. There were the tents of the white men and the *byut* of Arabs neatly arranged with almost military precision, and behind these the shelters of the negroes, lightly constructed of such materials as Nature had provided upon the spot.

Within the open front of an Arab beyt sat several white burnoused Beduins drinking the inevitable coffee; in the shade of a great tree before another tent four white men were engrossed in a game of cards; among the native shelters a group of stalwart

Galla warriors were playing at minkala. There were blacks of other tribes too—men of East Africa and Central Africa, with a sprinkling of West Coast negroes.

It might have puzzled an experienced African traveler or hunter to catalogue this motley aggregation of races and colors. There were far too many blacks to justify a belief that all were porters, for with all the impedimenta of the camp ready for transportation, there would not have been but a small fraction of the load for each of them, even after more than enough had been included among the askari, who do not carry any loads beside their rifles and ammunition.

Then too, there were more rifles than would have been needed to protect even a larger party. There seemed, indeed, to be a rifle for every man. But these were minor details which made no impression upon Nkima. All that impressed him was the fact that here were many strange Tarmangani and Gomangani in the country of his master, and as all strangers were, to Nkima, enemies, he was perturbed. Now, more than ever, he wished that he might find Tarzan.

A swarthy turbaned East Indian sat cross-legged upon the ground before a tent, apparently sunk in meditation, but could one have seen his dark, sensuous eyes, he would have discovered that their gaze was far from introspective—they were bent constantly upon another tent that stood a little apart from its fellows; and when a girl emerged from this tent, Raghunath Jafar arose and approached her. He smiled an oily smile as he spoke to her, but the girl did not smile as she replied. She spoke civilly, but she did not pause, continuing her way toward the four men at cards.

As she approached their table, they looked up, and upon the face of each was reflected some pleasurable emotion; but whether it was the same in each, the masks that we call faces, and which are trained to conceal our true thoughts, did not divulge. Evident it was, however, that the girl was popular.

"Hello, Zora!" cried a large, smooth-faced fellow. "Have a good nap?"

"Yes, comrade," replied the girl; "but I am tired of napping. This inactivity is getting on my nerves."

"Mine too," agreed the man.

"How much longer will you wait for the American, Comrade Zveri?" asked Raghunath Jafar.

The other shrugged. "I need him," he answered. "We might easily carry on without him, but for the moral effect upon the world of having a rich and high-born American identified actively with the affair, it is worth waiting."

"Are you quite sure of this gringo, Zveri?" asked a swarthy young Mexican sitting next to the big man, who was evidently the leader of the expedition.

"I met him in New York and again in San Francisco," replied Zveri. "He has been very carefully checked and favorably recommended."

"I am always suspicious of these fellows who owe everything they have to capitalism," insisted Romero. "It is in their blood—at heart they hate the proletariat, just as we hate them."

"This fellow is different, Miguel," insisted Zveri. "He has been won over so completely that he would betray his own father for the good of the cause—and already he is betraying his country."

A slight involuntary sneer, that passed unnoticed by the others, curled the lip of Zora Drinov as she heard this description of the remaining member of the party, who had not yet reached the rendezvous.

Miguel Romero, the Mexican, was still unconvinced. "I myself have no use for gringoes of any sort," he said.

Zveri shrugged his heavy shoulders. "Our personal animosities are of no importance," he said, "as against the interests of the workers of' the world. When Colt arrives, we must accept him as one of us; nor must we forget that however much we may detest America and all Americans, nothing of moment may be accomplished in the world of today without them and their filthy wealth."

"Wealth ground out of the blood and sweat of the working class!" growled Romero.

"Exactly," agreed Raghunath Jafar. "But how appropriate that this same wealth should be used to undermine and overthrow capitalistic America and bring the workers eventually into their own."

"That is precisely the way I feel about it," said Zveri. "I would rather use American gold in furthering the cause than any other—and after that British."

"But what do the puny resources of this single American mean to us?" demanded Zora. "A mere nothing compared to what America is already pouring into Soviet Russia. What is his treason compared with the treason of those others who are already doing more to hasten the day of world communism than the Third Internationale itself? It is nothing, not a drop in the bucket."

"What do you mean, Zora?" asked Miguel.

"I mean the bankers and manufacturers and engineers of America, who are selling their own country and the world to us in the hope of adding more gold to their already bursting coffers. Their manufacturers are vying with one another to furnish us with engines for countless thousands of airplanes; their engineers are selling us their brains and their skill to build a great modern manufacturing city—in which ammunition and engines of war may be produced. These are the traitors; these are the men who are hastening the day when Moscow shall dictate the policies of a world."

"You speak as though you regretted it," said a dry voice at her shoulder.

The girl turned quickly. "Oh, it is you, Sheik Abu Batu?" she said, as she recognized the swart Arab who had strolled over from his coffee. "Our own good fortune does not blind me to the perfidiousness of the enemy, nor cause me to admire treason in anyone, even though I profit by it."

"Does that include me?" demanded the young Mexican, Romero.

Zora laughed. "You know better than that, Miguel," she said. "You are of the working class; you are loyal to the workers of your own country; but these others are of the capitalistic class, their government is a capitalistic government that is so opposed to our beliefs that it has never recognized our government; yet, in their greed, these swine are selling out their own kind and their own country for a few more rotten dollars. I loathe them."

Zveri laughed. "You are a good Red, Zora," he cried; "you hate the enemy as much when he helps us as when he hinders."

"But hating and talking accomplish so little," said the girl. "I wish we might do something. Sitting here in idleness seems so futile."

"And what would you have us do?" demanded Zveri.

"We might at least make a try for the gold of Opar," she said. "If Kitembo is right, there should be enough there to finance a dozen expeditions such as you are planning; and we do not need this American—what do they call them, cake-eaters?—to assist us in that venture."

"I have been thinking along similar lines," said Raghunath Jafar.

Zveri scowled. "Perhaps some of the rest of you would like to run this expedition," he said crustily. "I know what I am doing, and I don't have to discuss all my plans with anyone. When I have orders to give, I'll give them. Kitembo has already received his, and preparations have been under way for several days for the expedition to Opar."

"The rest of us are as much interested and are risking as much as you, Zveri," snapped Romero. "We were to work together—not as master and slaves."

"You'll soon learn that I am master," snarled Zveri in an ugly tone.

"Yes," sneered Romero; "the Czar was master too—and Obregon. You know what happened to them?"

Zveri leaped to his feet and whipped out a revolver; and as he leveled it at Romero, the girl struck his arm up and stepped between them. "Are you mad, Zveri?" she cried.

"Do not interfere, Zora; this is my affair, and it might as well be settled now as later. I am chief here, and I am not going to have any traitors in my camp. Stand aside."

"No!" said the girl with finality. "Miguel was wrong, and so were you; but to shed blood—our own blood—now would utterly ruin any chance we have of success. It would sow the seed of fear and suspicion and cost us the respect of the blacks, for they would know that there was dissension among us. Furthermore Miguel is not armed—to shoot him would be cowardly murder that would lose you the respect of every decent man in the expedition."

She had spoken rapidly in Russian, a language that was understood by only Zveri and herself, of those who were present; then she turned again to Miguel and addressed him in English: "You were wrong, Miguel," she said gently. "There must be one responsible head, and Comrade Zveri was chosen for the responsibility. He regrets that he acted hastily. Tell him that you are sorry for what you said, and then the two of you shake hands and let us all forget the matter."

For an instant Romero hesitated; then he extended his hand toward Zveri. "I am sorry," he said.

The Russian took the proffered hand in his and bowed stiffly. "Let us forget it, Comrade," he said; but the scowl was still upon his face, though no darker than that which clouded the Mexican's.

LITTLE NKIMA yawned and swung by his tail from

a branch far overhead. His curiosity concerning these enemies was sated. They no longer afforded him entertainment, but he knew that his master should know about their presence and that thought, entering his little head, recalled his sorrow and his great yearning for Tarzan, to the end that he was again imbued with a grim determination to continue his search for the ape-man. Perhaps in half an hour some trivial occurrence might again distract his attention, but for the moment this was his life-work. Swinging through the forest, little Nkima held the fate of Europe in his pink palm, but he did not know it.

The afternoon was waning. In the distance a lion roared. An instinctive shiver ran up Nkima's spine. In reality, however, he was not much afraid, knowing, as he did, that no lion could reach him in the tree-tops.

A young man marching near the head of a safari cocked his head, listening. "Not very far away, Tony," he said.

"No sir; much too close," replied the Filipino.

"You'll have to learn to cut out that *sir* stuff, Tony, before we join the others," admonished the young man.

The Filipino grinned. "All right, Comrade," he assented. "I got so used calling everybody 'sir,' it hard for me to change."

"I'm afraid you're not a very good Red, then, Tony."

"Oh, yes, I am," insisted the Filipino emphatically. "Why else am I here? You think I like to come this God-forsaken country full of lion, ant, snake, fly, mosquito, just for the walk? No, I come lay down my life for Philippine independence."

"That's noble of you, all right, Tony," said the other; "but just how is it going to make the Philippines free?"

Antonio Mori scratched his head. "I don't know," he admitted; "but it make trouble for America."

High among the tree-tops a little monkey crossed their path. For a moment he paused and watched them; then he resumed his journey in the opposite direction.

A half hour later the lion roared again; and so disconcertingly close and unexpected rose the voice of thunder from the jungle beneath him that little Nkima nearly fell out of the tree through which he was passing. With a scream of terror he scampered as high aloft as he could go; and there he sat, scolding angrily.

The lion, a magnificent full-maned male, stepped into the open beneath the tree in which the trembling Nkima clung. Once again he raised his mighty voice until the ground itself trembled to the great, rolling volume of his challenge. Nkima looked down upon him, and suddenly ceased to scold. Instead he leaped about excitedly, chattering and grimacing. Numa the lion looked up, and then a strange thing occurred. The monkey ceased its chattering and voiced a low, peculiar sound. The eyes of the lion, that had been glaring balefully upward, took on a new and almost gentle expression. He arched his back and rubbed his side luxuriously against the bole of the tree, and from those savage jaws came a soft, purring sound. Then little Nkima dropped quickly downward through the foliage of the tree, gave a final nimble leap, and alighted upon the thick mane of the king of beasts.

CHAPTER II

THE HINDU

WITH the coming of a new day came a new activity to the camp of the conspirators. Now were the Bedauwy drinking no coffee in the muk'aad; the cards of the whites were put away, and the Galla warriors played no longer at minkala.

Zveri sat behind his folding camp-table directing his aides, and with the assistance of Zora and Raghunath Jafar issued ammunition to the file of armed men marching past them. Miguel Romero and the two remaining whites were supervising the distribution of loads among the porters. Savage black Kitembo moved constantly among his men, hastening laggards from belated breakfast fires and forming those who had received their ammunition into companies. Abu Batu the sheik squatted aloof with his sun-bitten warriors. They, always ready, now watched with contempt the disorderly preparations of their companions.

Zveri whipped out a revolver and leveled it at Romero. The girl struck up his arm.

"How many are you leaving to guard the camp?" asked Zora.

"You and Comrade Jafar will remain in charge here," replied Zveri. "Your boys and ten askaris also will remain as camp guard."

"That will be plenty," she agreed. "There is no danger."

"No," agreed Zveri, "not now; but if that Tarzan were here, it would be different. I took pains to assure myself as to that before I chose this region for our base camp, and I have learned that he has been absent for a great while—went on some fool dirigible expedition that has never been heard from. It is almost certain he is dead."

When the last of the blacks had received his issue of ammunition, Kitembo assembled his tribesmen at a little distance from the balance of the expedition and harangued them in a low voice. They were

Basembos; and Kitembo, their chief, spoke to them in the dialect of their people.

KITEMBO hated all whites. The British had occupied the land that had been the home of his people since before the memory of man; and because Kitembo, hereditary chief, had been irreconcilable to the domination of the invaders, they had deposed him, elevating a puppet to the chieftaincy.

To Kitembo the chief, savage, cruel and treacherous, all whites were anathema; but he saw in his connection with Zveri an opportunity to be avenged upon the British, and so he had gathered about him many of his tribes-men and enlisted in the expedition that Zveri promised him would rid the land forever of the British, and restore Kitembo to even greater power and glory than had formerly been the lot of Basembo chiefs.

It was not, however, always easy for Kitembo to hold the interest of his people in this undertaking. The British had greatly undermined his power and influence, so that warriors, who formerly might have been as subservient to his will as slaves, now dared openly to question his authority. There had been no demur so long as the expedition entailed no greater hardships than short marches, pleasant camps and plenty of food—with West Coast blacks, and members of other tribes less warlike than the Basembos; to act as porters, carry the loads and do all the heavy work. But now, with fighting looming ahead, some of his people had desired to know just what they were going to get out of it—having, apparently, little stomach for risking their hides for the gratification of the ambitions or hatreds of either the white Zveri or the black Kitembo.

It was for the purpose of mollifying these malcontents that Kitembo was now haranguing his warriors, promising them loot on the one hand and ruthless punishment on the other as a choice between obedience and mutiny. Some of the rewards he dangled before their imaginations might have caused Zveri and the other white members of the expedition considerable perturbation could they have understood the Basembo dialect; but perhaps a greater argument for obedience to his commands was the genuine fear that most of his followers still entertained for their pitiless chieftain.

Among the other blacks of the expedition were outlaw members of several tribes and a considerable number of porters hired in the ordinary manner to

A little monkey rode on the back of a great lion, shrilling insults at every other jungle creature.

accompany what was officially described as a scientific expedition.

Abu Batu and his warriors were animated to temporary loyalty to Zveri by two motives—a lust for loot, and a hatred for all Nasrany as represented by the British influence in Egypt and out into the desert, which they considered their hereditary domain.

The members of other races accompanying Zveri were assumed to be motivated by noble humanitarian aspirations, but it was, nevertheless, true that their leader spoke to them more often of the acquisition of personal riches and power than of the advancement of the brotherhood of man.

It was, then, such a loosely knit but none the less formidable expedition that set forth this lovely morning upon the sack of the treasure vaults of mysterious Opar.

AS Zora Drinov watched them depart, her beautiful, inscrutable eyes remained fixed steadfastly upon the person of Peter Zveri until he had disappeared from view along the river trail that led into the dark forest.

Was it a maid watching in trepidation the departure of her lover upon a mission fraught with danger, or—

"Perhaps he will not return," said an oily voice at her shoulder.

The girl turned her head to look into the half-closed eyes of Raghunath Jafar.

"He will return, Comrade," she said. "Peter Zveri always returns to—me."

"You are very sure of him," said the man.

"It is written," replied the girl as she started to move toward her tent.

"Wait," said Jafar, stretching forth a hand.

She stopped and turned toward him. "What do you want?" she asked.

"You," he replied. "What do you see in that uncouth swine, Zora? What does he know of love or beauty? I can appreciate you, beautiful flower of the morning. With me you may attain the transcendent bliss of perfect love, for I am an adept in love. A beast like Zveri would only degrade you."

The sickening disgust which the girl felt she hid from the eyes of the man, for she realized that the expedition might be gone for days, and that during that time she and Jafar would be practically alone together, except for a handful of savage black warriors whose attitude toward a matter of this nature between an alien woman and an alien man she could not anticipate; but she was none the less determined to put a definite end to his advances.

"You are playing with death, Jafar," she said quietly. "I am here upon no mission of love, and if Zveri should learn of what you have said to me, he would kill you. Do not speak to me again on this subject."

"It will not be necessary," replied the Hindu enigmatically. His half-closed eyes were fixed steadily upon those of the girl. For perhaps less than half a minute the two stood thus, while there crept through Zora Drinov a sense of growing weakness, a realization of approaching capitulation. She fought against it, pitting her will against that of the man. Suddenly she tore her eyes from his. She had won, but victory left her weak and trembling as might be one who had but just experienced a stubbornly contested physical encounter. Turning quickly away, she moved swiftly toward her tent, not daring to look back for fear that she might again encounter those twin pools of vicious and malignant power that were the eyes of Raghunath Jafar—and so she did not see the oily smile of satisfaction that twisted the sensuous lips of the Hindu, nor did she hear his whispered repetition:

"It will not be necessary."

AS the expedition wound along the trail that leads to the foot of the barrier cliffs that hem the lower frontier of the arid plateau beyond which stands the ancient ruins that are Opar, Wayne Colt, far to the west, pushed on toward the base camp of the conspirators.

To the south, a little monkey rode upon the back of a great lion, shrilling insults now with perfect impunity at every other jungle creature that crossed their path, while with equal contempt for all lesser creatures, the mighty carnivore strode haughtily down-wind, secure in the knowledge of his unquestioned might. A herd of antelope, grazing in his path, caught the acrid scent of the cat and moved nervously about, but when he came within sight of them, they trotted only a short distance to one side, making a path for him, and while he was still in sight, they resumed their feeding. For Numa the lion had fed well, and the herbivores knew, as creatures of the wild know many things that are beyond the dull sensibilities of man, and felt no fear of Numa with a full belly.

To others, yet far off, came the scent of the lion; and they too moved nervously, though their fear was less than had been the first fear of the antelopes. These others were the great apes of the tribe of To-yat, whose mighty bulls had little cause to fear even Numa himself, though their shes and their balus might well tremble.

As the cat approached, the Mangani became more restless and more irritable. To-yat, the king ape, beat his breast and bared his great fighting fangs. Ga-yat, his powerful shoulders hunched, moved to the edge of the herd nearest the approaching danger. Zu-tho thumped a warning menace with his calloused feet. The shes called their balus to them, and many took to the lower branches of the larger trees or sought positions close to an arboreal avenue of escape.

It was at this moment that an almost naked white man dropped from the dense foliage of a tree and alighted in their midst. Taut nerves and short tempers snapped. Roaring and snarling, the herd rushed upon the rash and hated man-thing. The king ape was in the lead.

"To-yat has a short memory," said the newcomer in the tongue of the Mangani.

For an instant the ape paused, perhaps surprised to hear the language of his kind issuing from the lips of a man-thing. "I am To-yat!" he growled. "I kill."

"I am Tarzan,' replied the man, "mighty hunter, mighty fighter. I come in peace."

"Kill! Kill!' roared To-yat, and the other great bulls advanced, bare-fanged, menacingly.

"Zu-tho! Ga-yat!" snapped the man. "It is I, Tarzan of the Apes!" But the scent of Numa was strong in their nostrils, and the shock of Tarzan's sudden appearance had plunged them into a panic.

"Kill! Kill!" they bellowed, though as yet they did not charge, but advanced slowly, working themselves into the necessary frenzy of rage that would terminate in a sudden blood-mad rush no living creature might withstand, and which would leave naught but torn and bloody fragments of the object of their wrath.

And then a shrill scream broke from the lips of a great hairy mother with a tiny balu on her back. "Numa!" she shrieked, and turning, fled into the safety of the foliage of a near-by tree.

Instantly the shes and balus remaining upon the ground took to the trees. The bulls turned their attention for a moment from the man to the new menace. What they saw upset what little equanimity remained to them. Advancing straight toward them, his round, yellow-green eyes blazing in ferocity, was a mighty yellow lion, and upon his back perched a little monkey, screaming insults at them. The sight was too much for the apes of To-yat, and the king was the first to break before it. With a roar, the ferocity of which may have salved his self-esteem, he leaped for the nearest tree, and instantly the others broke and fled, leaving the white giant to face the angry lion alone.

With blazing eyes the king of beasts advanced upon the man, his head lowered and flattened, his tail extended, the brush flicking. The man spoke a single word in a low tone that might have carried but a few yards. Instantly the head of the lion came up, the horrid glare died in his eyes, and at the same instant the little monkey, voicing a shrill scream of recognition and delight, leaped over Numa's head and in three prodigious bounds was upon the shoulder of the man, his little arms encircling the bronzed neck.

"Little Nkima!" whispered Tarzan, the soft cheek of the monkey pressed against his own.

The lion strode majestically forward. He sniffed the bare legs of the man, rubbed his head against his side and lay down at his feet.

"Jad-bal-ja!" greeted the ape-man.

The great apes of the tribe of To-yat watched from the safety of the trees. Their panic and their anger had subsided. "It is Tarzan," said Zu-tho.

"Yes, it is Tarzan," echoed Ga-yat.

To-yat grumbled. He did not like Tarzan, but he

feared him; and now, with this new evidence of the power of the great Tarmangani, he feared him even more.

For a time Tarzan listened to the glib chattering of little Nkima. He learned of the strange Tarmangani and the many Gomangani warriors who had invaded the domain of the Lord of the Jungle.

The great apes moved restlessly in the trees, wishing to descend; but they feared Numa, and the great bulls were too heavy to travel in safety upon the high-flung leafy trails along which the lesser apes might pass with safety, and so could not depart until Numa had gone.

"Go away!" cried To-yat the king. "Go away, and leave the Mangani in peace.

"We are going," replied the ape-man, "but you need not fear either Tarzan or the Golden Lion. We are your friends. I have told Jad-bal-ja that he is never to harm you. You may descend."

"We shall stay in the trees until he has gone," said To-yat; "he might forget."

"You are afraid," said Tarzan contemptuously. "Zu-tho or Ga-yat would not be afraid."

"Zu-tho is afraid of nothing," boasted that great bull.

Without a word Ga-yat climbed ponderously from the tree in which he had taken refuge, and if not with enthusiasm, at least with slight hesitation, advanced toward Tarzan and Jad-bal-ja the big Golden Lion. His fellows eyed him intently, momentarily expecting to see him charged and mauled by the yellow-eyed destroyer that lay at Tarzan's feet watching every move of the shaggy bull. The

The man spoke a single word. Instantly the head of the lion came up and the glare died from his eyes.

Lord of the Jungle also watched great Numa, for none knew better than he, that a lion, however accustomed to obey his master, is still a lion. The years of their companionship, since Jad-bal-ja had been a little spotted fluffy ball, had never given him reason to doubt the loyalty of the carnivore, though there had been times when he had found it both difficult and dangerous to thwart some of the beast's more ferocious hereditary instincts.

Ga-yat approached, while little Nkima scolded and chattered from the safety of his master's shoulder, and the lion, blinking lazily, finally looked away. The danger, if there had been any, was over—it is the fixed, intent gaze of the lion that bodes ill.

Tarzan advanced and laid a friendly hand upon the shoulder of the ape. "This is Ga-yat," he said, addressing Jad-bal-ja, "friend of Tarzan; do not harm him." He did not speak in any language of man. Per-

haps the medium of communication that he used
might not properly be called a language at all, but
the lion and the great ape and the little Manu understood him.

"Tell the Mangani that Tarzan is the friend of little Nkima," shrilled the monkey. "He must not harm
little Nkima."

"It is as Nkima has said," the ape-man assured
Ga-yat.

"The friends of Tarzan are the friends of Ga-yat,"
replied the great ape.

"It is well," said Tarzan; "and now I go. Tell To-
yat and the others what we have said, and tell them
also that there are strange men in this country which
is Tarzan's. Let them watch them, but do not let the
men see them, for these are bad men, perhaps, who
carry the thunder-sticks that hurl death with smoke
and fire and a great noise. Tarzan goes now to see
why these men are in his country."

ZORA DRINOV had avoided Jafar since the departure of the expedition to Opar. Scarcely had she left
her tent, feigning a headache as an excuse; nor had
the Hindu made any attempt to invade her privacy.
Thus passed the first day. Upon the morning of the
second Jafar summoned the head man of the askaris
that had been left to guard them and to procure
meat.

"Today," said Raghunath Jafar, "would be a good
day to hunt. The signs are propitious. Go, therefore,
into the forest, taking all your men, and do not return until the sun is low in the west. If you do this,
there will be presents for you, besides all the meat

you can eat from the carcasses of your kills. Do you understand?"

"Yes, Bwana," replied the black.

"Take with you the boy of the woman. He will not be needed here. My boy will remain to cook for us."

"Perhaps he will not come," suggested the negro.

"You are many; he is only one; but do not let the woman know that you are taking him."

"What are the presents?" demanded the head man.

"A piece of cloth and cartridges," replied Ja-far.

"And the curved sword that you carry when we are on the march."

"No," said Jafar.

"This is not a good day to hunt," replied the black, turning away.

"Two pieces of cloth and fifty cartridges," suggested Jafar.

"And the curved sword!" And thus, after much haggling, the bargain was made.

The head man gathered his askaris and bade them prepare for the hunt, saying that the brown bwana had so ordered, but he said nothing about any presents. When they were ready, he dispatched one to summon the white woman's servant.

"You are to accompany us on the hunt," he said to the boy.

"Who said so?" demanded Wamala.

"The brown bwana," replied Kahiya, the head man.

Wamala laughed. "I take my orders from my mistress, not from the brown bwana."

Kahiya leaped upon him and clapped a rough palm across his mouth as two of his men seized Wamala upon either side. "You take your orders from Kahiya," he said. Hunting spears were pressed against the boy's trembling body. "Will you go upon the hunt with us?" demanded Kahiya.

"I go," replied Wamala. "I did but joke."

AS Zveri led his expedition toward Opar, Wayne Colt, impatient to join the main body of the conspirators, urged his men to greater speed in their search for the camp. The principal conspirators had entered Africa at different points, that they might not arouse too much attention by their numbers. Pursuant to this plan, Colt had landed on the west coast and had traveled inland a short distance by train to the railhead, from which point he had had a long and arduous journey on foot, so that now, with his destination almost in sight, he was anxious to put a period to this phase of his adventure. Then too, he was curious to meet the other principals in this hazardous undertaking, Peter Zveri being the only one with whom he was acquainted.

The young American was not unmindful of the great risks he was inviting in affiliating himself with an expedition which aimed at the peace of Europe and at the ultimate control of a large section of northeastern Africa through the disaffection, by propaganda, of large and warlike native tribes— especially in view of the fact that much of their operation must be carried on within British territory, where British power was considerably more than a mere gesture.

But since Colt was young and enthusiastic, though misguided, these contingencies did not weigh heavily upon his spirits, which, far from being depressed, were upon the contrary eager and restless for action.

The tedium of the journey from the coast had been unrelieved by pleasurable or adequate companionship, since the childish mentality of Tony could not rise above a muddy conception of Philippine independence and a consideration of the fine clothes he was going to buy when, by some vaguely visualized economic process, he was to obtain his share of the capitalists' fortunes.

However, notwithstanding Tony's mental shortcomings, Colt was genuinely fond of the youth, and as between the companionship of the Filipino or Zveri, he would have chosen the former, his brief acquaintance with the Russian in New York and San Francisco having convinced him that as a playfellow he left everything to be desired; nor had he any reason to anticipate that he would find any more congenial associates among the conspirators.

Plodding doggedly onward, Colt was only vaguely aware of the now familiar sights and sounds of the jungle, both of which by this time, it must be admitted, had considerably palled upon him. Even had he taken particular note of the latter, it is to be doubted that his untrained ear would have caught the persistent chatter of a little monkey that followed in the trees behind him; nor would this have particularly impressed him, unless he had been able to know that this particular little monkey rode upon the shoulder of a bronzed Apollo of the forest, who moved silently in his wake along a leafy highway of the lower terraces.

Tarzan had guessed that perhaps this white man, upon whose trail he had come unexpectedly, was making his way toward the main camp of the party of strangers for which the Lord of the Jungle was searching; and so, with the persistence and patience of the savage stalker of the jungle, he followed Wayne Colt; while little Nkima, riding upon his shoulder, berated his master for not immediately destroying the Tarmangani and all his party; for little Nkima was a bloodthirsty soul when the spilling of blood was to be accomplished by some one else.

CHAPTER III

OUT OF THE GRAVE

WHILE Colt impatiently urged his men to greater speed, and Tarzan followed, and Nkima scolded, Raghunath Jafar approached the tent of Zora Drinov. As his figure darkened the entrance, casting a shadow across the book she was reading, the girl looked up from the cot upon which she was lying.

The Hindu smiled his oily, ingratiating smile. "I came to see if your headache was better," he said.

"Thank you, no," said the girl coldly. "But perhaps with undisturbed rest I may be better soon."

Ignoring the suggestion, Jafar entered the tent and seated himself in a camp-chair. "I find it lonely," he said, "since the others have gone. Do you not also?"

"No," replied Zora. "I am quite content to be alone and resting."

"Your headache developed very suddenly," said Jafar. "A short time ago you seemed quite well and animated."

The girl made no reply. She was wondering what had become of her boy Wamala, and why he had disregarded her explicit instructions to permit no one to disturb her. Perhaps Raghunath Jafar read her thoughts, for to East Indians are often attributed uncanny powers, however little warranted such a belief may be. However that may be, his next words suggested the possibility.

"Wamala has gone hunting with the askaris," he said.

"I gave him no such permission," said Zora.

"I took the liberty of doing so," said Jafar.

"You had no right," said the girl angrily, sitting up upon the edge of her cot. "You have presumed altogether too far, Comrade Jafar!"

"Wait a moment, my dear," said the Hindu soothingly. "Let us not quarrel! As you know, I love you; and love does not find confirmation in crowds. Perhaps I have presumed, but it was only for the purpose of giving me an opportunity to plead my cause without interruption. And then too, as you know, all is fair in love and war."

"Then we may consider this as war," said the girl, "for it certainly is not love, either upon your side or upon mine. There is another word to describe what animates you, Comrade Jafar; and that which animates me now is loathing. I could not abide you if you were the last man on earth; and when Zveri returns, I promise you that there shall be an accounting."

"Long before Zveri returns, I shall have taught you to love me," said the Hindu passionately. He arose and came toward her. The girl leaped to her feet, looking about quickly for a weapon of defense. Her cartridge-belt and revolver hung over the chair in which Jafar had been sitting, and her rifle was upon the opposite side of the tent.

"You are quite unarmed," said the Hindu: "I took particular note of that when I entered the tent; nor will it do you any good to call for help, for there is no one in camp but you and I and my boy; and he knows that if he values his life, he is not to come here unless I call him."

"You need not fear either Tarzan or the Golden Lion; we are your friends." Ga-yat climbed from the tree and advanced.

"You are a beast," said the girl.

"Why not be reasonable, Zora?" demanded Jafar. "It would not harm you any to be kind to me, and it will make it very much easier for you. Zveri need know nothing of it, and once we are back in civilization again, if you still feel that you do not wish to remain with me, I shall not try to hold you; but I am sure I can teach you to love me, and that we shall be very happy together."

"Get out!" ordered the girl. There was neither fear nor hysteria in her voice. It was very calm and level and controlled. To a man not entirely blinded by passion, that might have meant something—it might have meant a grim determination to carry self-defense to the very length of death; but Raghunath Jafar saw only the woman of his desire, and stepping quickly forward, he seized her.

Zora Drinov was young and lithe and strong; yet she was no match for the burly Hindu, whose layers of greasy fat belied the great physical strength beneath them. She tried to wrench herself free and escape from the tent, but he held her and dragged her back. She turned upon him in a fury and struck him repeatedly in the face, but he only held her more closely in his embrace. . . .

Wayne Colt's guide, who had been slightly in advance of the American, stopped suddenly and looked back with a broad smile.

Then he pointed ahead. "The camp, Bwana!" he exclaimed triumphantly.

"Thank the Lord!" exclaimed Colt with a sigh of relief.

"It is deserted," said the guide.

"It does look that way, doesn't it?" agreed Colt. "Let's have a look around." And followed by his men, Colt moved in among the tents. His tired porters threw down their loads and with the askaris, sprawled at full length beneath the shade of the trees; while Colt, followed by Tony, commenced an investigation of the camp.

Almost immediately the young American's attention was attracted by the violent shaking of one of the tents. "There is some one or something in there," he said to Tony, as he walked briskly toward the entrance.

The sight that met his eyes within brought a sharp ejaculation to his lips—a man and woman struggling, the former choking the bare throat of his victim, while the girl struck feebly at his face with clenched fists.

So engrossed was Jafar in his unsuccessful attempt to subdue the girl that he was unaware of Colt's presence until a heavy hand fell upon his shoulder, and he was jerked violently aside.

Consumed by maniacal fury, he leaped to his feet and struck at the American, only to be met with a blow that sent him reeling backward. Again he charged, and again he was struck heavily upon the face. This time he went to the ground; and as he staggered to his feet, Colt seized him, wheeled him around and hurled him through the entrance of the tent, accelerating his departure with a well-timed kick. "If he tries to come back, Tony, shoot him," he snapped at the Filipino, and then turned to assist the girl to her feet. Half carrying her, he laid her on the cot, and then, finding water in a bucket, bathed her forehead, her throat and her wrists.

Outside the tent, Raghunath Jafar saw the porters and the askaris lying in the shade of a tree. He also saw Antonio Mori with a determined scowl upon his face and a revolver in his hand; and with an angry imprecation Jafar turned and made his way toward his own tent.

Presently Zora Drinov opened her eyes and looked up into the solicitous face of Wayne Colt.

From the leafy seclusion of a tree above the camp, Tarzan of the Apes overlooked the scene below. A single whispered syllable had silenced Nkima's scolding. Tarzan had noted the violent shaking of the tent that had attracted Colt's attention, and he had seen the precipitate ejection of the Hindu from its interior and the menacing attitude of the Filipino preventing Jafar's return to the conflict. These matters were of little interest to the ape-man. The quarrelings and defections of these people did not even arouse his curiosity. What he wished to learn was the reason for their presence here; and for the purpose of obtaining this information he had two plans. One was to keep them under constant surveillance until their acts divulged that which he wished to know. The other was to determine definitely the head of the expedition and then to enter the camp and demand the information desired. But this he would not do until he had obtained sufficient knowledge to give him an advantage. What was going on within the tent he did not know; nor did he care.

For several seconds after she opened her eyes,

Zora Drinov gazed intently into those of the man bent upon her.

"You must be the American," she said finally.

"I am Wayne Colt," he replied, "and I take it from the fact that you guessed my identity that this is Comrade Zveri's camp."

She nodded. "You came just in time, Comrade Colt," she said.

"Thank God for that!" he said.

"There is no God," she reminded him.

Colt flushed. "We are creatures of heredity and habit," he explained.

Zora Drinov smiled. "That is true," she said; "but it is our business to break a great many bad habits not only for ourselves, but for the entire world."

Since he had laid her upon the cot, Colt had been quietly appraising the girl. He had not known that there was a white woman in Zveri's camp, but had he it is certain that he would not have anticipated one at all like this girl. He would rather have visualized a female agitator, capable of accompanying a band of men to the heart of Africa, as a coarse and unkempt peasant woman of middle age; but this girl, from her head of glorious, wavy hair to her small well-shaped foot, suggested the antithesis of a peasant origin, and far from being unkempt, she was as neat and smart as it was possible for woman to be under such circumstances.

"Comrade Zveri is absent from camp?" he asked.

"Yes, he is away on a short expedition."

"And there is no one to introduce us to one another?" he asked with a smile.

"Oh, pardon me," she said. "I am Zora Drinov."

"I had not anticipated such a pleasant surprise," said Colt. "And who was the fellow I interrupted?"

"That was Raghunath Jafar, a Hindu."

"He is one of us?" asked Colt.

"Yes," replied the girl, "but not for long—not after Peter Zveri returns."

"You mean—"

"I mean that Peter will kill him."

Colt shrugged. "It is what he deserves," he said. "Perhaps I should have done it."

"No," said the girl; "leave that for Peter."

"Were you left alone here in this camp without any protection?" demanded Colt.

"No. Peter left my boy and ten askaris, but in some way Jafar got them all out of camp."

"You will be safe now," he said. "I shall see to that until Comrade Zveri returns. I am going now to make my camp, and I shall send two of my askaris to stand guard before your tent."

"That is good of you," she said, "but I think now that you are here it will not be necessary."

"I shall do it anyway," he said. "I shall feel safer."

"And when you have made camp, will you come and have supper with me?" she asked, and then: "Oh, I forgot; Jafar has sent my boy away, too. There is no one to cook for me."

"Then perhaps, you will dine with me," he said. "My boy is a fairly good cook."

"I shall be delighted, Comrade Colt," she replied.

AS the American left the tent, Zora Drinov lay back upon the cot with half-closed eyes. How different the man had been from what she had expected! Recalling his features, and especially his eyes, it was difficult to believe that such a man could be a traitor to his father or to his country; but then, she realized, many a man has turned against his own for a principle. With her own people it was different. They had never had a chance. They had always been ground beneath the heel of one tyrant or another. What they were doing they believed implicitly to be for their own and for their country. Among those of them who were motivated by honest conviction, there could not fairly be brought any charge of treason, and yet, Russian though she was to the core, she could not help but look with contempt upon the citizens of other countries who turned against their governments to aid the ambitions of a foreign power. We may be willing to profit by the acts of foreign mercenaries and traitors, but we cannot admire them.

As Colt crossed from Zora's tent to where his men lay, to give the necessary instruction for the making of his camp, Raghunath Jafar watched him from the interior of his own tent. A malignant scowl clouded the countenance of the Hindu, and hatred smoldered in his eyes.

Tarzan, watching from above, saw the young American issuing instructions to his men. The personality of this young stranger had impressed Tarzan favorably. He liked him as well as he could like any stranger, for deeply ingrained in the fiber of the ape-man was the wild beast suspicion of all strangers, and especially of all white strangers. As he watched him now, nothing else within the range of his vision escaped him. It was thus that he saw

Raghunath Jafar emerge from his tent, carrying a rifle. Only Tarzan and little Nkima saw this, and only Tarzan placed any sinister interpretation upon it.

Raghunath Jafar walked directly away from camp and entered the jungle. Swinging silently through the trees, Tarzan of the Apes followed him. Jafar made a half-circle of the camp just within the concealing verdure of the jungle, and then he halted. From where he stood, the entire camp was visible to him, but his own position was concealed by foliage.

Colt was watching the disposition of his loads and the pitching of his tent. His men were busy with the various duties assigned to them by their headman. They were tired, and there was little talking. For the most part they worked in silence, and an unusual quiet pervaded the scene—a quiet that was suddenly and unexpectedly shattered by an anguished scream and the report of a rifle, blending so closely that it was impossible to say which had preceded the other. A bullet whizzed by Colt's head and nipped the lobe off the ear of one of his men standing behind him.

Instantly the peaceful activities of the camp were supplanted by pandemonium. For a moment there was a difference of opinion as to the direction from which the shot and the scream had come; then Colt saw a wisp of smoke rising from the jungle just beyond the edge of camp.

"There it is," he said, and started toward the point.

The headman of the askaris stopped him. "Do not go, Bwana," he said. "Perhaps it is an enemy. Let us fire into the jungle first."

"No," said Colt, "we will investigate first. Take

some of your men in from the right, and I'll take the rest in from the left. We'll work around slowly through the jungle until we meet."

"Yes, Bwana," said the headman; and calling his men, he gave the necessary instructions.

No sound of flight or any suggestion of a living presence greeted the two parties as they entered the jungle; nor had they discovered any signs of a marauder when, a few moments later, they made contact with one another. They were now formed in a half-circle that bent back into the jungle, and at a word from Colt, they advanced toward the camp.

It was Colt who found Raghunath Jafar lying dead just at the edge of camp. His right hand grasped his rifle. Protruding from his chest was the shaft of a sturdy arrow.

The negroes gathering around the corpse looked at one another questioningly and then back into the jungle and up into the trees. One of them examined the arrow. "It is not like any arrow I have ever seen," he said. "It was not made by the hand of man."

Immediately the blacks were filled with superstitious fears. "The shot was meant for the bwana," said one; "therefore the demon who fired the shot is a friend of our bwana. We need not be afraid."

THIS explanation satisfied the blacks, but it did not satisfy Wayne Colt. He was puzzling over it as he went back into camp, after giving orders that the Hindu be buried.

Zora Drinov was standing in the entrance of her tent and as she saw him she came to meet him. "What was it?" she asked. "What happened?"

"Comrade Zveri will not kill Raghunath Jafar," he said.

"Why?" she asked.

"Because Raghunath Jafar is already dead."

"Who could have shot the arrow?" she asked, after he had told her of the manner of the Hindu's death.

"I haven't the remotest idea," he admitted. "It is an absolute mystery, but it means that the camp is being watched, and that we must be very careful not to go into the jungle alone. The men believe that the arrow was fired to save me from an assassin's bullet, and while it is entirely possible that Jafar may have been intending to kill me, I believe that if I had gone into the jungle alone instead of him, it would have been I who would be lying out there dead now. Have you been bothered at all by natives since you made camp here, or have you had any unpleasant experiences with them at all?"

It was Colt who found Jafar lying dead. Protruding from his chest was the shaft of an arrow.

"We have not seen a native since we entered this camp. We have often commented upon the fact that the country seems to be entirely deserted and uninhabited, notwithstanding the fact that it is filled with game."

"This thing may help to account for the fact that it is uninhabited," suggested Colt, "or rather apparently uninhabited. We may have unintentionally invaded the country of some unusually ferocious tribe which takes this means of acquainting newcomers with the fact that they are *persona non grata.*"

"You say one of our men was wounded?" asked Zora.

"Nothing serious. He just had his ear nicked a little."

"Was he near you?"

"He was standing right behind me," replied Colt.

"I think there is no doubt but that Jafar meant to kill you," said Zora.

"Perhaps," said Colt, "but he did not succeed. He did not even kill my appetite—and now if I can calm the excitement of my boy, we shall have supper presently."

FROM a distance Tarzan and Nkima watched the burial of Raghunath Jafar, and a little later saw the return of Kahiya and his askaris, with Zora's boy Wamala, whc had been sent out of camp by Jafar.

"Where," said Tarzan to Nkima, "are all the many Tarmangani and Gomangani that you told me were in this camp?"

"They have taken their thundersticks and gone away," replied the little Manu. "They are hunting for

Nkima."

Tarzan of the Apes smiled one of his rare smiles. "We shall have to hunt them down and find out what they are about, Nkima," he said.

"But it grows dark in the jungle soon," pleaded Nkima, "and then will Sabor and Sheeta and Numa and Histah be abroad, and they too search for little Nkima."

Darkness had fallen before Colt's boy announced supper, and in the meantime Tarzan, changing his plans, had returned to the trees above the camp. He was convinced that there was something irregular in the aims of the expedition whose base he had discovered. He knew from the size of the camp that it had contained many men. Where they had gone, and for what purpose, were matters that he must ascertain. Feeling that this expedition whatever its purpose, might naturally be a principal topic of conversation in the camp, he sought a point of vantage wherefrom he might overhear the conversations that passed between the two white members of the party beneath him; and so it was that as Zora Drinov and Wayne Colt seated themselves at the supper table, Tarzan of the Apes crouched amid the foliage of a great tree just above them.

"You have passed through a rather trying ordeal today," said Colt, "but you do not appear to be any the worse for it. I should think that your nerves would be shaken."

"I have passed through too much already in my life, Comrade Colt, to have any nerves left at all," replied the girl.

"I suppose so," said Colt. "You must have passed

through the revolution in Russia."

"I was only a little girl at the time," she explained, "but I remember it quite distinctly."

Colt was gazing at her intently. "From your appearance," he ventured, "I imagine that you were not by birth of the proletariat."

"My father was a laborer. He died in exile under the Czarist regime. That was how I learned to hate everything monarchistic and capitalistic. And when I was offered this opportunity to join Comrade Zveri, I saw another field in which to encompass my revenge, while at the same time advancing the interests of my class throughout the world."

"WHEN I last saw Zveri in the United States," said Colt, "he evidently had not formulated the plans he is now carrying out, as he never mentioned any expedition of this sort. When I received orders to join him here, none of the details were imparted to me, and so I am rather in the dark as to what his purpose is."

"It is only for good soldiers to obey," the girl reminded him.

"Yes, I know that," agreed Colt, "but at the same time, even a poor soldier may act more intelligently sometimes if he knows the objective."

"The general plan, of course, is no secret to any of us here," said Zora, "and I shall betray no confidence in explaining it to you. It is a part of a larger plan to embroil the capitalistic powers in wars and revolutions to such an extent that they will be helpless to unite against us.

"Our emissaries have been laboring for a long

while toward a culmination of the revolution in India that will distract the attention and the armed forces of Great Britain. We are not succeeding so well in Mexico as we had planned, but there is still hope, while our prospects in the Philippines are very bright. The conditions in China you well know. She is absolutely helpless, and we have hope that with our assistance she will eventually constitute a real menace to Japan. Italy is a very dangerous enemy, and it is largely for the purpose of embroiling her in war with France that we are here."

"But just how can that be accomplished in Africa?" asked Colt.

"Comrade Zveri believes that it will be simple," said the girl. "The suspicion and jealousy that exist between France and Italy are well known. Their race for naval supremacy amounts almost to a scandal, and at the first overt act of either against the other, war might easily result; and a war between Italy and France would embroil all of Europe."

"But just how can Zveri, operating in the wilds of Africa, embroil Italy and France in war?" demanded the American.

"There are now in Rome a delegation of French and of Italian Reds engaged in this very business. The poor men know only a part of the plan, and unfortunately for them, it will be necessary to martyrize them in the cause for the advancement of our world plan. They have been furnished with papers outlining a plan for the invasion of Italian Somaliland by French troops. At the proper time, one of Comrade Zveri's secret agents in Rome will reveal the plot to the Fascist Government, and almost simultaneously a considerable number of our own blacks, disguised in the uniforms of French native troops, led by the white men of our expedition, uniformed as French officers, will invade Italian Somaliland.

"In the meantime our agents are carrying on in Egypt and Abyssinia and among the native tribes of North Africa, and already we have definite assurance that with the attention of France and Italy distracted by war, and Great Britain embarrassed by a revolution in India, the natives of North Africa will arise in what will amount almost to a holy war for the purpose of throwing off the yoke of foreign domination, and the establishment of autonomous Soviet states throughout the entire area."

"A daring and stupendous undertaking!" exclaimed Colt. "And it is one that will require enormous resources in money as well as men."

"It is Comrade Zveri's pet scheme," said the girl. "I do not know, of course, all the details of his organization and backing, but I do know that while he is already well financed for the initial operations, he is depending to a considerable extent upon this district for furnishing most of the necessary gold to carry on the tremendous operations that will be necessary to insure final success."

"Then I am afraid he is foredoomed to failure," said Colt, "for he surely cannot find enough wealth in this savage country to carry on any such stupendous program."

"Comrade Zveri believes to the contrary," said Zora; "in fact, the expedition that he is now engaged upon is for the purpose of obtaining the treasure he seeks."

Above them, in the darkness, the silent figure of the ape-man lay stretched at ease upon a great branch, his keen ears absorbing all that passed between them, while curled in sleep upon his bronzed back lay little Nkima, entirely oblivious of the fact that he might have listened to words well calculated to shake the foundations of organized government throughout the world.

"And where," demanded Colt, "if it is no secret, does Comrade Zveri expect to find such a great store of gold?"

"In the famous treasure vaults of Opar," replied the girl. "You certainly must have heard of them."

"Yes," replied Colt, "but I never considered them other than purely legendary. The folk-lore of the entire world is filled with these mythical treasure vaults."

"But Opar is no myth," replied Zora.

IF the startling information divulged to him affected Tarzan, it induced no outward manifestation. Listening in silence, imperturbable trained to the utmost refinement of self-control, he might have been part and parcel of the great branch upon which he lay, or of the shadowy foliage which hid him from view.

For a time Colt sat in silence, contemplating the stupendous possibilities of the plan that he had just heard unfolded. It seemed to him little short of the dream of a madman, and he did not believe that it had the slightest chance for success. What he did realize was the jeopardy in which it placed the members of the expedition, for he believed that there would be no escape for any of them once Great Britain, France and Italy were apprised of their activities; and without conscious volition, his fears seemed centered upon the safety of the girl.

He knew the type of people with whom he was working, and so he knew that it would be dangerous to voice a doubt as to the practicability of the plan— for scarcely without exception the agitators whom he had met had fallen naturally into two separate categories, the impractical visionary, who believed everything that he wanted to believe, and the shrewd knave, actuated by motives of avarice, who hoped to profit either in power or riches by any change that he might be instrumental in bringing about in the established order of things. It seemed horrible that a young and beautiful girl should have been enticed into such adesperate situation. She seemed far too intelligent to be merely a brainless tool and even his brief association with her made it most difficult for him to believe that she was a knave.

"The undertaking is certainly fraught with grave dangers," he said, "and as it is primarily a job for men, I cannot understand why you were permitted to face the dangers and hardships that must of necessity be entailed by the carrying out of such a perilous campaign."

"The life of a woman is of no more value than that of a man," she said, "and I was needed. There is always a great deal of important and confidential clerical work to be done which Comrade Zveri can only entrust to one in whom he has implicit confidence. He reposes such trust in me and, in addition, I am a trained typist and stenographer. Those reasons in themselves are sufficient to explain why I am here, but another very important one is that I desire to be with Comrade Zveri."

In the girl's words Colt saw the admission of a romance, but to his American mind this was all the greater reason why the girl should not have been brought along for he could not conceive of a man exposing the girl he loved to such dangers.

ABOVE them, Tarzan of the Apes moved silently. First he reached over his shoulder and lifted little Nkima from his back. Nkima would have objected, but the veriest shadow of a whisper silenced him. The ape-man had various methods of dealing with enemies—methods that he had learned and practiced long before he had been cognizant of the fact that he was not an ape. Long before he had ever seen another white man, he had terrorized the Gomangani, the black men of the forest and the jungle, and had learned that a long step toward defeating an enemy may be taken by first demoralizing its morale. He knew now that these people were not only the invaders of his own domain and, therefore, his own personal enemies, but that they threatened the peace of Great Britain, which was dear to him, and of the rest of the civilized world with which, at least, Tarzan had no quarrels. It is true that he held civilization in general in considerable contempt, but in even greater contempt he held those who interfered with the rights of others, or with the established order of jungle or city.

As Tarzan left the tree in which he had been hiding, the two below him were no more aware of his departure than they had been of his presence. Colt found himself attempting to fathom the mystery of love. He knew Zveri and it appeared inconceivable to him that a girl of Zora Drinov's type could be attracted by a man of Zveri's stamp. Of course, it was none of his affair, but it bothered him nevertheless because it seemed to constitute a reflection upon the girl and to lower her in his estimation. He was disappointed in her, and Colt did not like to be disappointed in people to whom he had been attracted.

"You knew Comrade Zveri in America?" asked Zora.

"Yes."

"What do you think of him?" she demanded.

"I found him a very forceful character," replied Colt. "I believe him to be a man who would carry on to a conclusion anything that he attempted. Perhaps no better man could have been selected for this mission."

If the girl had hoped to surprise Colt into an expression of personal like or dislike for Zveri, she had failed, and if such was the fact she was too wise to pursue the subject further. She realized that she was dealing with a man from whom she would get little information that he did not wish her to have; but on the other hand a man who might easily wrest information from others, for he was that type which seemed to invite confidences.

Their conversation drifted to various subjects—to their lives and experiences in their native lands—to the happenings that had befallen them since they had entered Africa, and finally, to the experiences of the day. And while they talked, Tarzan of the Apes returned to the tree above them, but this time he did not come alone.

"I wonder if we shall ever know," she said, "who killed Jafar."

"It is a mystery that is not lessened by the fact that none of the askaris could recognize the type of arrow with which he was slain, though that might be accounted for by the fact that none of them are of this district."

"It has considerably shaken the nerves of the men," said Zora, "and I sincerely hope that nothing similar occurs again. I have found that it does not take much to upset these natives; while most of them are brave in the face of known dangers, they are apt to be entirely demoralized by anything bordering on the supernatural."

"I think they felt better when they got the Hindu planted under ground," said Colt, "though some of them were not at all sure but what he might return anyway."

"There is not much chance of that," said the girl, laughing.

She had scarcely ceased speaking when the branches above them rustled, and a heavy body plunged downward to the table-top between them, crushing the flimsy piece of furniture to earth.

The two sprang to their feet, Colt whipping out his revolver, and the girl stifling a cry as she stepped back. Colt felt the hairs rise upon his head and gooseflesh form upon his arms and back—for there between them lay the dead body of Raghunath Jafar upon its back, the eyes rolled backward, staring up into the night!

CHAPTER IV

INTO THE LION'S DEN

N KIMA was angry. He had been awakened
from the depth of a sound sleep, which was
bad enough, but now his master had set out
upon foolish errands.

While Tarzan remained in the vicinity of the
camp, Nkima had not been particularly perturbed;
and when he had returned to the tree with his burden, the little Manu was sure that he was going to
remain there for the balance of the night; but instead he had departed immediately, and now was
swinging through the black forest with a determination that evidenced fixity of purpose.

Where Zveri and his party had started slowly
along winding jungle trails, Tarzan moved almost in
an air-line through the jungle toward his destination, which was the same as that of Zveri, with the
result that before Zveri reached the almost perpen-
dicular crag which formed the last and greatest
natural barrier to the forbidden valley of Opar, Tar-

zan and Nkima had disappeared beyond the summit
and were crossing the desolate valley, upon the far
side of which loomed the great walls and lofty spires
and turrents of ancient Opar.

No evidence of ruin was apparent at this great
distance; and once again, in imagination, he beheld
a city of magnificent beauty, its streets and temples
thronged with people; and once again his mind
toyed with the mystery of the city's origin, when
back somewhere in the dim vista of antiquity a race
of rich and powerful people had conceived and built
this enduring monument to a vanished civilization.

That its few inhabitants were direct descendants
of its once powerful builders seemed not unlikely, in
view of the rites and ceremonies of the ancient religion which they practiced as well as by the fact that
by scarcely any other hypothesis could the presence
of a white-skinned people be accounted for in this
remote and inaccessible African fastness.

Tarzan raised the body high above his head and cast it in the faces of the priests charging upon him.

The peculiar laws of heredity, which seemed operative in Opar as in no other portion of the world, suggested an origin differing materially from that of other men; for it is a peculiar fact that the men of Opar bear little or no resemblance to the females of their kind. The former are short, heavy-set, hairy, almost ape-like in their conformation and appearance; the women are slender, smooth-skinned and often beautiful.

There were certain physical and mental attributes of the men that had suggested to Tarzan the possibility that at some time in the past the colonists had, either by choice or necessity, interbred with the great apes of the district, and he also was aware that owing to the scarcity of victims for the human sacrifice which their rigid worship demanded it was the accepted practice among them to use for this purpose either males or females who deviated considerably from the standard time had established for each sex, with the result that through the law of nat-

ural selection an overwhelming majority of the
males would be grotesque and the females normal
and beautiful.

It was with such reveries that the mind of the
ape-man was occupied as he crossed the desolate
valley of Opar which lay shimmering in the bright
sunlight that was relieved only by the shade of an
occasional gnarled and stunted tree. Ahead of him
and to his right was the small rocky hillock, upon
the summit of which was located the outer entrance
to the treasure vaults of Opar. But with this he was
not now interested, his sole object being to forewarn
La of the approach of the invaders, that she might
prepare her defense.

It had been long since Tarzan had visited Opar,
but upon that last occasion, when he had restored La
to her loyal people and reëstablished her supremacy
following the defeat of the forces of Cadj, the high
priest, and the death of the latter beneath the fangs
and talons of Jad-bal-ja, he had carried away with
him for the first time a conviction of the friendliness
of all of the people of Opar. He had for years known
that La was secretly his friend, but her savage, grotesque retainers always heretofore had feared and
hated him, and so it was now that he approached
Opar as one might approach any citadel of one's
friends, without stealth and without any doubt but
that he would be received in friendship.

Nkima, however, was not so sure. The gloomy
ruins terrified him. He scolded and pleaded, but all
to no avail, and at last terror overcame his love and
loyalty so that, as they were approaching the outer
wall, which loomed high above them, he leaped

from his master's shoulder and scampered away from the ruins that confronted him. As Tarzan approached the narrow fissure which alone gave entrance through the massive outer walls of Opar, he was conscious, as he had been years before on the occasion of his first approach to the city, of unseen eyes upon him, and momentarily he expected to hear a greeting when the watchers recognized him.

Without hesitation, therefore, and with no apprehensiveness, Tarzan entered the narrow cleft and descended a flight of concrete steps that led to the winding passage through the thick outer wall. The narrow court, beyond which loomed the inner wall, was silent and deserted; nor was the silence broken as he crossed it to another narrow passage which led through it; at the end of this he came to a broad avenue upon the opposite side of which stood the crumbling ruins of the great temple of Opar.

IN silence and solitude he entered the frowning portal, flanked by rows of stately pillars, from the capitals of which grotesque birds stared down upon him as they had stared through all the countless ages since forgotten hands had carved them from the solid rock of the monoliths.

On through the temple toward the inner courtyard, where he knew the activities of the city were carried on, Tarzan made his way in silence. He had not sought to approach Opar stealthily and he knew he had not arrived unseen. Why a greeting was delayed he did not know, unless it was that they were waiting, after carrying word of his coming to, La for her instructions.

Through the main corridor Tarzan made his way, noting again the tablets of gold with their ancient and long undeciphered hieroglyphics. Through the chamber of the seven golden pillars he passed and across the golden floor of an adjoining room—and still only silence and emptiness, yet with vague suggestions of figures moving in the galleries that overlooked the apartment through which he was passing; then at last he came to a heavy door beyond which he was sure he would find either priests or priestesses of this great temple of the Flaming God.

Fearlessly he pushed it open and stepped across the threshold—and at that instant a knotted club descended heavily upon his head, felling him senseless to the floor.

INSTANTLY he was surrounded by a score of gnarled and knotted men. Their matted beards fell low upon their hairy chests as they rolled forward upon their short, crooked legs. They chattered in low growling gutturals as they bound their victim's wrists and ankles with stout thongs. Then they lifted him and carried him along other corridors and through the crumbling glories of magnificent apartments to a great tiled room, at one end of which a dark-browed young woman sat upon a massive throne resting upon a dais a few feet above the level of the floor.

Standing beside the girl upon the throne was another of the gnarled and knotted men. Upon his arms and legs were bands of gold and about his throat many necklaces. Upon the floor beneath these two was a gathering of men and women—the priests and priestesses of the Flaming God of Opar.

Tarzan's captors carried their victim to the foot of the throne and tossed his body upon the tile floor. Almost simultaneously the ape-man regained consciousness and opening his eyes looked about him.

"Is it he?" demanded the girl upon the throne.

One of Tarzan's captors saw that he had regained consciousness and with the help of others dragged him roughly to his feet.

"It is he, Oah," exclaimed the man at her side.

An expression of venomous hatred convulsed the face of the woman. "God has been good to His high priestess," she said. "I have prayed for this day to come, as I prayed for the other—and as the other came, so has this."

Tarzan looked quickly from the woman to the man at her side. "What is the meaning of this, Dooth?" he demanded of the man. "Where is La? Where is your high priestess?"

The girl rose angrily from her throne. "Know, man of the outer world, that *I* am high priestess! I, Oah, am high priestess of the Flaming God."

Tarzan ignored her. "Where is La?" he demanded again of Dooth.

Oah flew into a frenzy of rage. "She is dead!" she screamed, advancing to the edge of the dais as though to leap upon Tarzan, the jeweled handle of her sacrificial knife gleaming in the sunlight which poured through a great aperture where a portion of the ancient roof of the throne-room had fallen in. "She is dead!" she repeated. "Dead—as you will be, when next we honor the Flaming God with the life-blood of a man! La was weak. She loved you and thus she betrayed her god who had chosen you for sacrifice. But Oah is strong—strong with the hate she has nursed in her breast since Tarzan and La stole the throne of Opar from her. . . . Take him away!" she screamed to his captors. "And let me not see him again until I behold him bound to the altar in the court of sacrifice."

They cut the bonds that secured Tarzan's ankles so that he might walk, but even though his wrists were tied behind him it was evident that they still held him in great fear, for they put ropes about his neck and his arms and led him as man might lead a lion. Down into the familiar darkness of the pits of Opar they led him, lighting the way with torches, and when finally they had brought him to the dungeon in which he was to be confined it was some time before they could muster sufficient courage to cut the bonds that held his wrists; even then they did not do so until they had again bound his ankles securely so that they might escape from the chamber and bolt the door before he could release his feet and pursue them, for thus greatly had the prowess of Tarzan impressed itself upon the brains of the crooked priests of Opar.

Tarzan had been in the dungeons of Opar before—and, before, he had escaped; so he set to work immediately seeking for a means of escape from his present predicament, for he knew the chances were that Oah would not long delay the moment for which she had prayed—the instant when she should plunge the gleaming sacrificial knife into his breast.

Quickly removing the thongs from his ankles, Tarzan groped his way carefully along the walls of his cell until he had made a complete circuit of it; then, similarly, he examined the floor. He discovered that he was in a rectangular chamber about ten feet long and eight wide and that by standing upon his tiptoes he could just reach the ceiling. The only opening was the door through which he had entered. A small opening in this, protected by iron bars, gave the cell its only ventilation, but as it opened upon a dark corridor it admitted no light.

Tarzan examined the bolts and the hinges of the door, but they were, as he had conjectured, too substantial to be forced. Then, for the first time, he saw that a priest sat on guard in the corridor without, thus putting a definite end to any idea of surreptitious escape.

FOR three days and nights priests relieved each other at intervals; but upon the morning of the fourth day Tarzan discovered that the corridor was empty and once again he turned his attention actively to thoughts of escape.

It had so happened that at the time of Tarzan's capture his hunting-knife had been hidden by the tail of the leopard-skin which formed his loin-cloth, and in their excitement the ignorant, half-human priests of Opar had overlooked it when they took his other weapons away from him. Doubly thankful was Tarzan for this good fortune, since for sentimental reasons he cherished the hunting-knife of his long-dead sire—the knife that had started him upon the upward path to ascendancy over the beasts of the jungle that day,—now long gone,—when more by accident than intent he had plunged it into the heart

of Bolgani the gorilla. But for more practical reasons
it was indeed a gift from the gods, since it afforded
him not only a weapon of defense, but an instrument wherewith he might seek to make good his escape.

YEARS before Tarzan of the Apes had escaped from
the pits of Opar; he well knew the construction of
their massive walls. Granite blocks of various sizes,
hand-hewn to fit with perfection, were laid in
courses without mortar, the one wall that he had
passed through having been fifteen feet in thickness.
Fortune had favored him upon that occasion in that
he had been placed in a cell which, unknown to the
present inhabitants of Opar, had a secret entrance,
the opening of which was closed by a single layer of
loosely laid courses that the ape-man had been able
to remove without great effort.

Naturally he sought for a similar condition in the
cell in which he now found himself, but his search
was not crowned with success. No single stone could
he budge from its place, anchored as each was by
the tremendous weight of the temple walls they
supported. And so, perforce, he turned his attention
toward the door.

He knew that there were few locks in Opar, since
the present degraded inhabitants of the city had not
developed sufficient ingenuity either to repair old
ones or construct new. Those locks that he had seen
were ponderous affairs opened by huge keys and
were, he guessed, of an antiquity that reached back
to the days of Atlantis; but for the most part, heavy
bolts and bars secured such doors as might be fas-

tened at all and he surmised that it was such a crude contrivance which now barred his way to freedom.

Groping his way to the door, he examined the small opening that let in air. It was about shoulder high and perhaps ten inches square and was equipped with four vertical iron bars half an inch square, set an inch and a half apart—too close to permit him to insert his hands between them; but this fact did not entirely discourage the ape-man. Perhaps there was another way.

His steel-thewed fingers closed upon the center of one of the bars. With his left hand he clung to another and bracing one knee high against the door he slowly flexed his right elbow. Rolling like plastic steel, the muscles of his forearm and his biceps swelled; gradually the bar bent inward.

The ape-man smiled as he took a new grip upon the iron bar. Then he surged backward with all his weight and all the strength of that mighty arm, and the bar bent to a wide U as he wrenched it from its sockets.

He tried to insert his arm through the new opening, but it still was too small. A moment later another bar was torn away and now, his arm thrust through the aperture to its full length, he groped for the bar or bolts that held him prisoner.

At the fullest extent to which he could reach his finger-tips downward against the door, he just touched the top of the bar, which was a timber about three inches in thickness. Its other dimensions, however, he was unable to ascertain, nor whether it would release by raising one end or must be drawn back through keepers.

To have freedom almost within one's grasp and yet to be denied it was maddening; but if the ape-man felt any such reaction he did not show it, so perfect was his self-control.

Withdrawing his arm from the aperture, he removed his hunting-knife from his scabbard and, again reaching outward, pressed the point of the blade into the wood of the bar. At first he tried lifting the bar by this means, but his knife-point only pulled out of the wood. Next, he attempted to move the bar backward in a horizontal plane. In this he was successful, and though the distance that he moved it in one effort was small, he was satisfied, for he knew that patience would win its reward.

Never more than a quarter of an inch, sometimes only a sixteenth of an inch at a time, Tarzan slowly worked the bar backward. He worked methodically and carefully, never hurrying, never affected by nervous anxiety, although he knew not at what moment a savage warrior-priest of Opar might make his rounds. At last his efforts were rewarded, and the door swung upon its hinges.

Stepping quickly out, Tarzan shot the bar behind him; then, knowing no other avenue of escape, he turned back up the corridor along which his captors had conducted him to his prison cell. Faintly in the distance he discerned a lessening darkness and toward this he moved upon silent feet. As the light increased slightly he saw that the corridor was about ten feet wide and that at irregular intervals it was pierced by doors, all of which were closed and secured by bolts or bars.

A hundred yards from the cell in which he had

been incarcerated he crossed a transverse corridor and here he paused an instant to investigate with palpitating nostrils and keen eyes and ears. In neither direction could he discern any light, but faint sounds came to his ears indicating that life existed somewhere behind the doors along this corridor, and his nostrils were assailed by a medley of scents—the sweet aroma of incense, the odor of human bodies and the acrid scent of carnivores. But there was nothing there to attract his further investigation, so he continued on his way along the corridor toward the rapidly increasing light ahead.

He had advanced but a short distance when his keen ears detected the sound of approaching footsteps. Here was no place to risk discovery; slowly he fell back toward the transverse corridor, intending to take concealment there until the danger had passed. But it was already closer than he had imagined—an instant later half a dozen priests of Opar turned into the corridor from one just ahead of him. They saw him instantly and halted, peering through the gloom:

"It is the ape-man," said one: "He has escaped!" And with their knotted cudgels and their wicked knives they advanced upon him.

That they came slowly evidenced the respect in which they held his prowess, but still they came; and Tarzan fell back, for even he, armed only with a knife, was no match for six of these savage half-men with their heavy cudgels. As he retreated, a plan formed quickly in his alert mind and when he reached the transverse corridor he backed slowly into it. Knowing that now that he was hidden from them they would come very slowly, fearing that he might be lying in wait for them, he turned and ran swiftly along the corridor. He passed several doors, not because he was looking for any door in particular, but because he knew that the more difficult it was for them to find him the greater his chances of eluding them. At last he paused before one secured by a huge wooden bar. Quickly he raised it, opened the door and stepped within, just as the leader of the priests stepped into view at the intersection of the corridor.

The instant that Tarzan stepped into the dark and gloomy chamber beyond he knew that he had made a fearful blunder. Strong in his nostrils was the acrid scent of Numa the lion; the silence of the pit was shattered by a savage roar. In the dark background Tarzan saw two yellow-green eyes flaming with hate.

And then the lion charged.

CHAPTER V

BEFORE THE WALLS OF OPAR

PETER ZVERI established camp at the edge of the at the foot of the barrier cliff that guards the desolate valley of Opar. Here he left his porters and a few askari as guards; then, with his fighting-men, guided by Kitembo, he commenced the arduous climb of the summit.

None of them had ever come this way before, not even Kitembo,—though he knew the exact location of Opar from one who had seen it,—and so when the first view of the distant city broke upon them they were filled with awe, and vague questionings arose in the primitive minds of the black men.

It was a silent party which filed across the dusty plain toward Opar; nor were the blacks the only members of the expedition to be assailed with doubt, for in their black tents on distant deserts the Arabs had imbibed with the milk of their mothers the fear of jân and ghrôl, and they had heard, too, of the fabled city of Nimmr, which it was not well for men to approach. With such thoughts and forebodings were the minds of the men filled as they approached the towering ruins of the ancient Atlantian city. From the top of the great boulder that guards the outer entrance to the treasure vaults of Opar a little monkey watched the progress of the expedition across the valley. He was a much-distraught little monkey, for in his heart he knew that his master should be warned of the coming of these many Gomangani and Tarmangani with their thundersticks—but fear of the forbidding ruins gave him pause and so he danced about upon the top of the

In the distance Romero saw the dust of the fleeing expedition; and he started in pursuit.

rock, chattering and scolding. But the warriors of Peter Zveri marched right past and never paid any attention to him—and as they marched other eyes were upon them, peering from out of the foliage of the trees that grew rank among the ruins.

If any member of the party saw a little monkey scampering quickly past upon their right, or saw him clamber up the ruined outer wall of Opar, he gave the matter no thought. The minds of all were occupied by speculation as to what lay within that gloomy pile.

Kitembo did not know the location of the treasure-vaults of Opar. He had only agreed to guide Zveri to the city; but, like Zveri, he entertained no doubt that it would be easy to discover the vaults if they were unable to wring the location from any of the inhabitants of the city. Surprised, indeed, would they have been had they known that no living Oparian knew either of the location of the treasure-vaults or of their existence—and that among all living men, only Tarzan and some of his Waziri warriors knew their location or how to reach them.

"The place is nothing but a deserted ruin," said Zveri to one of his white companions.

"It is an ominous-looking place, though," replied the other, "and it has already had its effect upon the men."

Zveri shrugged. "This might frighten them at night," he said, "but not in broad daylight."

THEY were close to the ruined outer wall now, which frowned down upon them menacingly; here they halted while several searched for an opening.

Abu Batu was the first to find it—the narrow crevice with the flight of concrete steps leading upward. "Here is a way through, Comrade," he called to Zveri.

"Take some of your men with you and reconnoiter," ordered Zveri.

Abu Batu summoned half a dozen of his black men, who advanced with evident reluctance.

Gathering the skirt of his thob about him, the sheik entered the crevice. At the same instant a piercing screech broke from the interior of the ruined city—a long-drawn, high-pitched shriek that ended in a series of low moans. The Bedaùwy halted; the blacks froze in terrified rigidity.

"Go on!" yelled Zveri. "A scream can't kill you!"

"Wullah," exclaimed one of the Aarabs; "but jân can."

"Get out of there, then!" cried Zveri angrily. "If you damned cowards are afraid to go, I'll go in myself!"

There was no argument. The Aarabs stepped aside. And then a little monkey, screaming with terror, appeared upon the top of the wall from the inside of the city. His sudden and noisy appearance brought every eye to bear upon him. They saw him turn an affrighted glance backward over his shoulder and then, with a loud scream, leap far out to the ground below. It scarcely seemed he could survive the jump—yet it barely sufficed to interrupt his flight, for he was on his way again in an instant as, with prodigious leaps and bounds, he fled screaming out across the barren plains.

It was the last straw. The shaken nerves of the

Oah flew into a frenzy of rage. "La is dead!" she screamed. "Dead—as you will be, when next we honor the Flaming God with the lifeblood of a man!"

blacks gave to the sudden strain and almost with one accord they turned and fled the dismal city, while close upon their heels were Abu Batu and his desert warriors.

Peter Zveri and his three white companions, finding themselves suddenly deserted, looked at one another questioningly.

"The dirty cowards!" exclaimed Zveri angrily. "You go back, Mike, and see if you can rally them. We are going on in, now that we are here."

Michael Dorsky, only too glad of any assignment that took him further away from Opar, started at a brisk run after the fleeing warriors, while Zveri turned again to the fissure with Miguel Romero and Paul Ivitch at his heels.

The three men passed through the outer wall and entered the courtyard, across which they saw the lofty inner wall rising before them. Romero was the first to find the opening that led to the city proper and, calling to his fellows, he stepped boldly into the narrow passage, when once again the hideous scream shattered the brooding silence of the ancient temple.

The three men halted. Zveri wiped the perspiration from his brow. "I think we have gone as far as we can, alone," he said. "Perhaps we had all better go back and rally the men. There is no sense in doing anything foolhardy."

Miguel Romero threw him a contemptuous sneer, but Ivitch assured Zveri that the suggestion met with his entire approval.

The two men crossed the court quickly without waiting to see whether the Mexican followed them or not, and were soon once again outside the city.

"Where is Miguel?" asked Ivitch suddenly.

Zveri looked around. "Romero!" he shouted in a loud voice, but there was no reply.

"It must have got him," said Ivitch, with a shudder.

"Small loss!" grumbled Zveri.

But whatever the thing was that Ivitch feared, it had not as yet gotten the young Mexican, who, after watching his companions' precipitate flight, had continued on through the opening in the inner wall, determined to have at least one look at the interior of the ancient city of Opar which he had traveled so far to see.

Before his eyes spread a magnificent panorama of stately ruins. At the sight the young and impressionable Latin-American stood spellbound. Again

the eerie wail rose from the interior of a great building before him, but if he was frightened Romero
gave no evidence of it. Perhaps he grasped his rifle a
little more tightly; perhaps he loosened his revolver
in his holster; but he did not retreat. He was awed by
the stately grandeur of the scene before him, where
age and ruin seemed only to enhance its pristine
magnificence.

A movement within the temple caught his attention. He saw a figure emerge from somewhere,—the
figure of a gnarled and knotted man that rolled on
short crooked legs,—and then another and another
came, until there were fully a hundred of the savage
creatures approaching slowly toward him. He saw
their knotted bludgeons and their knives and he realized that here was a menace more effective than
an unearthly scream.

With a shrug he backed into the passageway. "I
cannot fight an army single-handed," he muttered.
Rapidly he crossed the outer court, passed through
the first great wall and stood again upon the plain
outside the city. In the distance he saw the dust of
the fleeing expedition and, with a grin he started in
pursuit, swinging along at an easy walk as he puffed
upon a cigarette. From the top of the rocky hill at
his left a little monkey saw him pass—a little monkey which still trembled from fright, but whose terrified screams had now become only low, pitiful
moans. It had been a hard day for little Nkima.

SO rapid had been the retreat of the expedition that
Zveri, with Dorsky and Ivitch, did not overtake the
main party until the majority of it was already de-

scending the barrier cliffs—nor could any threats or promises stay the retreat, which ended only when camp was reached.

Immediately Zveri called Abu Batu, together with Dorsky and Ivitch, into council. The affair had been Zveri's first reverse; and it was a serious one, inasmuch as he had banked so heavily upon the inexhaustible store of gold to be found in the treasure-vaults of Opar. He berated Abu Batu, Kitembo, their ancestors, and all their followers, for cowardice—but all that he accomplished was to arouse the anger and resentment of these two leaders.

"We came with you to fight the white men, not demons and ghosts," said Kitembo. "I am not afraid. I would go into the city; but my men will not accompany me—and I cannot fight the enemy alone."

"Nor I," said Abu Batu.

"I know," said Zveri with a sneer, "you are both brave men, but you are much better runners than you are fighters. Look at us—we were not afraid; we went in, and we were not harmed."

"Where is Comrade Romero?" demanded Abu Batu.

"Well, perhaps *he* is lost,"

admitted Zveri. "What do you expect? To win a battle without losing a man?"

"There was no battle," said Kitembo, "and the man who went farthest into the accursed city did not return."

Dorsky looked up suddenly. "There he is now!" he exclaimed, and as all eyes turned up the trail toward Opar they saw Miguel Romero strolling jauntily into camp, unharmed.

"Greeting, my brave comrades!" he cried to them. "I am glad to find you alive. I feared that you might all succumb to heart-failure."

Sullen silence greeted his raillery and no one

Drawing the door quickly inward, Tarzan slipped behind it as the lion charged.

spoke until he had approached and seated himself near them.

"What detained you?" demanded Zveri presently.

"I wanted to see what was beyond the inner wall," replied the Mexican.

"And you saw?" asked Abu Batu.

"I saw magnificent buildings in splendid ruins," replied Romero.

"And what else?" asked Kitembo.

"I saw a company of strange warriors—short heavy men on crooked legs, with long powerful arms and hairy bodies. They came out of a great building that might have been a temple. There were too many of them for me. I could not fight them alone, so I came away."

"Did they have weapons?" asked Zveri.

"Clubs and knives," replied Romero.

"You see?" exclaimed Zveri. "Just a band of savages armed with clubs! We could take the city without the loss of a man."

"What did they look like?" demanded Kitembo. "Describe them to me." And when Romero had done so, with careful attention to details, Kitembo shook his head. "It is as I thought," he said. "They are not men; they are demons."

"Men or demons, we are going back and take their city," said Zveri angrily. "We must have the gold of Opar."

"You may go, white man," said Kitembo, "but you will go alone. I know my men and I tell you that they will not follow you there. Lead us against white men, or brown men, or black men, and we will follow you. But we will not follow you against demons and ghosts."

"And you, Abu Batu?" demanded Zveri.

"I have talked with my men on the return from the city and they tell me that they will not go back there. They will not fight the jân and ghrôl. They heard the voice of the jin warning them away, and they are afraid."

Zveri stormed and threatened and cajoled, but all to no effect. Neither the Aarab sheik nor the African chief could be moved.

"There is still a way," said Romero.

"And what is that?" asked Zveri.

"When the gringo comes with the Philippine, there will be six of us who are neither Aarabs nor Africans. We six can take Opar."

Paul Ivitch made a wry face and Zveri cleared his throat.

"If we are killed," said the latter, "our whole plan is wrecked. There will be no one left to carry on."

Romero shrugged. "It was only a suggestion," he said; "but of course if you are afraid—"

"I am not afraid!" stormed Zveri. "But neither am I a fool."

An ill-concealed sneer curved Romero's lips. "I am going to eat," he said, and, rising, he left them. . .

The day following his advent into the camp of his fellow-conspirators, Wayne Colt wrote a long message in cipher and dispatched it to the Coast by one of his boys.

From her tent Zora Drinov had seen the message given to the boy. She had seen him place it in the end of a forked stick and start off upon his long journey. Shortly afterward, Colt joined her in the shade of a great tree beside her tent.

"You sent a message this morning, Comrade Colt," she said.

He looked up at her quickly. "Yes," he said.

"Perhaps you should know that only Comrade Zveri is permitted to send messages from the expedition," she told him.

"I did not know," he said. "This was merely in relation to some funds that were to have been awaiting me when I reached the Coast. They were not there. I sent the boy back after them."

"Oh!" she said; then their conversation drifted to other topics.

That afternoon he took his rifle and went out to look for game and Zora went with him. That evening they had supper together again, but this time she was the hostess.

And so the days passed, until an excited native aroused the camp one day with an announcement that the expedition was returning. No words were necessary to apprise those who had been left behind that victory had not perched upon the banner of their little army. Failure was clearly written upon the faces of the leaders.

Zveri greeted Zora and Colt, introducing the latter to his companions, and when Tony had been similarly presented the returning warriors threw themselves down upon cots or upon the ground to rest.

That night, as they gathered around the supper-table, each party narrated the adventures that had befallen them since the expedition had left camp. Colt and Zora were thrilled by the stories of weird

Opar, but no less mysterious was their tale of the death of Raghunath Jafar and his burial and uncanny resurrection.

"Not one of the boys would touch the body after that," said Zora. "Tony and Comrade Colt had to bury him themselves."

"I hope you made a good job of it this time," said Miguel.

"He hasn't come back again," said Colt with a grin.

"Who could have dug him up in the first place?" demanded Zveri.

"None of the boys, certainly," said Zora. "They were all too much frightened by the peculiar circumstances surrounding his death."

"It must have been the same creature that killed him," said Colt; "and whoever or whatever it was must have been possessed of almost superhuman strength to have carried away that heavy corpse into a tree and drop it upon us."

"The most uncanny feature of it to me," said Zora, "is the fact that it was accomplished in absolute silence. I'll swear that not even a leaf rustled until just before the body hurtled down upon our table."

"It could have been only a man," said Zveri.

"Unquestionably," said Colt. "But what a man!"

As the company broke up later, repairing to their various tents, Zveri detained Zora with a gesture. "I want to talk to you a minute, Zora," he said, and the girl sank back into the chair she had just quitted. "What do you think of this American?" asked Zveri softly. "You have had a good opportunity to size him up."

"He seems to be all right. He is a very likable fellow," replied the girl.

"He said or did nothing, then, that might arouse your suspicion?" demanded Zveri.

"No," said Zora, "nothing at all."

"You two have been alone here together for a number of days," continued Zveri. "Did he treat you with perfect respect?"

"He was certainly much more respectful than your friend Raghunath Jafar!"

"Don't mention that dog to me," said Zveri. "I wish that I had been here to kill him myself."

"I told him that you would when you got back; but some one beat you to it."

They were silent for several moments. It was evident that Zveri was trying to frame into words something that was upon his mind. At last he spoke. "Colt is a very prepossessing young man," he said. "See that you don't fall in love with him, Zora."

"And why not?" she demanded. "I have given my mind and my strength and my talent to the cause and, perhaps, most of my heart. But there is a corner of it that is mine to do with as I wish."

"You mean to say that you are in love with him?" demanded Zveri.

"Certainly not; nothing of the kind. Such an idea had not entered my head. I just want you to know, Peter, that in matters of this kind you may not dictate to me."

"Listen, Zora—you know perfectly well that I love you; and what is more, I am going to have you. I get what I go after."

"Don't bore me, Peter. I have no time now for anything so foolish as love. When we are through with this undertaking, perhaps I shall give it a little thought."

"I want you to give it a lot of thought right now, Zora," he insisted. "There are some details in relation to this expedition that I have not told you. I have not divulged them to anyone—but I am going to tell you now, because I love you and you are going to become my wife. There is more at stake in this for us than you dream. After all the risks and the hardships, I do not intend to surrender the power and wealth that I shall have gained, to anyone."

"You mean not even to the cause?" she asked.

"I mean not even to the cause—except that I shall use them both for the cause."

"Then what do you intend? I do not understand you."

"I intend to make myself Emperor of Africa," he said, "and I intend to make you my Empress."

"Peter!" she cried. "Are you crazy?"

"Yes, I am crazy for power, for riches—and for you."

"You can never do it, Peter. You know how far-reaching are the tentacles of the power we serve. If you fail it, if you turn traitor, those tentacles will reach you and drag you down to destruction."

"When I win my goal, my power will be as great as theirs, and then I may defy them."

"But how about these others with us, who are serving loyally the cause which they think you represent? They will tear you to pieces, Peter!"

The man laughed. "You do not know them, Zora.

They are all alike; all men and women are alike. If I offered to make them Grand Dukes and give them each a palace and a harem, they would slit their own mothers' throats to obtain such a prize."

The girl arose. "I am astounded, Peter! I thought that you, at least, were sincere."

He arose quickly and grasped her by the arm. "Listen, Zora," he hissed in her ear, "I love you—and because I love you I have put my life in your hands. But understand this; If you betray me, I shall kill you! Do not forget that."

"You did not have to tell me that, Peter. I was quite well aware of it."

"And you will not betray me?" he demanded.

"I never betray a friend, Peter," she said. . . .

The next morning Zveri was engaged in working out the details of a second expedition to Opar, based upon Romero's suggestions. It was decided that this time they would call for volunteers, and as the Europeans, the two Americans and the Filipino had already indicated their willingness to take part in the adventure, it remained now only to seek to enlist the services of some of the blacks and Aarabs.

For this purpose Zveri summoned the entire company to a palaver. Here he explained just what they proposed doing. He stressed the fact that Comrade Romero had seen the inhabitants of the city and that they were only stunted savages, armed with sticks. Eloquently he explained how easily they might be overcome with rifles.

Practically the entire party was willing to go as far as the walls of Opar, but there were only ten warriors who would agree to enter the city with the white men; all of these were from the askaris who had been left behind to guard camp and from those who had accompanied Colt from the Coast, none of whom had been subjected to the terrors of Opar. Not one of those who had heard the weird screams issuing from the ruins would agree to enter the city and it was admitted among the whites that it was not at all unlikely that their ten volunteers might suddenly develop a change of heart when they actually stood before the frowning portals of Opar and heard the weird warning cry from its defenders.

SEVERAL days were spent in making careful preparations for the new expedition, but at last the final detail was completed and early one morning Zveri and his followers set out once more upon the trail to Opar.

Zora Drinov had wished to accompany them, but as Zveri was expecting messages from various agents throughout Northern Africa, it was necessary to leave her behind. Abu Batu and his warriors were left to guard the camp and these, with a few black servants, were all who did not accompany the expedition.

Since the failure of the first expedition and the fiasco at the gates of Opar, the relations between Abu Batu and Zveri had been strained. The sheik and his warriors smarted under the charges of cowardice, and though they would not volunteer to enter the city of Opar, they still resented the affront of being selected to remain behind as camp guards; and so it was that as the others departed the Aarabs sat whispering over their thick coffee, their swart scowling faces half-hidden by their thorribs.

They did not deign even to glance at their departing comrades; but the eyes of Abu Batu were fixed meditatively upon the slender figure of Zora Drinov.

CHAPTER VI

BETRAYED

THE heart of little Nkima had been torn conflicting emotions, as from the vantage-point of the rocky hillock he watched the hasty departure of Miguel Romero from the city of Opar. Seeing these brave Tarmangani, armed with death-dealing thunder-sticks, driven away from the ruins, he was convinced that something terrible must have befallen his master within the grim recesses of that crumbling pile. His loyal heart prompted him to return and investigate, but Nkima was only a very little Manu—a little Manu who was much afraid—and though he started twice again toward Opar he could not muster his courage to the sticking-point; and at last, whimpering pitifully, he turned back across the plains toward the grim forest, where at least the dangers were familiar ones. . . .

The door of the gloomy chamber which Tarzan had entered swung inward and his hands were still upon it as the menacing roar of the lion apprised him of the danger of his situation.

Agile and quick is Numa the lion, but with even greater celerity functioned the mind and muscles of Tarzan of the Apes. In the instant that the lion sprang toward him a picture of the whole scene flashed to the mind of the ape-man. He saw the gnarled priests of Opar advancing along the corridor in pursuit of him; he saw the heavy door that swung inward; he saw the charging lion—and he pieced these various factors together to create a situation far more to his advantage than they normally presented.

Drawing the door quickly inward, he slipped behind it as the lion charged—with the result that the beast, either carried forward by his own momentum or sensing escape, sprang into the corridor full in the faces of the advancing priests; and at the same instant Tarzan closed the door behind him.

Just what happened in the corridor without he could not see, but from the growls and screams that receded quickly into the distance he was able to picture a scene which brought a quiet smile to his lips— and an instant later a piercing shriek of agony and terror announced the fate of at least one of the fleeing Oparians.

Realizing that he would gain nothing by remaining where he was, Tarzan decided to leave the cell and seek a way out of the labyrinthine mazes of the pits beneath Opar. He knew that the lion upon its prey would doubtless bar his passage along the route he had been following when his escape had been interrupted by the priests and though, as a last resort, he might face Numa, he was of no mind to invite

"Listen, Zora," Zveri hissed. "If you betray me, I shall kill you! Do not forget that!"

such an unnecessary risk.

But when he sought to open the heavy door he found that he could not budge it, and in an instant he realized what had happened—he was once again in prison in the dungeons of Opar!

The bar that secured this particular door was not of the sliding type, but, working upon a pin at the inner end, dropped into heavy wrought-iron keepers bolted to the door itself and to its frame. When he had entered he had raised the bar, and in slamming the door to it had dropped into place of its own weight, imprisoning him as effectually as though the work had been done by the hand of man.

The darkness of the corridor without was less intense than that upon which his former cell had been located and though not enough light entered the cell to illuminate its interior, there was sufficient to show him the nature of the ventilating opening in the door, which he found to consist of a number of small round holes, none of which was of sufficient diameter to permit him to pass his hand through in an attempt to raise the bar.

AS Tarzan stood in momentary contemplation of this new predicament, the sound of stealthy movement came to him from the black recesses at the rear of the cell. He wheeled quickly, drawing his hunting-knife from its sheath.

He did not have to ask himself what the author of this sound might be, for he knew that the only other living creature that might have occupied this cell with its former inmate was another lion. Why it had not joined in the attack upon him, he could not guess, but that it would eventually seize him was a foregone conclusion. Probably even now it was preparing to sneak upon him. He wished that his eyes might penetrate the darkness, for if he could see the lion as it charged, he might be better prepared to meet it. In the past he had met the charges of other lions, but always before he had been able to see their swift spring and to elude the sweep of their mighty claws as they reared upon their hind legs to seize him. Now it would be different and for once in his life, Tarzan of the Apes felt death was inescapable.

He was not afraid, but he did not wish to die and he knew that the price at which he would sell his life would cost his antagonist dearly. In silence he waited. Again he heard that faint, yet ominous sound. The foul air of the cell reeked with the stench of carnivores; from a distant corridor he heard the growling of a lion at its kill.

And then a voice broke the silence.

"Who are you?" it asked. It was the voice of a woman and it came from the back of the cell in which the ape-man was imprisoned.

"Where are you?" demanded Tarzan.

"I am here at the back of the cell," replied the woman.

"Where is the lion?"

"He went out when you opened the door," she replied.

"Yes, I know," said Tarzan. "But the other one—where is he?"

"There is no other one. There was but one lion here and it is gone. —Ah, now I know you!" she exclaimed. "I know the voice. It is Tarzan!"

"La!" exclaimed the ape-man, advancing quickly across the cell. "How could you be here with the lion and still live?"

"I am in an adjoining cell that is separated from this one by a door made of iron bars," replied La. Tarzan heard metal hinges creak. "It is not locked," she said. "It was not necessary to lock it, for it opened into this other cell where the lion was."

Groping forward through the dark, the two advanced until their hands touched one another.

La pressed close to Tarzan. She was trembling. "I have been afraid," she said; "but I shall not be afraid now."

"I shall not be of much help to you," said Tarzan. "I also am a prisoner."

"I know it," replied La. "But I always feel safe

when you are near."

"Tell me what has happened," demanded Tarzan. "How is it that Oah is posing as high priestess, and you are a prisoner in your own dungeons?"

"I forgave Oah her former treason—when she conspired with Cadj to wrest my power from me," explained La. "But she could not exist without intrigue and duplicity. To further her ambitions, she made love to Dooth, who has been high priest since Jad-bal-ja killed Cadj. They spread stories about me through the city—and as my people have never forgiven me for my friendship for you, they succeeded in winning enough to their cause to overthrow and imprison me. All the ideas were Oah's, for Dooth and the other priests, as you well know, are stupid beasts. It was Oah's idea to imprison me thus, with a lion for company, merely to make my suffering more terrible, until the time should come when she might prevail upon the priests to offer me in sacrifice to the Flaming God. In that she has had some difficulty, I know, as those who have brought my food have told me."

"How could they bring food to you here?" asked Tarzan. "No one could pass through the outer cell while the lion was there."

"There is another opening in the lion's cell, that leads into a low, narrow corridor into which they can drop meat from above. Thus they would entice the lion from this outer cell, after which they would lower a gate of iron bars across the opening of the small corridor into which he went, and while he was thus imprisoned they brought my food to me. But they did not feed him much. He was always hungry, often growling and pawing at the bars of my cell. Perhaps Oah hoped that some day he would batter them down."

"Where does this other corridor, in which they fed the lion, lead?" asked Tarzan.

"I do not know," replied La, "but I imagine that it is only a blind tunnel built in ancient times for this very purpose."

"We must have a look at it," said Tarzan. "It may offer a means of escape."

"Why not escape through the door by which you entered?" asked La, and when the ape-man had explained why this was impossible, she pointed out the location of the entrance to the small tunnel.

"We must get out of here as quickly as possible, if it is possible at all," said Tarzan, "for if they are able to capture the lion, they will certainly return him to this cell."

"They will capture him," said La. "There is no question as to that."

"Then I had better hurry and make my investiga-

"Silence!" said the ape-man. "Do as you are told—and you will not be harmed."

tion of the tunnel," said Tarzan, "for it might prove embarrassing were they to return him to the cell while I was in the tunnel, if it proved to be a blind one."

"I will listen at the outer door while you investigate," said La. "Make haste."

GROPING his way toward the section of the wall La had indicated, Tarzan found a heavy grating of iron closing an aperture leading into a low, narrow corridor. Lifting the barrier, Tarzan entered and with his hands extended before him, moved forward in a crouching position, since the low ceiling would not permit him to stand erect. He had progressed but a short distance when he discovered that the corridor made an abrupt right-angle turn to the left and beyond the turn he saw at a short distance a faint luminosity. Moving quickly forward, he came to the end of the corridor, at the bottom of a vertical shaft, the interior of which was illuminated by subdued daylight. The shaft was constructed of the usual rough-hewn granite of the foundation walls of the city, but here set with no great nicety or precision, giving the interior of the shaft a rough and uneven surface.

As Tarzan was examining it he heard La's voice coming along the tunnel from the cell in which he had left her. Her tone was excited, and her message one that presaged a situation wrought with extreme danger to them both.

"Make haste, Tarzan! They are returning with the lion!"

The ape-man hurried quickly back to the mouth

of the tunnel.

"Quick!" he cried to La, as he raised the gate that had fallen behind him after he had passed through.

"In there?" she demanded in an affrighted voice.

"It is our only chance of escape," replied the ape-man.

Without another word La crowded into the corridor beside him. Tarzan lowered the grating and, with La following closely behind him, returned to the opening leading into the shaft.

Without a word, he lifted La in his arms and raised her as high as he could. Nor did she need be told what to do; with little difficulty she found both hand- and foot-holds upon the rough surface of the shaft's interior and with Tarzan just below, assisting and steadying her, she made her way slowly aloft.

The shaft led directly upward into a room in the tower, which overlooked the entire city of Opar, and here, concealed by the crumbling walls, they paused to formulate their plans.

They both knew that their greatest danger lay in discovery by one of the numerous monkeys which infest the ruins of Opar, with which the inhabitants of the city are able to converse. Tarzan was anxious to be away from Opar that he might thwart the plans of the white men who had invaded his domain. But first he wished to bring about the downfall of La's enemies and reinstate her upon the throne of Opar, or if that should prove impossible, to insure the safety of her flight.

As he viewed her now in the light of day he was struck again by the matchlessness of her deathless beauty, that neither time nor care nor danger seemed capable of dimming—and he wondered what he should do with her, where he could take her: where this savage priestess of the Flaming God could find a place in all the world, outside the walls of Opar, with the environment of which she would harmonize. And as he pondered he was forced to admit to himself that no such place existed. La was of Opar—a savage queen born to rule a race of savage half-men; as well introduce a tigress to the salons of civilization as La of Opar! Two or three thousand years earlier she might have been a *Cleopatra* or a *Sheba*, but today she could be only La of Opar.

For a time they had sat in silence, the beautiful eyes of the high priestess fixed upon the stern profile of the forest god.

"Tarzan!" she said at last.

The man looked up. "What is it, La?" he asked.

"I still love you, Tarzan," she said in a low voice.

A troubled expression came into the eyes of the ape-man. "Let us not speak of that," he said.

"I like to speak of it," she said. "It gives me sorrow, but it is a sweet sorrow—the only sweetness that has ever come into my life."

Tarzan extended a bronzed hand and laid it upon her slender fingers. "You have always possessed my heart, La," he said, "up to the point of love. If my affection goes no further than this, it is through no fault of mine nor yours."

La laughed. "It is certainly through no fault of mine, Tarzan," she said; "but I know that such things are not ordered by ourselves. Love is a gift of the gods. Sometimes it is awarded as a recompense;

sometimes as a punishment. For me it has been a punishment, perhaps—but I would not have it otherwise. I have nurtured it in my breast since first I met you and without that love, however hopeless it may be, I should not care to live."

Tarzan made no reply and the two relapsed into silence, waiting for night to fall that they might descend into the city unobserved. Tarzan's alert mind was occupied with plans for reinstating La upon her throne, and presently they fell to discussing these.

"Just before the Flaming God goes to his rest at night," said La, "the priests and the priestesses all gather in the throne-room. There they will be to-night before the throne upon which Oah will be seated. Then may we descend to the city."

"And then what?" asked Tarzan.

"If we can kill Oah in the throne-room," said La, "and Dooth at the same time, they would have no leaders—and without leaders they are lost."

"I cannot kill a woman," said Tarzan.

"*I* can," said La; "and you can attend to Dooth. You certainly would not object to killing him?"

"If he attacked I would kill him," said Tarzan, "but not otherwise. Tarzan kills only in self-defense and for food, or when there is no other way to thwart an enemy."

In the floor of the ancient room in which they were waiting were two openings; one was the mouth of the shaft through which they had ascended from the dungeons; the other opened into a similar but larger shaft, to the bottom of which ran a long wooden ladder set in the masonry of its sides. It was this shaft which offered them a means of escape

from the tower; and as Tarzan sat with his eyes resting idly upon the opening, an unpleasant thought
suddenly obtruded itself upon his consciousness.

He turned toward La. "We had forgotten," he
said, "that whoever casts the meat down the shaft to
the lion must ascend by this other shaft. We may not
be as safe from detection here as we had hoped."

"They do not feed the lion very often," said La;
"not every day."

"When did they feed him last?" asked Tarzan.

"I do not recall," said La. "Time drags so heavily
in the darkness of the cell that I lost count of days."

"*S-st!*" cautioned Tarzan. "Some one is ascending
now."

Silently the ape-man arose and crossed the floor
to the opening, where he crouched upon the side
opposite the ladder. La moved stealthily to his side,
so that the ascending man, whose back would be toward them, as he emerged from the shaft, would not
see them.

Slowly the man ascended. They could hear his
shuffling progress coming nearer and nearer to the
top. He did not climb as the ape-like priests of Opar
are wont to climb. Tarzan thought perhaps he was
carrying a load either of such weight or cumber-
someness as to retard his progress, but when finally
his head came into view the ape-man saw that he
was an old man, which accounted for his lack of agility. Then powerful fingers closed about the throat of
the unsuspecting Oparian, and he was lifted bodily
out of the shaft.

"Silence!" said the ape-man. "Do as you are told—
and you will not be harmed."

La had snatched a knife from the girdle of their victim, and now Tarzan forced him to the floor of the room and slightly released his hold upon the fellow's throat, turning him around so that he faced them.

An expression of incredulity and surprise crossed the face of the old priest as his eyes fell upon La.

"Darus!" exclaimed La.

"All honor to the Flaming God who has ordered your escape!" exclaimed the priest joyfully.

La turned to Tarzan. "You need not fear Darus," she said. "He will not betray us. Of all the priests of Opar, there never lived one more loyal to his queen."

"That is right," said the old man, shaking his head.

"Are there many more loyal to the high priestess, La?" demanded Tarzan.

"Yes, very many," replied Darus; "but they are afraid. Oah is a she-devil and Dooth is a fool. Between the two there is no longer either safety or happiness in Opar."

"How many are there whom you absolutely know may be depended upon?" demanded La.

"Oh, very many," replied Darus.

"Gather them in the throne-room tonight then, Darus, and as the Flaming God goes to his couch be ready to strike at the enemies of La, your priestess."

"You will be there?" asked Darus.

"I shall be there," replied La. "This, your dagger, shall be the signal. When you see La of Opar plunge it into the breast of Oah the false priestess, fall upon those who are the enemies of La."

"It shall be done, just as you say," Darus assured her; "and now I must throw this meat to the lion and be gone."

Slowly the old priest descended the ladder, gibbering and muttering to himself, after he had cast a few bones and scraps of meat into the other shaft to the lion.

"You are quite sure you can trust him, La?" demanded Tarzan.

"Absolutely," replied the girl. "Darus would die for me—and I know that he hates Oah and Dooth."

The slow remaining hours of the afternoon dragged on; the sun was low in the west and now the two must take their greatest risk, that of descending into the city while it was still light and making their way to the throne-room—although the risk was greatly minimized by the fact that the inhabitants of the city were all supposed to be congregated in the throne-room at this time, performing the age-old rite with which they speeded the Flaming God to his night of rest. Without interruption they descended to the base of the tower, crossed the court-yard and entered the temple. Through devious and round-about passages, La led the way to a small doorway that opened into the throne-room at the back of the dais upon which the throne stood. Here she paused, listening to the services being conducted within the great chamber, waiting for the cue that would bring them to a point when all within the room, except the high priestess, were prostrated, with their faces pressed against the floor.

When that instant arrived, La swung open the door and leaped silently upon the dais, behind the throne in which her victim sat. Close behind her came Tarzan—and in that first instant both realized that they had been betrayed, for the dais was swarming with priests ready to seize them.

Already one had caught La by an arm, but before he could drag her away Tarzan sprang upon him, seized him by the neck and jerked his head backward so suddenly and with such force that the sound of his snapping vertebræ could be heard across the room. Then he raised the body high above his head and cast it in the faces of the priests charging upon him. As they staggered back, he seized La and swung her into the corridor along which they had approached the throne-room.

It was useless to stand and fight, for he knew that even though he might hold his own for awhile, they must eventually overcome him and that once they laid their hands upon La they would tear her limb from limb.

Down the corridor behind them came the yelling horde of priests, and in their wake, screaming for the blood of her victim, was Oah.

"Make for the outer walls by the shortest route, La," directed Tarzan, and the girl sped on winged feet, leading him through the labyrinthine corridors of the ruins until they broke suddenly into the chamber of the seven pillars of gold, and then Tarzan knew the way.

No longer needing his guide, and—realizing that the priests were overtaking them—being fleeter of foot than La, he swept the girl into his arms and sped through the echoing chambers of the temple toward the inner wall. Across the courtyard and through the outer wall he ran; still the priests pursued, urged on by the screaming Oah. Out across the deserted valley they fled and now the priests were losing ground, for their short, crooked legs could not compete with the speed of Tarzan's clean-limbed stride, even though he was burdened by the weight of La.

The sudden darkness of the near tropics that follows the setting of the sun soon obliterated the pursuers from their sight and a short time thereafter the sounds of pursuit ceased and Tarzan knew that the chase had been abandoned, for the men of Opar have no love for the darkness of the outer world.

Then Tarzan paused and lowered La to the ground; but as he did so her soft arms

"I am crying for joy," La said. "—joy that perhaps I shall be with you for a long time."

encircled his neck and she pressed close to him, her cheek against his breast, and burst into tears.

"Do not cry, La," he said. "We shall come again to Opar and when we do you shall be seated upon your throne again."

"I am not crying for that," she replied.

"Then why do you cry?" he asked.

"I am crying for joy," she said, "—joy that perhaps I shall be alone with you now for a long time."

In pity, Tarzan pressed her to him for a long moment, and then they set off once more toward the barrier cliff.

That night they slept in a great tree in the forest at the foot of the cliff. Tarzan constructed a rude couch for La between two branches, while he settled himself in a crotch of the tree a few feet below her.

It was dawn when Tarzan awoke. The sky was overcast and he sensed an approaching storm. No food had passed his lips for many hours and he knew that La had not eaten since the morning of the previous day. Food, therefore, was a prime essential; he must find it and return to La before the storm broke. Since it was meat he craved he knew he must be able to make a fire and cook it before La could eat it, though as for himself he still preferred it raw.

He looked into La's cot and saw that she was still asleep. Knowing she must be exhausted from all she had passed through the previous day, he let her sleep on,—and swinging to a near-by tree, he set out upon his search for food.

AS Tarzan moved up-wind through the middle terrace, every faculty of his delicately attuned senses was alert. Like the lion, Tarzan particularly relished the flesh of Pacco the zebra, though either Bara the antelope or Horta the boar would have proven an acceptable substitute; but the forest seemed to be deserted by every member of the herds he sought.

Only the scent-spoor of the great cats assailed his nostrils, mingled with the lesser and more human odor of Manu the monkey.

Time means little to a hunting beast; it meant little to Tarzan who, having set out in search of meat, would return only when he had found meat.

When La awakened it was some time before she could place her surroundings, but when she did a slow smile of happiness and contentment parted her lovely lips, revealing an even row of perfect teeth. She sighed; then she murmured the name of the man she loved.

"Tarzan!" she called.

There was no reply. Again she spoke his name, but this time louder. Again the only answer was silence. Slightly troubled, she arose upon an elbow and leaned over the side of her sleeping couch.

The tree beneath her was empty.

She thought, correctly, that perhaps he had gone to hunt, but still she was troubled by his absence and the longer she waited the more troubled she became. She knew that he did not love her and that she must be a burden to him. She knew too that he was as much a wild beast as the lions of the forest and that the same desire for freedom, which animated them, must animate him. Perhaps he had been unable to withstand the temptation longer and while she slept, he had left her.

There was not a great deal in the training or ethics of La of Opar that could have found exception to such conduct, for the life of her people was a life of ruthless selfishness and cruelty. They entertained few of the finer sensibilities of civilized man, or the great nobility of character that marked so many of the wild beasts.

La's love for Tarzan had been the only soft spot in her savage life, and realizing that she would think nothing of deserting a creature she did not love, she was fair enough to cast no reproaches upon Tarzan for having done the thing that she might have done in similar circumstances—nor to her mind did it ill accord with her conception of his nobility of character.

As she descended to the ground she sought to determine some plan of action for the future, but in this moment of loneliness and depression she saw no alternative but to return to Opar. And so it was toward the city of her birth that she turned her steps; but she had not gone far before she realized the danger and futility of this plan, which could but lead to certain death while Oah and Dooth ruled in Opar.

She felt bitter toward the old priest Darus, whom she believed had betrayed her, and accepting his treason as an index of what she might expect from others whom she had believed to be friendly to her, she realized the utter hopelessness of her position in so far as regaining the throne of Opar without outside help was concerned. La had no happy life to which she might look forward, but the will to live was yet strong within her—more the result, perhaps, of the courageousness of her spirit than of any fear of death, which to her was but another word for defeat.

She paused in the trail that she had reached a short distance from the tree in which she had spent the night and there, with almost nothing to guide her, she sought to determine in what direction she should break a new trail into the future—for wherever she went, other than back to Opar, it would be a new trail, leading among peoples and experiences as foreign to her as though she had suddenly stepped from another planet, or from the long-lost continent of her progenitors.

It occurred to her that perhaps there might be other people in this strange world as generous and chivalrous as Tarzan. At least in this direction there lay hope. In Opar there was none; so she turned back away from Opar and above her black clouds rolled and billowed as the storm king marshaled his forces—and behind her a great tawny beast with gleaming eyes slunk through the underbrush beside the trail that she followed.

CHAPTER VII

IN FUTILE SEARCH

TARZAN of the Apes, ranging far in search of
food, caught at length the welcome scent of
Horta the boar. The man paused and with a
deep inhalation filled his lungs with air until his
great bronzed chest expanded to the full. The blood
coursed through his veins, as every fiber of his being
reacted to the exhilaration of the moment—the keen
delight of the hunting beast that has scented its
quarry! Then swiftly and silently he sped in the direction of his prey.

Presently he came upon it, a young tusker, powerful and agile, his wicked tusks gleaming as he tore
bark from a young tree. The ape-man was poised
just above him, concealed by the foliage of a great
tree.

A vivid flash of lightning broke from the billow-
ing black clouds above. The storm broke; at the
same instant the man launched himself on the boar,
grasping in one hand the hunting knife of his long-

dead sire.

The weight of the man's body crushed the boar to the earth; before he could struggle to his feet again, the keen blade had severed his jugular. His life-blood gushing from the wound, the boar sought to rise and turn to fight, but the steel thews of the ape-man dragged him down and an instant later, with a last convulsive shudder, Horta died.

Leaping to his feet, Tarzan placed a foot upon the carcass of his kill and raising his face to the heavens, gave voice to the victory-cry of the bull-ape.

Faintly to the ears of marching men came the hideous scream. The blacks in the party halted, wide-eyed.

"What the devil was that?" demanded Zveri.

"It sounded like a panther," said Colt.

"That was no panther," said Kitembo. "It was the cry of a bull-ape who has made a kill, or—"

"Or what?" demanded Zveri.

Kitembo looked fearfully in the direction from which the sound had come. "Let us get away from here," he said.

Again the lightning flashed and the thunder crashed and as the torrential rain deluged them, the party staggered on in the direction of the barrier cliffs of Opar. . . .

Cold and wet, La of Opar crouched beneath a great tree that only partially protected her almost naked body from the fury of the storm. In the dense underbrush a few yards from her a tawny carnivore lay with unblinking eyes fixed steadily upon her.

The storm, titanic in its brief fury, passed on, leaving the deep worn trail a tiny torrent of muddy water and La, thoroughly chilled, hastened onward in an effort to woo new warmth to her chilled body.

She knew that trails must lead somewhere and in her heart she hoped that this one would lead to the country of Tarzan. If she could live there, seeing him occasionally, she would be content. Even knowing that he was near her would be better than nothing. Of course she had no conception of the immensity of the world she trod. A knowledge even of the extent of the forest that surrounded her would have

The great apes of To-yat were engaged in the death-dance of the Dum Dum.

appalled her.

In her imagination she visualized a small world, dotted with the remains of ruined cities like Opar, in which dwelt creatures like those she had known— gnarled and knotted men like the priests of Opar, white men like Tarzan, black men such as she had seen, and great shaggy gorillas like Bolgani, who had ruled in the Valley of the Palace of Diamonds.

Thinking these thoughts, she came at last to a clearing into which the unbroken rays of the warm sun poured without interruption. Near the center of the clearing was a small boulder and toward this she made her way with the intention of basking in the warm rays of the sun until she should be dried and warmed, for the dripping foliage had kept her wet and cold even after the rain had ceased.

As she seated herself she saw a movement at the edge of the clearing ahead of her and an instant later a great leopard bounded into view. The beast paused at sight of the woman, evidently as much surprised as she, and then, apparently realizing the defenselessness of this unexpected prey, the creature crouched and with twitching tail slowly wormed itself forward.

La rose and drew the knife that she had taken from Darus from her girdle. She knew that flight was futile. In a few bounds the great beast could overtake her and even had there been a tree that she could have reached before she was overtaken, it would have proven no sanctuary from a leopard.

Defense she knew to be also futile, but surrender without battle was not within the fiber of La of Opar.

The metal discs, elaborately wrought by the hands of some long-dead goldsmith of ancient Opar, rose and fell above her firm breast as her heart beat, perhaps a bit more rapidly, beneath them. On came the leopard. She knew that in an instant he would charge; then of a sudden he rose to his feet, his back arched, his mouth grinning in a fearful snarl, and simultaneously a tawny streak whizzed by her from behind and she saw a great lion leap upon her would-be destroyer.

At the last instant, but too late, the leopard had turned to flee. The lion seized him by the back of the neck and with his jaws and one great paw he twisted the head back until the spine snapped. Then, almost contemptuously, he cast the body from him and turned toward the girl.

In an instant La realized what had happened. The lion had been stalking her and seeing another about to seize his prey, he had leaped to battle in its defense. She had been saved, though only to fall victim immediately to another and more terrible beast.

The lion stood looking at her. She wondered why he did not charge and claim his prey. She did not know that within that little brain the scent of the woman had aroused the memory of another day, when Tarzan had lain bound upon the sacrificial altar of Opar with Jad-bal-ja, the Golden Lion, standing guard above him. A woman had come—this same woman. Tarzan his master had told him not to harm her—and she had approached and cut the bonds that secured him.

This Jad-bal-ja remembered and he remembered too that he was not to harm this woman and if he was not to harm her, then nothing must harm her. For this reason he had killed Sheeta the leopard.

But all this La of Opar did not know, for she had not recognized Jad-bal-ja. She merely wondered how much longer it would be—and when the lion came closer she steeled herself, for still she meant to fight; yet there was something in his attitude that she could not understand. He was not charging; he was merely walking toward her, and when he was a couple of yards from her he half turned away and lay down and yawned.

For what seemed an eternity to the girl she stood there watching him. He paid no attention to her. Could it be that, sure of his prey and not yet hungry, he merely waited until he was quite ready to make his kill? The idea was horrible and even La's iron nerves commenced to weaken beneath the strain.

She knew she could not escape, and so better instant death than this suspense. She determined, therefore, to end the matter quickly and to discover once and for all whether the lion considered her already his prey or would permit her to depart.

Gathering all the forces of self-control that she possessed, she placed the point of her dagger to her heart and walked boldly past the lion. Should he attack her she would end the agony instantly by plunging the blade into her heart.

Jad-bal-ja did not move, but with lazy, half-closed eyes he watched the woman cross the clearing and disappear beyond the turn of the trail that wound its way back into the jungle. . . .

All that day La moved on with grim determination, looking always for a ruined city like Opar, astonished by the immensity of the forest, appalled by its loneliness. Surely, she thought, she must soon come to the country of Tarzan! She found fruits and tubers to allay her hunger and as the trail descended a valley in which a river ran, she did not want for water. But night came again and still no sight of man or city. Once again she crept into a tree to sleep, but this time there was no Tarzan to fashion a couch for her or to watch over her safety.

AFTER Tarzan had slain the boar, he cut off the hind-quarters and started back to the tree in which he had left La. The storm made his progress slower than it otherwise would have been, but notwithstanding this he realized long before he reached his destination that his hunting had taken him much farther afield than he had imagined.

When at last he reached the tree and found that La was not there, he was slightly disconcerted, but thinking that perhaps she had descended to stretch her limbs after the storm he called her name aloud several times. Receiving no answer, he became genuinely apprehensive for her safety, and dropping to the ground sought some trace of her. It so happened that beneath the tree her footprints were still visible, not having been entirely obliterated by the rain, and he saw that they led back in the direction of Opar, so that, although he lost them when they reached the trail, in which water still was running, he was none the less confident that he knew her intended destination and so he set off in the direction of the barrier cliff.

It was not difficult for him to account for her absence and for the fact that she was returning to Opar and he reproached himself for his thoughtlessness in having left her for so long a time without first telling her of his purpose. He guessed, rightly, that she had imagined herself deserted and had turned back to the only home she knew, to the only place in the world where La of Opar might hope to find friends; but that she would find them even there Tarzan doubted and he was determined that she must not go back until she could do so with a force of warriors sufficiently great to insure the overthrow of her enemies.

It had been Tarzan's plan first to thwart the scheme of the party whose camp he had discovered in his dominion and then to return with La to the country of his Waziri, where he would gather a sufficient body of those redoubtable warriors to insure the safety and success of La's return to Opar.

Never communicative, he had neglected to explain his purpose to La and this he now regretted, since he was quite certain that had he done so she would not have felt it necessary to have attempted to return alone to Opar.

But he was not much concerned with the outcome, since he was confident that he could overtake her long before she reached the city and, inured as he was to the dangers of the forest and the jungle, he minimized their importance, as we do those which confront us daily in the ordinary course of our seemingly humdrum existence, where death threatens us quite as constantly as it does the denizens of the jungle.

MOMENTARILY expecting to catch sight of La, Tarzan slowly traversed the back trail to the foot of the rocky escarpment that guards the plain of Opar. Now he commenced to have his doubts for it did not seem possible that La could have covered so great a distance in so short a time. He scaled the cliff and came out upon the summit of the flat mountain that overlooked distant Opar. Here only a light rain had fallen the storm having followed the course of the valley below. Plain in the trail were the footprints of himself and La where they had passed down from Opar the night before, but nowhere was there any sign of spoor to indicate that the girl had returned, nor, as he looked out across the valley, was there any moving thing in sight.

What had become of her? Where could she have gone? In the great forest that spread below him there were countless trails. Somewhere below her spoor must be plain in the freshly wet earth, but he realized that even for him it might prove a long and difficult task to pick it up again.

Rather sorrowfully he turned back to descend the barrier cliff and as he did so his attention was attracted by a movement at the edge of the forest below. Dropping to his belly behind a low bush, Tarzan watched the spot to which his attention had been attracted. Warily he gazed as the head of a column of men debouched from the forest and moved toward the foot of the cliff.

Behind her a tawny beast with gleaming eyes slunk through the underbrush beside the trail.

Tarzan had known nothing of what had transpired upon the occasion of Zveri's first expedition to Opar, which had occurred while he had been incarcerated in the cell beneath the city. The apparent mysterious disappearance of the party that he had known to have been marching on Opar had mystified him; but here it was again—where it had been in the meantime was of no moment.

Tarzan wished that he had his bow and arrow that the Oparians had taken from him and which he had not had an opportunity to replace since he had escaped from them. But if he did not have them there were other ways of annoying the invaders.

From his position he watched them approach the cliff and commence the ascent.

Tarzan selected a large boulder, many of which were strewn about the flat top of the mountain, and when the leaders of the party were about halfway to the summit and the others were strung out below them, the ape-man pushed the rock over the edge of the cliff just above them.

In its descent it just grazed Zveri, struck a protuberance beyond him, bounded over Colt's head and carried two of Kitembo's warriors to death at the base of the escarpment.

The ascent stopped instantly. Several of the blacks who had accompanied the first expedition started a hasty retreat and utter disorganization and rout faced the expedition, whose nerves had become more and more sensitive the nearer they approached Opar.

"Stop the damn' cowards!" shouted Zveri to Dorsky and Ivitch, who were bringing up the rear. "Who will volunteer to go over the top and investigate?"

"I'll go," said Romero.

"And I'll go with him," said Colt.

"Who else?" demanded Zveri; but no one else volunteered. Already the Mexican and the American were climbing upward.

"Cover our advance with a few rifles," Colt shouted back to Zveri. "That ought to keep them away from the edge."

Zveri issued instructions to several of the askaris who had not joined in the retreat. When their rifles commenced popping it put new heart into those who had started to flee, and presently Dorsky and Ivitch had rallied the men and the ascent was resumed.

Quite aware that he could not stop the advance single-handed, Tarzan had withdrawn quickly along the edge of the cliff to a spot where tumbled masses of granite offered concealment and where he knew there existed a precipitous trail to the bottom of the cliff. Here he could remain and watch, or, if necessary, make a hasty retreat. He saw Romero and Colt reach the summit and immediately recognized the latter as the man he had seen in the base camp of the invaders. Tarzan had previously been impressed by the appearance of the young American and now he acknowledged his unquestioned bravery and that of his companion in leading a party over the summit of the cliff in the face of an unknown danger.

Romero and Colt looked quickly about them, but there was no enemy in sight and this word they passed back to the ascending company.

From his point of vantage Tarzan watched the

expedition surmount the summit of the cliff and start upon its march toward Opar. He believed that they could never find the treasure-vaults and now that La was not in the city, he was not concerned with the fate of those who had turned against her. Upon the bare and inhospitable Oparian plain, or in the city itself, they could accomplish little in furthering the objects of the expedition he had overheard Zora Drinov explaining to Colt. He knew that eventually they must return to their base camp and in the meantime he would prosecute his search for La; and so as Zveri led his expedition once again toward Opar, Tarzan of the Apes slipped over the edge of the barrier cliff and descended swiftly to the forest below.

Just inside the forest and upon the bank of the river was an admirable camp site and having noticed that the expedition was accompanied by no porters, Tarzan naturally assumed that they had established a temporary camp within striking distance of the city. It occurred to him that in this camp he might find La a prisoner.

AS he had expected, he found the camp located upon the spot where upon other occasions he had camped with his Waziri warriors.

And old thorn *boma* that had encircled it for years had been repaired by the newcomers and within it a number of rude shelters had been erected while in the center stood the tents of the white men. Porters were dozing in the shade of the trees; a single askari made a pretense of standing guard, while his fellows lolled at their ease, their rifles at their sides. But nowhere could he see La of Opar.

He moved down-wind from the camp, hoping to catch her scent spoor if she was there, but so strong was the smell of smoke and the body odors of the blacks that he could not be sure but that these drowned La's scent if she was a prisoner in the

Before the boar could struggle to his feet,
the keen blade severed his jugular.

camp. He decided therefore to wait until darkness had fallen when he might make a more careful investigation and he was further prompted to this decision by the sight of weapons, which he sorely needed. All of the warriors were armed with rifles, but some, clinging through force of ancient habit to the weapons of their ancestors, carried also bows and arrows and in addition there were many spears.

As a few mouthfuls of the raw flesh of Horta had constituted the only food that had passed Tarzan's lips for almost two days, he was ravenously hungry. With the discovery that La had disappeared, he had cached the hind-quarter of the boar in the tree in which they had spent the night, before setting out upon his fruitless search for her. So now, while he waited for darkness, he hunted again and this time Bara the antelope fell a victim to his prowess, nor did he leave the carcass of his kill until he had satisfied his hunger. Then he lay up in a near-by tree and slept.

THE anger of Abu Batu against Zveri was rooted deeply in his inherent racial antipathy for Europeans and their religion, and its growth was stimulated by the aspersions which the Russian had cast upon the courage of the Aarab and his followers.

"Dog of a Nasrâny!" ejaculated the Sheik. "He called us cowards, we Bedaùwy, and he left us here like old men and boys to guard the camp and the woman!"

"He is but an instrument of Allah," said one of the Aarabs, "in the great cause that will rid Africa of all Nastâny."

"Wellah-billah!" ejaculated Abu Batu. "What proof have we that these people will do as they promise? I would rather have my freedom on the desert and what wealth I can gather by myself than to lie longer in the same camp with these Nasrâny pigs."

"There is no good in them," muttered another.

"I have looked upon their woman," said the Sheik, "and I find her good. I know a city where she would bring many pieces of gold."

"In the trunk of the chief Nasrâny there are many pieces of gold and silver," said one of the men. "His boy told that to a Galla, who repeated it to me."

"The plunder of the camp is rich beside," suggested a swarthy warrior.

"If we do this thing, perhaps the great cause will be lost," suggested the one who had first answered the Sheik.

"It is the cause of the Nasrâny," said Abu Batu, "and it is only for profit. Is not the huge pig always reminding us of the money and the women and the power that we shall have when we have thrown out the English? Man is moved only by his greed. Let us take our profits in advance and be gone."

Wamala was preparing the evening meal for his mistress. "Before, you were left with the brown Bwana," he said, "and he was no good; nor do I like any better the Sheik Abu Batu. He is no good. I wish that Bwana Colt was here."

"So do I," said Zora. "It seems to me that the Aarabs have been sullen and surly ever since the expedition returned from Opar."

"They have sat all day in the tent of their chief talking together," said Wamala; "and often Abu Batu looked at you."

"That is your imagination, Wamala," replied the girl. "He would not dare to harm me."

"Who would have thought that the brown Bwana would have dared to?" Wamala reminded her.

"Hush, Wamala—the first thing you know you will have me frightened," said Zora, and then suddenly: "Look, Wamala! Who is that?"

The black boy turned his eyes in the direction toward which his mistress was looking. At the edge of the camp stood a figure that might have rung an exclamation of surprise from a stoic. A beautiful woman stood there regarding them intently. She had halted just at the edge of camp—an almost naked woman whose gorgeous beauty was her first and most striking charactertistic. Two golden discs covered her firm breasts and a narrow stomacher of gold and precious stones encircled her hips, supporting in front and behind a broad strip of soft leather, studded with gold and jewels, which formed the pattern of a pedestal on the summit of which was seated a grotesque bird. Her feet were shod in sandals that were covered with mud, as were her shapely legs upward to above her knees. A mass of wavy hair, shot with golden bronze lights by the rays of the setting sun, half surrounded an oval face, and from beneath narrow brows fearless gray eyes regarded them.

Some of the Aarabs had caught sight of her, too, and they were coming forward now toward her. She looked quickly from Zora and Wamala toward the others. Then the European girl arose quickly and approached her that she might reach her before the

Aarabs did, and as she came near the stranger with outstretched hands, Zora smiled. La of Opar came quickly to meet her, as though sensing in the smile of the other an index to the friendly intent of this stranger.

"Who are you?" asked Zora. "And what are you doing here alone in the jungle?"

La shook her head and replied in a language that Zora did not understand.

Zora Drinov was an accomplished linguist but she exhausted every language in her repertoire, including a few phrases from various Bantu dialects, and still found no means of communicating with the stranger.

The Aarabs addressed her in their own tongue and Wamala in the dialect of his tribe, but all to no avail. Then Zora put an arm about her and led her toward her tent and there, by means of signs, La of Opar indicated that she desired to bathe. Wamala was directed to prepare a tub in Zora's tent and by the time supper was prepared the stranger reappeared, washed and refreshed.

As Zora Drinov seated herself opposite her strange guest, she was impressed with the belief that never before had she looked upon so beautiful a woman and she marveled that one who must have felt so utterly out of place in her surroundings should still retain a poise that suggested the majestic bearing of a queen rather than of a stranger ill at ease.

By signs and gestures, Zora sought to converse with her guest until even the regal La found herself laughing. Then La tried it too, until Zora knew that her guest had been threatened with clubs and knives and driven from her home, that she had walked a long way, that either a lion or a leopard had attacked her and that she was very tired.

When supper was over, Wamala prepared another cot for La in the tent with Zora, for something in the faces of the Aarabs had made the European girl fear for the safety of her beautiful guest.

"You must sleep outside the tent door tonight, Wamala," she said. "Here is an extra pistol."

In his goat-hair beyt Abu Batu, the Sheik, talked long into the night with the principal men of his tribe. "The new one," he said, "will bring a price such as has never been paid before!"

TARZAN awoke and glanced upward through the foliage at the stars. He saw that the night was half gone and he arose and stretched himself. He ate again sparingly of the flesh of Bara and slipped silently into the shadows of the night. . . .

The camp at the foot of the barrier cliff slept. A single askari kept guard and tended the beast-fire. From a tree at the edge of the camp two eyes watched him, and when he was looking away a figure dropped silently into the shadows. Behind the huts of the porters it crept, pausing occasionally to test the air with dilated nostrils. It came at last, among the shadows, to the tents of the Europeans and one by one it ripped a hole in each rear wall and stealthily entered.

It was Tarzan searching for La, but he did not find her and, disappointed, he turned to another matter.

Making a half circuit of the camp, moving sometimes only inch by inch as he wormed himself along on his belly, lest the askari upon guard might see him, he made his way to the shelters of the other askaris and there he selected a bow and arrow and a stout spear. But even yet he was not done.

For a long time he crouched waiting—waiting until the askari by the fire should turn in a certain direction.

Presently the sentry arose and threw some dry wood upon the fire, after which he walked toward the shelter of his fellows to awaken the man who was to relieve him. It was this moment for which Tarzan had been waiting. The path of the askari brought him close to where Tarzan lay in hiding. The man approached and passed and in the same instant Tarzan leaped to his feet and sprang upon the unsuspecting black. A strong arm encircled the fellow from behind and swung him to a broad, bronzed shoulder. As Tarzan had anticipated a scream of terror burst from the man's lips, awakening his fellows, and then he was borne swiftly through the shadows of the camp away from the beast-fire as, with his prey struggling futilely in his grasp, the ape-man leaped the thorn *boma* and disappeared into the black jungle beyond.

So sudden and violent the attack, so complete the man's surprise, that he had loosened his grasp upon his rifle in an effort to clutch his antagonist as he was thrown lightly to the shoulder of his captor.

His screams, echoing through the forest, brought his terrified companions from their shelters in time to see an indistinct form leap the *boma* and vanish into the darkness. They stood temporarily paralyzed by fright, listening to the diminishing cries of their comrade. Presently these ceased suddenly. Then the headman found his voice.

"Simba! " he said.

"It was not Simba," said another. "It ran high upon two legs, like a man. I saw it."

PRESENTLY from the dark jungle came a hideous, long-drawn cry. "That is the voice of neither man nor lion," said the headman.

"It is a demon," said another, and then they huddled about the fire, throwing dry wood upon it until its blaze had crackled high into the air.

In the darkness of the jungle Tarzan paused and laid aside his spear and bow, possession of which had permitted him to use but one hand in his abduction of the sentry. Now the fingers of his free hand closed upon the throat of his victim, putting a sudden period to his screams. Only for an instant did Tarzan choke the man and when he relaxed his grasp upon the fellow's throat, the black made no further outcry, fearing to invite again the ungentle grip of those steel fingers. Quickly Tarzan jerked the fellow to his feet, relieved him of his knife and, grasping him by his thick wool, pushed him ahead of him into the jungle, after stooping to retrieve his spear and bow. It was then that he voiced the victory cry of the bull-ape, for the value of the effect that it would have not only upon his victim, but upon his fellows in the camp behind him.

Tarzan had no intention of harming the fellow. His quarrel was not with the innocent black tools of

the white men and, while he would not have hesitated to take the life of the black had it been necessary, he knew well enough that he might effect his
purpose with them as well without bloodshed as
with it.

The whites could not accomplish anything without their black allies and if Tarzan could successfully
undermine the morale of the latter, the scheme of
their masters would be as effectually thwarted as
though he had destroyed them, since he was confident that they would not remain in a district where
they were constantly reminded of the presence of a
malign, supernatural enemy. Furthermore, this pol-
icy accorded better with Tarzan's grim sense of humor, and therefore amused him, which the taking of
life never did.

For an hour he marched his victim ahead of him
in an utter silence, which he knew would have its effect upon the nerves of the black man.

Finally he halted him, stripped his remaining
clothing from him, and taking the fellow's loin-cloth
bound his wrists and ankles together loosely. Then
Tarzan left his captive, taking his cartridge-belt and
other belongings with him, knowing the man would
soon free himself from his bonds and believing that
he had made his escape, would remain for life convinced that he had narrowly eluded a terrible fate.

Satisfied with his night's work, Tarzan returned
to the tree in which he had cached the carcass of
Bara, ate once more and lay up in sleep until morning, when he again took up his search for La, seeking
trace of her up the valley beyond the barrier cliff of
Opar, in the general direction her spoor had indi-

cated she had gone, though, in fact, she had gone in precisely the opposite direction, down the valley.

CHAPTER VIII

THE TREACHERY OF ABU BATU

NIGHT was falling when a frightened little monkey took refuge in a tree-top. For days he had been wandering through the jungle, seeking in his little mind a solution for his problem during those occasional intervals that he could concentrate his mental forces upon it. But in an instant he might forget it to go swinging and scampering through the trees; or again a sudden terror would drive it from his consciousness, as one or another of the hereditary menaces to his existence appeared within the range of his perceptive faculties.

While his grief lasted it was real and poignant, and tears welled in the eyes of little Nkima as he thought of his absent master. Lurking always within him upon the border-land of conviction was the thought that he must obtain succor for Tarzan. In some way he must fetch aid to his master. The great black Gomangani warriors, who were also the servants of Tarzan, were many darknesses away, but

yet it was in the general direction of the country of
the Waziri that he drifted. Time was in no sense of
the essence of the solution of this or any other problem in the mind of Nkima. He had seen Tarzan enter Opar alive. He had not seen him destroyed, nor
had he seen him come out of the city; therefore by
the standards of his logic logic must still be alive and
in the city, but because the city was filled with enemies Tarzan must be in danger. As conditions were
they would remain. Nkima could not readily visual-
ize any change that he did not actually witness, so,
whether he found and fetched the Waziri today or
tomorrow would have little effect upon the result.
They would go to Opar and kill Tarzan's enemies,
and then little Nkima would have his master once
more and he would not have to be afraid of Sheeta,
or Sabor, or Histah.

Night fell and in the forest Nkima heard a gentle
tapping. He aroused himself and listened intently.
The tapping grew in volume until it rolled and
moved through the jungle. Its source was at no great
distance and as Nkima became aware of this, his excitement grew.

The moon was well up in the heavens, but the
shadows of the jungle were dense and Nkima was
upon the horns of a dilemma, between his desire to
go to the place from which the drumming emanated
and his fear of the dangers that might lie along the
way. But at length the urge prevailed over his terror
and keeping well up in the relatively greater safety
of the tree-tops he swung quickly in the direction
from which the sound was coming, to halt at last
above a little natural clearing that was roughly circu-

A tawny streak whizzed by her from behind, and she saw a great lion leap upon her would-be destroyer.

lar in shape.

Below him in the moonlight he witnessed a scene that he had spied upon before, for here the great apes of To-yat were engaged in the death-dance of the Dum-Dum. In the center of the amphitheater, was one of those remarkable earthen drums, which from time immemorial primitive man has heard, but which few have seen. Before the drum were seated two old shes, who beat upon its resounding surface with short sticks. There was a rough rhythmic cadence to their beating and to it, in a savage circle, danced the bulls, while encircling them in a thin outer line the females and the young squatted upon their haunches, enthralled spectators of the savage scene.

Close beside the drum lay the dead body of Sheeta the leopard, to celebrate whose killing the Dum-Dum had been organized.

Presently the dancing bulls would rush in upon the body and beat it with heavy sticks and, leaping out again, resume their dance. When the hunt, and the attack and the death had been depicted at length, they would cast away their bludgeons and with bared fangs leap upon the carcass, tearing and rending it as they fought among themselves for large pieces or choice morsels.

Now Nkima and his kind are noted neither for their tact nor judgment. One wiser than little Nkima would have remained silent until the dance and the feast were over, until a new day had come and the great bulls of the tribe of To-yat had recovered from the hysterical frenzy that the drum and the dancing always induced within them.

But little Nkima was only a monkey. What he wanted, he wanted immediately, not being endowed with that mental poise which results in patience, and so he swung by his tail from an overhanging branch and scolded at the top of his voice in an effort to attract the attention of the great apes below.

"To-yat! Ga-yat! Zutho!" he cried. "Tarzan is in danger! Come with Nkima and save Tarzan!"

A great bull stopped in the midst of the dancing and looked up. "Go away, Manu," he growled. "Go away or we kill!" But little Nkima thought that they could not catch him and so he continued to swing from the branch and yell and scream at them until finally To-yat sent a young ape, who was not too heavy, to clamber into the upper branches of the tree, to catch little Nkima and kill him.

Here was an emergency which Nkima had not foreseen. Like many people, he had believed that every one would be interested in what interested him, and when he had first heard the booming of

"Look, Wamala," said Zora. "Who is that?" At the edge of camp a beautiful woman stood regarding them intently.

the drums of the Dum-Dum he thought that the moment the apes learned of Tarzan's peril they would set out upon the trail to Opar.

Now, however, he knew differently and as the real menace of his mistake became painfully apparent with the leaping of a young ape into the tree below him, little Nkima emitted a loud shriek of terror and fled through the night; nor did he pause until, panting and exhausted, he had put a good mile between himself and the tribe of To-yat.

WHEN La of Opar awoke in the tent of Zora Drinov she looked about her, taking in the unfamiliar objects that surrounded her. Presently her gaze rested upon the face of her sleeping hostess.

These, indeed, she thought, must be the people of Tarzan, for had they not treated her with kindness and courtesy? They had offered her no harm and had fed her and given her shelter. A new thought crossed her mind now and her brows contracted, as did the pupils of her eyes into which there came a sudden, savage light. Perhaps this woman was Tarzan's mate! La of Opar grasped the hilt of Darus' knife where it lay ready beside her.

But then, as suddenly as it had come, the mood passed, for in her heart she knew that she could not return evil for good, nor could she harm one whom Tarzan loved; and so when Zora opened her eyes La greeted her with a smile.

If the European girl was a cause for astonishment to La, she herself filled the other with profoundest wonder and mystification. Her scant, yet rich and gorgeous apparel harked back to an ancient age and the gleaming whiteness of her skin seemed as much out of place in the heart of an African jungle as did her trappings in the twentieth century. Here was a mystery that nothing in the past experience of Zora Drinov could assist in solving. How she wished that they could converse, but all she could do was to smile back at the beautiful creature regarding her so intently.

La, accustomed as she had been to being waited upon all her life by the lesser priestesses of Opar, was surprised by the facility with which Zora Drinov attended to her own needs as she rose to bathe and dress, the only service she received being in the form of a pail of hot water which Wamala fetched and poured into her folding tub. Yet though La had never before been expected to lift a hand in the making of her toilet, she was far from helpless, and perhaps she found pleasure in the new experience of doing for herself.

Unlike the customs of the men of Opar, those of its women required scrupulous bodily cleanliness and in the past much of La's time had been devoted to her toilet, to the care of her nails and her teeth and her hair and to the massaging of her body with aromatic unguents—customs handed down from a cultured civilization of antiquity, to take on in ruined Opar the significance of religious rites.

By the time the two girls were ready for breakfast, Wamala was prepared to serve it. As they sat outside the tent beneath the shade of a tree, eating the coarse fare of the camp, Zora noted unwonted activity about the byût of the Aarabs, but she gave the matter little thought as they had upon other occasions moved their tents from one part of the camp to another.

Breakfast over, Zora took down her rifle, wiped out the bore and oiled the breech-mechanism, for today she was going out after fresh meat, the Aarabs having refused to hunt. La watched her with evident interest and later saw her depart with Wamala and two of the black porters, but she did not attempt to accompany her, since she had received no sign to do so.

Ibn Dammuk was the son of a sheik of the same tribe as Abu Batu and upon this expedition he was the latter's right-hand man. With the fold of his thôb drawn across the lower part of his face, leaving only his eyes exposed, he had been watching the two girls from a distance. He saw Zora Drinov quit the camp with a gun-bearer and two porters and knew that she had gone to hunt.

For some time after she had departed he sat in silence with two companions. Then he arose and sauntered across the camp toward La of Opar, where she sat buried in reverie in a camp chair before Zora's tent. As the three men approached La eyed them with level gaze, her natural suspicion of strangers aroused in her breast. As they came closer and their features became distinct, she felt a sudden distrust of them. They were crafty, malign-looking men—not at all like Tarzan—and instinctively she distrusted them.

They halted before her and Ibn Dammuk, the son of a sheik, addressed her.

La eyed him haughtily. She did not understand him and she did not wish to, for the message that she read in his eyes disgusted her. She shook her head to indicate that she did not understand and turned away to indicate that the interview was terminated. Ibn Dammuk stepped closer and laid a hand familiarly upon her naked shoulder.

Her eyes flaming with anger, La leaped to her feet, one hand moving swiftly to the hilt of her dagger. Ibn Dammuk stepped back, but one of his men attempted to seize her. Misguided fool! Like a tigress La was upon him, and before his friends could intervene the sharp blade of the knife of Darus, the priest of the Flaming God, had sunk thrice into his breast—and with a gasping scream he had slumped to the ground dead.

With flaming eyes and bloody knife, the high

priestess of Opar stood above her kill, while Abu Batu and the other Aarabs, attracted by the death-cry of the stricken man, ran hurriedly toward the little group.

"Stand back!" cried La. "Lay no profaning hand upon the person of the high priestess of the Flaming God!"

They did not understand her words, but they understood her flashing eyes and her dripping blade. Jabbering volubly, they gathered around her, but at a safe distance.

"What means this, Ibn Dammuk?" demanded Abu Batu.

"Dogman did but touch her and she flew at him like *el adrea*. lord of the broad head."

"A lioness she may be," said Abu Batu, "but she must not be harmed."

"Wullah!" exclaimed Ibn Dammuk. "But she must be tamed."

"Her taming we may leave to him who will pay many pieces of gold for her," replied the Sheik. "It is necessary only for us to cage her. Surround her, my children, and take the knife from her. Make her wrists secure behind her back, and by the time the other returns we shall have struck camp and be ready to depart."

A dozen brawny men leaped upon La simultaneously. "Do not harm her! Do not harm her!" screamed Abu Batu, as, fighting like a lioness indeed, La sought to defend herself. Slashing right and left with her dagger, she drew blood more than once before they overpowered her, nor did they accomplish it before another Aarab fell with a pierced heart; but at length they succeeded in wrenching the blade from her and securing her wrists.

Leaving two warriors to guard her, Abu Batu turned his attention to gathering up the few black servants that remained in camp. These he forced to prepare loads of such of the camp equipment and provisions as he required, and while this work was going on under Ibn Dammuk's supervision, the Sheik ransacked the tents of the Europeans, giving special attention to those of Zora Drinov and Zveri, where he expected to find the gold that the leader of the expedition was reputed to have in large quantities; nor was he entirely disappointed since he found in Zora's tent a box containing a considerable amount of money, though by no means the great quantity that he had expected, a fact which was due to the foresight of Zveri, who had personally buried the bulk of his funds beneath the floor of his tent. . . .

Zora met with unexpected success in her hunting, for within a little more than an hour of her departure from camp she had come upon antelope, and two quick shots had dropped as many members of the herd. She waited while the porters skinned and dressed them, and then returned leisurely toward camp. Her mind was occupied to some extent with the disquieting attitude of the Aarabs, but she was not at all prepared for the reception that she met when she approached the camp about noon.

She was walking in advance, immediately followed by Wamala, who was carrying both of her rifles, while behind them were the porters, staggering under their heavy loads, when, just as she was about to enter the clearing, Aarabs leaped from the underbrush on either side of the trail. Two of them seized Wamala and wrenched the rifles from his grasp, while others laid heavy hands upon Zora. She tried to free herself from them and draw her revolver, but the attack had taken her so by surprise that before she could accomplish anything in defense, she was overpowered, her hands drawn behind her and bound at her back.

"What is the meaning of this?" she demanded. "Where is Abu Batu, the Sheik?"

The men laughed at her. "You shall see him presently," said one. "He has another guest whom he is entertaining, so he could not come to meet you,"—at which they all laughed again.

As she stepped into the clearing where she could obtain an unobstructed view of the camp, she was

"Stand back!" cried La. "Lay no profaning hand upon the person of the high priestess of the Flaming God!"

astounded by what she saw. Every tent had been struck. The Aarabs were leaning on their rifles ready to march, each of them burdened with a small pack, while the few black men who had been left in camp, were lined up before heavy loads. All the balance of the paraphernalia of the camp, which Abu Batu had not men enough to transport, was heaped in a pile in the center of the clearing, and even as she looked she saw men setting torches to it.

As she was led across the clearing toward the waiting Aarabs, she saw her erstwhile guest between two warriors, with wrists confined by thongs even as Zora's own. Near her, scowling malevolently, was Abu Batu.

"Why have you done this thing, Abu Batu?" demanded Zora.

"Allah was wroth that we should betray our land to the Nasrâny," said the Sheik. "We have seen the light and we are going back to our own people."

"What do you intend to do with this woman and with me?" asked Zora.

"We shall take you with us for a little way," replied Abu Batu. "I know a kind man who is very rich, who will give you both a good home."

"You mean that you are going to sell us to some black sultan?" demanded the girl.

The Sheik shrugged. "I would not put it that way," he said. "Rather let us say that I am making a present to a great and good friend and saving you and this other woman from certain death in the jungle should we depart without you."

"Abu Batu, you are a hypocrite and a traitor," said Zora, her voice vibrant with contempt.

"The Nasrâny like to call names," said the Sheik with a sneer. "Perhaps if the pig Zveri had not called us names this would not have happened."

"So this is your revenge," asked Zora, "because he reproached you for your cowardice at Opar?"

"Enough!" snapped Abu Batu. "Come, my children, let us be gone."

As the flames licked at the edges of the great pile of provisions and equipment that the Aarabs were forced to leave behind, the deserters started upon their march westward.

The girls marched near the head of the column, the feet of the Aarabs and the carriers behind them totally obliterating their spoor from the motley record of the trail. They might have found some comfort in their straits had they been able to converse with one another, but La could understand no one and Zora found no pleasure in speaking to the Aarabs, while Wamala and the other blacks were so far toward the rear of the column that she could not have communicated with them.

To pass the time away, Zora conceived the idea of teaching her companion in misery some European language and because in the original party there had been more who were familiar with English than with any other tongue, she selected that language for her experiment.

She began by pointing to herself and saying "woman" and then to La and repeating the same word; after which she pointed to several of the Aarabs in succession and said "man" in each instance.

It was evident that La understood her purpose immediately, for she entered into the spirit of it with eagerness and alacrity, repeating the two words again and again, each time indicating either a man or a woman.

Next the European girl again pointed to herself and said "Zora." For a moment La was perplexed; then she smiled and nodded.

"Zora," she said, pointing to her companion and then, swiftly, she touched her own breast with a slender forefinger and said, "La."

And this was the beginning. Each hour La learned new words, all nouns at first, that described each familiar object that appeared oftenest to their view. She learned with remarkable celerity, evidencing an alert and intelligent mind and a retentive memory.

Her pronunciation was not always perfect for she had a decidedly foreign accent that was like nothing Zora Drinov ever had heard before, and so altogether captivating that the teacher never tired of hearing her pupil recite.

As the march progressed Zora realized that there was little likelihood that they would be mistreated by their captors, it being evident to her that the Sheik was impressed with the belief that the better the condition in which they could be presented to their prospective purchaser the more handsome the return that Abu Batu might hope to receive.

Their route lay to the northwest through a section of the Galla country of Abyssinia and from scraps of conversation Zora overheard she learned that Abu Batu and his followers were apprehensive of danger during this portion of the journey.

And well they may have been apprehensive since for ages the Aarabs have conducted raids in Galla

With his prey struggling futilely in his grasp,
the ape-man disappeared into the jungle.

territory for the purpose of capturing slaves, and
among the negroes with them was a Galla slave that
Abu Batu had brought with him from his desert
home.

After the first day the prisoners had been allowed the freedom of their hands, but always Aarab guards surrounded them, though there seemed little likelihood that an unarmed girl would take the risk of escaping into the jungle where she would be surrounded by the dangers of wild beasts or almost certain starvation.

However, could Abu Batu have read their thoughts he might have been astonished to learn that in the mind of each was a determination to escape to any fate rather than to march docilely on to an end that the European girl was fully conscious of and which La of Opar unquestionably surmised in part.

La's education was progressing nicely by the time the party neared the border of the Galla country; but in the meantime both girls had become aware of a new menace threatening La.

Ibn Dammuk marched often beside her and in his eyes, when he looked at her, was a message that needed no words to convey. But when Abu Batu was near, Ibn Dammuk ignored the fair prisoner and this caused Zora the most apprehension, for it convinced her that the wily Ibn was but biding his time until he might find conditions favorable to the carrying out of some scheme that he already had decided upon. Nor did Zora harbor any doubts as to the general purpose of his plan.

At the edge of the Galla country they were halted by a river in flood. They could not go north into Abyssinia proper and they dared not go south where they might naturally have expected pursuit to follow. So perforce they were compelled to wait impatiently, where they were.

And while they waited Ibn Dammuk struck.

CHAPTER IX

IN THE DEATH-CELL OF OPAR

ONCE again Peter Zveri stood before the walls of Opar and once again the courage of his black soldiers was dissipated by the weird cries of the inmates the city of mystery. The ten warriors, who had not been to Opar before and who had volunteered to enter the city, halted, trembling, as the first of the blood-curdling screams rose, shrill and piercing, from the forbidding ruins.

Miguel Romero once more led the invaders and directly behind him was Wayne Colt. According to the plan the blacks were to have followed closely behind these two, with the balance of the whites bringing up the rear where they might rally and encourage the negroes, or if necessary, force them on at the points of their pistols. But the blacks would not even enter the opening of the outer wall, so demoralized were they by the uncanny warning screams which their superstitious minds attributed to malignant demons against which there could be no defense and whose animosity meant almost certain death for those who disregarded their wishes.

"In with you, you dirty cowards!" cried Zveri, menacing the blacks with his revolver.

One of the warriors raised his rifle threateningly. "Put away your weapon, white man," he said. "We will fight men, but we will not fight the spirits of the dead."

"Lay off, Peter," said Dorsky. "You will have the whole bunch on us in a minute and we shall all be killed. Every black in the outfit is in sympathy with these men."

Zveri lowered his pistol and commenced to plead with the warriors, promising them rewards that amounted to riches to them if they would accompany the whites into the city. But the volunteers were obdurate—nothing could induce them to venture into Opar.

Seeing failure once again imminent and with a mind already obsessed by the belief that the treasures of Opar would make him fabulously wealthy and insure the success of his secret scheme of empire, Zveri determined to follow Romero and Colt with the balance of his aides, which consisted only of Dorsky, Ivitch and the Filipino boy.

"Come on," he said, "we will have to make a try at it alone, if these yellow dogs won't help us."

By the time the four men had passed through the outer wall, Romero and Colt were already out of sight beyond the inner wall. Once again the warning scream broke menacingly upon the brooding silence of the ruined city.

"God!" ejaculated Ivitch. "What do you suppose it

"Put down the she," Tarzan demanded. "No!" bellowed To-yat. "She is mine!"

could be?"

"Shut up!" exclaimed Zveri irritably. "Stop thinking about it, or you'll go yellow like those damn' blacks."

SLOWLY they crossed the court toward the inner wall, nor was there much enthusiasm manifest among them other than for an evident desire in the breast of each to permit one of the others the glory of leading the advance. Tony had reached the opening when a bedlam of noise from the opposite side of the wall burst upon their ears—a hideous chorus of war-cries, mingled with the sound of rushing feet. There was a shot, and then another and another.

Tony turned to see if his companions were following him. They had halted and were listening with blanched faces.

Then Ivitch turned. "To hell with the gold!" he said, and started back toward the outer wall at a run.

"Come back, you lousy cur!" cried Zveri, and took after him with Dorsky at his heels. Tony hesitated for a moment and then scurried in pursuit, nor did any of them halt until they were beyond the outer wall. There Zveri overtook Ivitch and seized him by the shoulder.

"I ought to kill you!" he cried in a trembling voice.

"You were as glad to get out of there as I was," growled Ivitch. "What was the sense of going in there? We would only have been killed like Colt and Romero. There were too many of them. Didn't you hear them?"

"I think Ivitch is right," said Dorsky. "It's all right to be brave, but we have got to remember the cause—if we are killed everything is lost."

"But the gold!" exclaimed Zveri. "Think of the gold!"

"Gold is no good to dead men," Dorsky reminded

him curtly.

"How about our comrades?" asked Tony. "Are we to leave them to be killed?"

"To hell with the Mexican," said Zveri; "and as for the American I think his funds will still be available as long as we can keep the news of his death from getting back to the Coast."

"You are not even going to try to rescue them?" asked Tony.

"I cannot do it alone," said Zveri.

"I will go with you," said Tony.

"Little good two of us can accomplish," mumbled Zveri. Then, in one of his sudden rages, he advanced menacingly upon the Filipino.

"Who do you think you are, anyway?" he demanded. "I am in command here—remember that! When I want your advice I'll ask for it!"

WHEN Romero and Colt had passed through the inner wall, that part of the temple interior which they could see appeared deserted and yet they were conscious of movement in the darker recesses and the apertures of the ruined galleries that looked down into the courtway.

Colt glanced back. "Shall we wait for the others?" he asked.

Romero shrugged. "I think we are going to have this glory all to ourselves, comrade," he said with a grin.

Colt smiled back at him. "Then let's get on with the business," he said. "I don't see anything very terrifying yet."

"There was something in there though," said

Romero. "I've seen things moving."

"So have I," said Colt.

With their rifles ready, they advanced boldly into the temple; but they had not gone far when, from shadowy archways and from numerous gloomy doorways there rushed a horde of horrid men and the silence of the ancient city was shattered by hideous war-cries.

Colt was in advance and now he kept on moving forward, firing a shot above the heads of the grotesque warrior priests of Opar. Romero saw a number of the enemy running along the side of the great room which they had entered, with the evident intention of cutting off their retreat. He swung about and fired, but not over their heads. Realizing the gravity of their position, he shot to kill, and now Colt did the same, with the result that the screams of a couple of wounded men mingled now with the war-cries of their fellows.

Romero was forced to drop back a few steps to prevent the Oparians from surrounding him. He shot rapidly now and succeeded in checking the advance around their flank. A quick glance at Colt showed him standing his ground and at the same instant he saw a hurled club strike the American on the head. The man dropped like a log and instantly his body was covered by the terrible little men of Opar.

Miguel Romero realized that his companion was lost and even if not now already dead, he could accomplish nothing single-handed, toward Colt's rescue. Indeed, if he escaped with his own life he would be fortunate; and so, keeping up a steady fire, he fell back toward the aperture in the inner wall.

Having captured one of the invaders, seeing the other falling back and hesitant to further risk the devastating fire of the terrifying weapon in the hand of their single antagonist, the Oparians hesitated.

Meanwhile Romero passed through the inner wall, turned and ran swiftly to the outer and a moment later had joined his companions upon the plain.

"Where is Colt?" demanded Zveri.

"They knocked him out with a club and captured him," said Romero. "He is probably dead by this time."

"And you deserted him?" asked Zveri.

The Mexican turned upon his chief in fury. "You ask me that?" he demanded. "You turned pale and ran even before you saw the enemy! If you fellows had backed us up, Colt might not have been lost— but to let us go in there alone— The two of us didn't have a Chinaman's chance with that bunch of wild men. And you accuse me of cowardice?"

"I didn't do anything of the kind," said Zveri sullenly. "I never said you were a coward."

"You meant to imply it, though," snapped Romero; "but let me tell you, Zveri, that you can't get away with that with me or anyone else who has been to Opar with you."

From beyond the walls rose a savage cry of victory and while it still rumbled through the tarnished halls of Opar, Zveri turned dejectedly away from the city.

"It's no use," he said. "I can't capture Opar alone. We are returning to camp."

THE little priests, swarming over Colt, stripped him of his weapons and secured his hands behind his back. He was still unconscious and so they lifted him to the shoulder of one of their fellows and bore him away into the interior of the temple.

When Colt regained consciousness he found himself lying on the floor of a large chamber. It was the throne-room of the temple of Opar, where he had been fetched that Oah the high priestess might see the prisoner.

Perceiving that their captive had regained consciousness his guards jerked him roughly to his feet and pushed him forward toward the foot of the dais upon which stood Oah's throne.

The effect of the picture bursting suddenly upon him imparted to Colt the definite impression that he was the victim of an hallucination or a dream. The outer chamber of the ruin, in which he had fallen, had given no suggestion of the size and magnificence of this great chamber, the grandeur of which was scarcely dimmed by the ruin of ages.

He saw before him, upon an ornate throne, a young woman of exceptional physical beauty, surrounded by the semi-barbaric grandeur of an ancient civilization. Grotesque, hairy men and beautiful maidens formed her entourage. Her eyes, resting upon him, were cold and cruel—her mien haughty and contemptuous. A squat warrior, more ape-like in his conformation than human, was addressing her in a language unfamiliar to the American.

When he had finished, the girl rose from the throne and drawing a long knife from her girdle raised it high above her head as she spoke rapidly and almost fiercely, her eyes fixed upon the prisoner.

From among a group of priestesses at the right of Oah's throne, a girl, just come into womanhood, regarded the prisoner through half-closed eyes and beneath the golden plates that confined her smooth white breasts, the heart of Nao palpitated to the thoughts that contemplation of this strange warrior engendered within her.

When Oah had finished speaking, Colt was led away, quite ignorant of the fact that he had been listening to the sentence of death imposed upon him by the high priestess of the Flaming God. His guards conducted him to a cell just within the entrance of a tunnel leading from the sacrificial court to the pits beneath the city and because it was not entirely below ground, fresh air and light had access to it through a window and the grated bars of its doorway. Here the escort left him, after removing the bonds from his wrists.

Through the small window in his cell Wayne Colt looked out upon the inner court of the Temple of the Sun of Opar. He saw the surrounding galleries rising tier upon tier to the summit of a lofty wall. He saw the stone altar standing in the center of the court, and the brown stains upon it and upon the pavement at its foot told him what the unintelligible words of Oah had been unable to convey. For an instant he felt his heart sink within his breast and a shudder passed through his frame as he contemplated the inescapability of the fate which confronted him. There could be no mistaking the purpose of that altar when viewed in connection with the grinning skulls of former human sacrifices which stared through eyeless sockets upon him from their niches in the surrounding walls.

Fascinated by the horror of his situation, he stood staring at the altar and skulls. Presently he gained control of himself and shook the terror from him, yet the hopelessness of his situation continued to depress him. His thoughts turned to his companion. He wondered what Romero's fate had been. There, indeed, had been a brave and gallant comrade; in fact, the only member of the party who had impressed Colt favorably, or in whose society he had found pleasure. The others had seemed either ignorant fanatics or avaricious opportunists; but the manner and speech of the Mexican had stamped him as a light-hearted soldier of fortune, who might gayly offer his life in any cause which momentarily seized his fancy with an eye more singly for excitement and adventure than for any serious purpose. He did not know, of course, that Zveri and the others had deserted him, but he was confident that Romero had not before his cause had become utterly hopeless, or until the Mexican himself had been killed or captured.

IN lonely contemplation of his predicament, Colt spent the balance of the long afternoon. Darkness fell and still there came no sign from his captors. He wondered if they intended leaving him there without food or water, or if, perchance, the ceremony that was to see him offered in sacrifice upon that grim, brown-stained altar was scheduled to commence so soon that they felt it unnecessary to minister to his physical needs.

He had lain down upon the hard cement-like surface of the cell floor and was trying to find momentary relief in sleep when his attention was attracted by the shadow of a sound coming from the courtyard where the altar stood. As he listened he was positive that some one was approaching and rising quietly he went to the window and looked out. In the shadowy darkness of the night, relieved only by the faint light of distant stars, he saw something moving across the courtyard toward his cell, but whether man or beast he could not distinguish—and then, from somewhere high up among the lofty ruins, there pealed out upon the silent night the long-drawn scream, which seemed now to the American as much a part of the mysterious city of Opar as the crumbling ruins themselves.

IT was a sullen and discouraged party that made its way back to the camp at the edge of the forest below the barrier cliffs of Opar, and when they arrived late in the evening it was to find only still further disorganization and discouragement.

No time was lost in narrating to the members of the returning expedition the story of the sentry who had been carried off into the jungle at night by a demon, from whom the man had managed to escape before being devoured. Still fresh in their minds was the uncanny affair of the death of Raghunath Jafar. Nor were the nerves of those who had been before the walls of Opar inclined to be at all steadied by that experience; so it was a nervous company which bivouacked that night beneath the dark trees at the edge of the gloomy forest and, with sighs of relief, witnessed the coming of the next dawn.

Later, after they had taken up the march toward the base camp, the spirit of the blacks gradually returned to normal and presently the tension under which they had been laboring for days was relieved by song and laughter.

But the whites were gloomy and sullen. Zveri and Romero did not speak to one another, while Ivitch, like all weak characters, nursed a grievance against everyone because of his own display of cowardice during the fiasco at Opar.

From the interior of a hollow tree in which he had been hiding, little Nkima saw the column pass and after it was safely by he emerged from his retreat and dancing up and down upon a limb of the tree, shouted dire threats after them and called them many names. . . .

Tarzan of the Apes lay stretched upon the back of Tantor the elephant, his elbows upon the broad head, his chin resting in his cupped hand. Futile had been his search for the spoor of La of Opar. Had the earth opened and swallowed her she could not more effectually have disappeared.

Today Tarzan had come upon Tantor, and as had been his custom from childhood, he had tarried for that silent communion with the sagacious old patriarch of the forest which seemed always to impart to the man something of the beast's great strength of character and poise. There was an atmosphere of restful stability about Tantor which filled the ape-man with a peace and tranquillity that he found restful, while Tantor, upon his part, welcomed the companionship of the Lord of the Jungle, whom alone of all two-legged creatures he viewed with friendship and affection.

The beasts of the jungle acknowledge no master, least of all the cruel tyrant that drives civilized man throughout his headlong race from the cradle to the grave—Time, the master of countless millions of slaves. Time, the measurable aspect of duration, was measureless to Tarzan and Tantor.

Of all the vast resources Nature had placed at their disposal, she had been most profligate with time, since she had awarded to each all that he could use during his lifetime, no matter how extravagant of it he might be. So great was the supply of it that it could not be wasted, since there was always more, even up to the moment of death, after which it ceased, with all things, to be essential to the individual. Tantor and Tarzan, therefore, were wasting no time as they communed together in silent meditation. But though time and space go on forever, whether in curves or straight lines, all other things must end—and so it was that the quiet and the peace the two friends were enjoying was suddenly shattered by the excited screams of a diminutive monkey in the foliage of a great tree above them.

It was Nkima. He had found his Tarzan, and his relief and joy aroused the jungle to the limit of his small shrill voice. Lazily Tarzan rolled over and looked up at the jabbering simian above him and then Nkima, satisfied now beyond peradventure of a doubt that this was indeed his master, launched himself downward to alight upon the bronzed body of the ape-man. Slender, hairy little arms went around Tarzan's neck as Nkima snuggled close to this haven of refuge which imparted to him those brief moments in his life when he might enjoy the raptures of a temporary superiority complex. Upon Tarzan's shoulder he felt almost fearless, and could with impunity insult the entire world.

"Where have you been, Nkima?" asked Tarzan.

"Looking for Tarzan," replied the monkey.

"What have you seen since I left you at the walls of Opar?" demanded the ape-man.

"I have seen many things. I have seen the great Mangani dancing in the moonlight around the dead body of Sheeta. I have seen the enemies of Tarzan marching through the forest. I have seen Histah, gorging himself on the carcass of Bara."

"Have you seen a Tarmangani she?" demanded Tarzan.

"No," replied Nkima. "There were no shes among the Gomangani and Tarmangani enemies of Tarzan. Only bulls, and they marched back toward the place where Nkima first saw them."

"When was this?" asked Tarzan.

"Kudu had climbed into the heavens but a short distance out of the darkness when Nkima saw the enemies of Tarzan marching back to the place where he first saw them."

"Perhaps we had better see what they are up to," said the ape-man. He slapped Tantor affectionately with his open palm in farewell, leaped to his feet and swung nimbly into the overhanging branches of a tree, while far away Zveri and his party plodded through the jungle toward their base camp.

Tarzan of the Apes follows no earth-bound trails where the density of the forest offers him the freedom of leafy highways, and thus he moves from point to point with a speed that has often been disconcerting to his enemies.

Now he moved in an almost direct line so that he overtook the expedition as it made camp for the night. As he watched them from behind a leafy screen of high-flung foliage, he noticed, though with no surprise, that they were not burdened with any treasure from Opar.

AS the success and happiness of jungle-dwellers—even life itself—is largely dependent upon their powers of observation, Tarzan had developed his to a high degree of perfection. At his first encounter with this party he had made himself familiar with the face, physique and carriage of each of its principals and of many of its humble warriors and porters—with the result that he was now immediately aware that Colt was no longer with the expedition. Experience permitted Tarzan to draw a fairly accurate picture of what had happened at Opar and the probable fate of the missing member of the expedition.

Years ago he had seen his own courageous Waziri turn and flee upon the occasion of their first experience of the weird warning screams from the ruined city and he could easily guess that Colt, attempting to lead the invaders into the city, had been deserted, and had found either death or capture within the gloomy interior. This, however, did not greatly concern Tarzan. While he had been rather drawn toward Colt by that tenuous and invisible power known as personality, he still considered him as an enemy, and if Colt were either dead or captured Tarzan's cause was advanced by just that much.

Tarzan noticed the constrained and sullen manner of the remainder of the whites and guessed that all was not well among them.

From Tarzan's shoulder Nkima looked down upon the camp, but he kept silent, as Tarzan had instructed him to do. Nkima saw many things that he should have liked to possess and particularly he coveted a red calico shirt worn by one of the askari. This, he thought, was very grand indeed, being set off as it was by the unrelieved nakedness of the majority of the blacks. Nkima wished that his master would descend and slay them all, but particularly the man with the red shirt—for at heart Nkima was bloodthirsty, which made it fortunate for the peace of the jungle that he had not been born a gorilla. But Tarzan's mind was not set upon carnage. He had other means for thwarting the activities of these strangers. During the day he had made a kill and now he withdrew to a safe distance from the camp and satisfied his hunger, while Nkima searched for birds' eggs, fruit and insects.

And so night fell and when it had enveloped the jungle in impenetrable darkness, relieved only by the beast-fires of the camp, Tarzan returned to a tree where he could overlook the activities of the bivouacked expedition. He watched them in silence for a long time; then suddenly he raised his voice in a long scream that mimicked perfectly the hideous warning cry of Opar's defenders.

The effect upon the camp was instantaneous. Conversation, singing and laughter ceased. For a moment the men sat as in a paralysis of terror. Then, seizing their weapons, they came closer to the fire.

With the shadow of a smile upon his lips, Tarzan slipped away into the jungle.

CHAPTER X

THE LOVE OF A PRIESTESS

IBN DAMMUK had bided his time and now, in the camp by the swollen river at the edge of the Galla country, he at last found the opportunity he had so long awaited. The surveillance over the two prisoners had somewhat relaxed, due largely to the belief entertained by Abu Batu that the women would not dare to invite the perils of the jungle by attempting to escape from captors who were, at the same time, their protectors from even greater dangers. He had, however, reckoned without just estimation of the courage and resourcefulness of his two captives who, had he but known it, were constantly awaiting the first opportunity for escape; and it was this fact as well that played into the hands of Ibn Dammuk.

With great cunning he enlisted the services of one of the blacks who had been forced to accompany them from the base camp and who was virtually a prisoner, and by promising him his liberty he easily gained the man's acquiescence in the plan that Ibn Dammuk had evolved.

A separate tent had been pitched for the two women and before it sat a single sentry, whose presence Abu Batu considered more than sufficient for the purpose, which was even more to protect the women from his own followers than to prevent a remotely possible attempt at escape.

This night, which Ibn Dammuk had chosen for his villainy, was one for which he had been waiting, since it found upon duty before the tent of the captives one of his own men, a member of his tribe, who was bound by laws of hereditary loyalty to serve and obey him. In the forest just beyond the camp, Ibn Dammuk waited, with two more of his own tribesmen, four slaves that they had brought from the desert and the black porter who was to win his liberty by this night's work.

The interior of the tent that had been pitched for Zora and La was illuminated by a paper lantern, in which a candle burned dimly, and in this subdued light the two sat talking in La's newly acquired English, which was at best most fragmentary and broken. However, it was far better than no means of communication and gave the two girls the only pleasure that they enjoyed. Perhaps it was not a remarkable coincidence that this night they were speaking of escape and planning to cut a hole in the back of their tent through which they might sneak away into the jungle after the camp had settled down for the night and their sentry should be dozing at his post, for frequently much of their conversation was upon the topic of escape. While they conversed, the sentry before their tent rose and strolled away and a moment later they heard a scratching upon the back of the tent. Their conversation ceased and they sat with eyes riveted upon the point where the fabric of the tent moved to the pressure of the scratching without.

Presently a voice spoke in a low whisper. "Memsahib Drinov!"

"Who is it? What do you want?" asked Zora in a low voice.

"I have found a way to escape. I can help you if you wish."

"Who are you?" demanded Zora.

"I am Bukula"—and Zora at once recognized the name as that of one of the blacks that Abu Batu had forced to accompany him from the base camp.

"Put out your lantern," whispered Bukula. "The sentry has gone away. I will come in and tell you my plans."

Zora arose and blew out the candle and a moment later the two captives saw Bukula crawling into the interior of the tent. "Listen, Memsahib," he said, "the boys that Abu Batu stole from Bwana Zveri are running away tonight. We are going back to the safari. We will take you two with us, if you want to come."

"Yes," said Zora, "we will come."

"That is good," said Bukula. "And now listen well to what I tell you. The sentry will not come back, but we cannot all go out at once. First I will take this other Memsahib with me out into the jungle where the boys are waiting; then I will return for you. You can make talk to her. Tell her to follow me and to make no noise."

Zora turned to La. "Follow Bukula," she said. "We are going tonight. I will come after you."

"I understand," replied La.

"It is agreed, Bukula," said Zora. "She understands."

Bukula stepped to the entrance to the tent and looked quickly about the camp. "Come!" he said; and followed by La, he disappeared quickly from Zora's view.

The European girl fully realized the risk that they ran of going into the jungle alone with these half-savage blacks, yet she trusted them more implicitly than she did the Aarabs and, too, she felt that she and La together might circumvent any treachery upon the part of any of the negroes, the majority of whom she knew would be loyal and faithful. Waiting in the silence and loneliness of the darkened tent, it seemed to Zora that it took Bukula an unnecessarily long time to return for her; and when minute after minute dragged slowly past until she felt that she had waited for hours and there was no sign either of the black or the sentry, her fears were aroused in earnest. Presently she determined not to wait any longer for Bukula, but to go out into the jungle in search of the escaping party. She thought that perhaps Bukula had been unable to return without risking detection and that they were all waiting just beyond the camp for a favorable opportunity to return to her. As she arose to put her decision into action, she heard footsteps approaching the tent and thinking that they were Bukula's she waited, but instead she saw the flapping robe and the long-barreled

musket of an Aarab silhouetted against the lesser
darkness of the exterior as the man stuck his head
inside the tent. "Where is Hajellan?" he demanded,
giving the name of the departed sentry.

"How should we know?" retorted Zora in a sleepy
voice. "Why do you awaken us thus in the middle of
the night?"

The fellow grumbled something in reply and
then, turning, called aloud across the camp, an-
nouncing to all who might hear that Hajellan was
missing and inquiring if any had seen him. Other
warriors strolled over then and there was a great
deal of speculation as to what had become of Hajellan. The name of the missing man was called aloud
many times, but there was no response, and finally
the Sheik came and questioned every one. "The
women are in the tent yet?" he demanded of the
new sentry.

"Yes," replied the man. "I have talked with them."

"It is strange," said Abu Batu and then, "Ibn Dammuk!" he cried. "Where art thou, Ibn? Hajellan was
one of thy men." There was no answer. "Where is
Ibn Dammuk?"

"He is not here," said a man standing near the
Sheik.

"Nor are Fodil and Dareyem," said another.

"Search the camp and see who is missing," demanded Abu Batu, and when the search had been
made they found that Ibn Dammuk, Hajellan, Fodil
and Dareyem were missing with five of the blacks.

"Ibn Dammuk has deserted us," said Abu Batu.
"Well, let it go. There will be fewer with whom to
share the reward we shall reap when we are paid for

the two women!" And thus reconciling himself to
the loss of four good fighting men, Abu Batu repaired to his tent and resumed his interrupted
slumber.

Weighed down by apprehension as to the fate of
La and disappointment occasioned by her own failure to escape, Zora spent an almost sleepless night;
yet fortunate for her peace of mind was it that she
did not know the truth. . . .

Bukula moved silently into the jungle, followed
by La, and when they had gone a short distance
from the camp the girl saw the dark forms of men
standing in a little group ahead of them.

The Aarabs, in their telltale thôbs, were hidden in
the underbrush, but their slaves had removed their
own white robes and, with Bukula, were standing
naked but for gee-strings, thus carrying conviction
to the mind of the girl that only black prisoners of
Abu Batu awaited her.

When she came among them she learned her
mistake, but too late to save herself—for she was
quickly seized by many hands and effectually
gagged before she could give the alarm. Then Ibn
Dammuk and his Aarab companions appeared and
silently the party moved on down the river through
the dark forest.

All night they fled, for Ibn Dammuk well guessed
what the wrath of Abu Batu would be when in the
morning he discovered the trick that had been
played upon him. When morning dawned they were
far away from camp, but still Ibn Dammuk pushed
on, after a brief halt for a hurried breakfast.

Long since had the gag been removed from La's

mouth and now Ibn Dammuk walked beside her, gloating upon his prize. He spoke to her, but La could not understand him. She only strode on in haughty disdain, biding her time against the moment when she might be revenged, and inwardly sorrowing over her separation from Zora, for whom a strange affection had been aroused in her savage breast.

Toward noon the party withdrew from the game trail which they had been following and made camp near the river. It was here that Ibn Dammuk made a fatal blunder.

Goaded to passion by close proximity to the beautiful woman for whom he had conceived a mad infatuation, the Aarab gave way to his desire to be alone with her. Leading her along a little trail that paralleled the river, he took her away out of sight of his companions and when they had gone perhaps a hundred yards from camp, he seized her in his arms and sought to kiss her.

With equal safety might Ibn Dammuk have embraced a lion. In the heat of his passion he forgot many things, among them the dagger that hung always at his side. But La of Opar did not forget. With the coming of daylight she had noticed that dagger and ever since she had coveted it; now, as the man pressed her close, her hand sought and found its hilt. For an instant she seemed to surrender. She let her body go limp in his arms, while her own, firm and beautifully rounded, crept about him, one to his right shoulder, the other beneath his left arm. But as yet she did not give him her lips; and as he struggled to possess them the hand upon his shoulder seized him suddenly by the throat. The long, tapered fingers that seemed so soft and white were suddenly claws of steel that closed upon his windpipe, and simultaneously the hand that had crept so softly beneath his left arm drove his own long dagger into his heart from beneath his shoulder-blade.

The single cry that he might have given was choked in his throat. For an instant the tall form of Ibn Dammuk stood rigidly erect; then it slumped forward and the girl let it slip to the earth. She spurned it once with her foot, then she removed from it the girdle and sheath for the dagger, wiped the bloody blade upon the man's thôb and hurried on up the little river trail until she found an open-ing in the underbrush that led away from the stream. On and on she went until exhaustion overtook her; then, with her remaining strength, she climbed into a tree in search of much-needed rest. . . .

In far-away Opar Wayne Colt watched the shadowy figure approach the corridor where his cell lay. He wondered if this was a messenger of death, coming to lead him to sacrifice. Nearer and nearer it came until presently it stopped before the bars of his cell door; then a soft voice spoke to him in a low whisper and in a tongue which he could not understand, and he knew that his visitor was a woman.

Prompted by curiosity, he came close to the bars. A small soft hand reached in and touched him, almost caressingly.

A full moon rising above the high walls that surround the sacrificial court suddenly flooded the mouth of the corridor and the entrance to Colt's cell in silvery light and in it the American saw the figure of a young girl pressed against the cold iron bars of the grating. She handed him food; when he took it she caressed his hand and drawing it to the bars pressed her lips against it.

Wayne Colt was nonplused. He could not know that Nao, the little priestess, had been the victim of love at first sight—that to her eyes, accustomed to the sight of males only in the form of the hairy grotesque priests of Opar, this stranger appeared a god indeed.

A slight noise attracted Nao's attention toward the court and, as she turned, the moonlight flooded her face and the American saw that she was very lovely. Then she turned back toward him, her dark eyes wells of adoration, her full, sensitive lips trembling with emotion as, still clinging to his hand, she spoke rapidly in low liquid tones.

She was trying to tell Colt that at noon of the second day he was to be offered in sacrifice to the Flaming God; that she did not wish him to die and if it were possible she would help him, but that she did not know how that would be possible.

Colt shook his head. "I cannot understand you, little one," he said, and Nao, though she could not interpret his words, sensed the futility of her own. Then, raising one of her hands from his, she made a great circle in a vertical plane from east to west with a slender index finger, indicating the path of the sun across the heavens, and then she started a second circle, which she stopped at zenith, indicating high noon of the second day. For an instant her raised hand poised dramatically aloft and then, the fingers closing as though around the hilt of an imaginary sacrificial knife, she plunged the invisible point deep into her bosom.

"Thus will Oah destroy you," she said, reaching through the bars and touching Colt over the heart.

The American thought that he understood the meaning of her pantomime, which he then repeated, plunging the imaginary blade into his own breast and looking questioningly at Nao.

In reply she nodded sadly and the tears welled to her eyes.

As plainly as though he had understood her words, Colt realized that here was a friend who would help him if she could and reaching through the bars, he drew the girl gently toward him and pressed his lips against her forehead. With a low sob Nao encircled his neck with her arms and pressed her face to his. Then as suddenly she released him and turning, hurried away on silent feet, to disappear in the gloomy shadows of an archway at one side of the court of sacrifice.

Colt ate the food that she had brought him and for a long time lay pondering the inexplicable forces which govern the acts of men. What train of circumstances leading down out of a mysterious past had produced this single human being in a city of enemies in whom all unsuspecting, there must always have existed a germ of potential friendship for him, an utter stranger and alien, of whose very existence she could not possibly have dreamed before this day? He tried to convince himself that the girl had been prompted to her act by pity for his plight, but he knew in his heart that a more powerful motive must have impelled her.

Colt had been attracted to many women but he had never loved, and he wondered if that was the way that love came and if some day it would seize him as it had seized this girl, and he wondered also if, had conditions been different, he might have been as strongly attracted to her. If not, then there seemed to be something wrong in the scheme of things. . . . And still puzzling over this riddle of the ages he fell asleep upon the hard floor of his cell.

WITH morning a hairy priest came and gave him food and water, and during the day others came and gazed at him, as though he were a wild beast in a menagerie. And so the long day dragged on and once again night came—his last night.

He tried to picture what the final ceremony would be like. It seemed almost incredible that in the Twentieth Century he was to be offered as a human sacrifice to some heathen deity, but the pantomime of the girl, and the concrete evidence of the bloody altar and the grinning skulls assured him that such must be the very fate awaiting him upon the morrow. He thought of his family and his friends at home. They would never know what had become of him. He weighed his sacrifice against the mission that he had undertaken and he had no regret, for he knew that it had not been in vain. Far away, already near the Coast, was the message he had dispatched by the runner. It would insure that he had not failed in his part for the sake of a great principle for which, if necessary, he was glad to lay down his life. He was glad that he had acted promptly and sent the message when he did—for now, upon the morrow, he could go to his death without vain regrets. But he did not wish to die, and during the day he made many plans to seize upon the slightest opportunity that might be presented to him to escape.

He wondered what had become of the girl and if she would come again now that it was dark. He wished that she would, for he craved the companionship of a friend during his last hours, but as the night wore on he gave up the hope and sought to forget the morrow in sleep. . . .

As Wayne Colt moved restlessly upon his hard couch Firg, a lesser priest of Opar, snored upon his pallet of straw in the small dark recess that was his bedchamber. Firg was the keeper of the keys and so impressed was he with the importance of his duties that he never would permit anyone even to touch the sacred emblems of his trust. Because it was well known that Firg would die in defense of them was probably the reason that they were intrusted to him. Not with justice could Firg have laid any claim to intellectuality, if he had known that such a thing existed. He was only an abysmal man and, like many men, far beneath the so-called brutes in most of his activities of mind. When he slept all his faculties were asleep—which is not true of wild beasts when they sleep.

Firg's cell was in one of the upper stories of the ruins that still remained intact. It was upon a corridor that encircled the main temple court—a corridor that was now in dense shadow, since the moon, touching it early in the night, had passed on; so the figure creeping stealthily toward the entrance to Firg's chamber would have been noticeable only to one who happened to be quite close. It moved silently but without hesitation, until it came to the entrance beyond which Firg lay. There it paused, listening, and when it heard Firg's noisy snoring, it entered quickly. Straight to the side of the sleeping man it moved and there it knelt, searching with one hand lightly over his body, while the other grasped a long sharp knife that hovered constantly above the hairy chest of the priest.

Presently it found what it wanted—a great ring, upon which were strung several enormous keys. A leather thong fastened the ring to Firg's girdle and with the keen blade of the dagger the nocturnal visitor sought to sever the thong. Firg stirred and instantly the creature at his side froze to immobility. Then the priest moved restlessly and commenced to snore again and once more the dagger sawed at the leather thong. It passed through the strand unexpectedly and touched the metal of the ring lightly, but just enough to make the keys jangle ever so slightly.

Instantly Firg was awake; but he did not rise. He was never to rise again—silently, swiftly, before the stupid creature could realize his danger, the keen blade of the dagger had pierced his heart.

Soundlessly Firg collapsed. His slayer hesitated a moment with poised dagger as though to make certain that the work had been well done. Then, wiping the telltale stains from the dagger's blade with the victim's loin-cloth, the figure arose and hurried from the chamber, carrying in one hand the great keys upon their golden ring.

Colt stirred uneasily in his sleep and then awakened with a start. In the waning moonlight he saw a figure beyond the grating of his cell. He heard a key turn in the massive lock. Could it be that they were coming for him? He rose to his feet, the urge of his last conscious thought strong upon him—escape. And then as the door swung open a soft voice spoke and he knew that the girl had returned.

She entered the cell and threw her arms about Colt's neck, drawing his lips down to hers. For a moment she clung to him; then she released him and, taking one of his hands in hers, urged him to follow her; nor was the American loath to leave the depressing interior of the death-cell.

On silent feet Nao led the way across the corner of the sacrificial court, through a dark archway into a gloomy corridor. Winding and twisting, keeping always in dark shadows, she led him along a circuitous route through the ruins until, after what seemed an eternity to Colt, the girl opened a low, strong, wooden door and led him into the great entrance-hall of the temple, through the mighty portal of which he could see the inner wall of the city.

Here Nao halted, and coming close to the man looked up into his eyes. Again her arms stole about his neck and again she pressed her lips to his. Her cheeks were wet with tears and her voice broke with little sobs that she tried to stifle as she poured her love into the ears of the man who could not understand. She had brought him here to offer him his freedom, but she could not let him go yet. She clung to him, caressing him and crooning to him.

FOR long minutes she held him there and Colt had

not the heart to tear himself away. At last she released him and pointed toward the opening in the inner wall.

"Go—taking the heart of Nao with you!" she said. "I shall never see you again, but at least I shall always have the memory of this hour to carry through life with me."

Wayne Colt stooped and kissed her hand, the slender, savage little hand that had but just now killed, that her lover might live—though of that Wayne knew nothing.

She pressed her dagger with its sheath upon him that he might not go out into the savage world unarmed; then he turned away from her and moved slowly toward the inner wall. At the entrance to the opening he paused and turned about. Dimly, in the moonlight, he saw the figure of the little priestess standing very erect in the shadows of the ancient ruins. He raised his hand and waved a final, silent farewell.

A great sadness depressed Colt as he passed through the inner wall and crossed the court to freedom, for he knew that he had left behind him a sad and hopeless heart in the bosom of one who must have risked death, perhaps, to save him—a perfect friend of whom he could but carry a vague memory of a half-seen lovely face, a friend whose name he did not know, the only token of whom he had carried away with him were the memory of hot kisses and a slender dagger.

And thus, as Wayne Colt walked across the moonlit plain of Opar, the joy of his escape was tempered by sadness as he recalled the figure of the forlorn little priestess standing in the shadows of the ruins.

CHAPTER XI

LOST IN THE JUNGLE

IT was some time after the uncanny scream had disturbed the camp of the conspirators before the men could settle down to rest again.

Zveri believed that they had been followed by a band of Oparian warriors, who might be contemplating a night attack, and so he placed a heavy guard about the camp; but his blacks were confident that that unearthly cry had broken from no human throat.

Depressed and dispirited, the men resumed their march the following morning. They made an early start and by dint of much driving arrived at the base camp just before dark. The sight that met their eyes there filled them with consternation. The camp had disappeared and in the center of the clearing where it had been pitched a pile of ashes suggested that disaster had overtaken the party which had been left behind.

This new disaster threw Zveri into a maniacal

rage, but there was no one present upon whom he might lay the blame, and so he was reduced to the expedient of tramping back and forth while he cursed his luck in loud tones and several languages.

From a tree Tarzan watched him. He too was at a loss to understand the nature of the disaster that seemed to have overtaken the camp during the absence of the main party, but he saw that it caused the leader intense anguish and the ape-man was pleased.

The blacks were confident that this was another manifestation of the anger of the malign spirit that had been haunting them and they were all for deserting this ill-starred white man, whose every move ended in failure or disaster.

Zveri's powers of leadership deserve full credit, since from the verge of almost certain mutiny he forced his men by means of both cajolery and threat to remain with him. He set them to building shelters for the entire party and immediatelyhe dispatched messengers to his various agents, urging them to forward necessary supplies immediately. He knew that certain things he needed already were on the way from the Coast—uniforms, rifles, ammunition. But now he particularly needed provisions and trade-goods.

To insure discipline, he kept the men working constantly, either in adding to the comforts of the camp, enlarging the clearing or hunting fresh meat.

And so the days passed and became weeks; meanwhile Tarzan watched in waiting. He was in no hurry, for hurry is not a characteristic of the beasts. He roamed the jungle often at a considerable distance from Zveri's camp, but occasionally he would return, though not to molest them, preferring to let them lull themselves into a stupor of tranquil security, the shattering of which in his own good time would have dire effect upon their morale. . . .

To the camp of Abu Batu, on the border of the Galla country, word had come from spies he had sent out that Galla warriors were gathering to prevent his passage through their territory. The Sheik, weakened by the desertion of so many men, dared not defy the bravery and numbers of the Galla warriors, but he knew that he must make some move, since it seemed inevitable that pursuit must overtake him from the rear if he remained where he was much longer.

At last scouts whom he had sent far up the river on the opposite side returned to report that a way to the west seemed clear along a more northerly route, and so breaking camp, Abu Batu moved north with his lone prisoner.

Great had been his rage when he discovered that lbn Dammuk had stolen La, and now he redoubled his precaution to prevent the escape of Zora Drinov.

So closely was she guarded that any possibility of escape seemed almost hopeless. She had learned the fate for which Abu Batu was reserving her and now, depressed and melancholy, her mind was occupied with plans for self-destruction. For a time she had harbored the hope that Zveri would overtake the Aarabs and rescue her, but this she had long since discarded, as day after day passed without bringing the hoped-for succor.

She could not know, of course, the straits in which Zveri had found himself. He had not dared to detach a party of his men to search for her, fearing that in their mutinous state of mind they might murder any of his lieutenants that he placed in charge of them and return to their own tribe, where, through the medium of gossip, word of his expedition and its activities might reach his enemies; nor could he lead all of his force upon such an expedition in person, since he must remain at the base camp to receive the supplies he knew would presently be arriving.

Perhaps, had he known definitely the danger that was confronting Zora, he would have cast aside every other consideration and gone to her rescue, but being naturally suspicious of the loyalty of all men, he persuaded himself that Zora had deliberately deserted him—a half-hearted conviction that had at least the effect of rendering his naturally unpleasant disposition infinitely more unbearable, so that those who should have been his companions and his support in his hour of need contrived to keep out of his way as much as possible.

And while these things were transpiring, little Nkima sped through the jungle upon a mission. In the service of his beloved master, little Nkima could hold to a single thought and a line of action for considerable periods of time at a stretch, but eventually his attention was certain to be attracted by some extraneous matter and then, for hours perhaps, he would forget all about whatever duty had been imposed upon him, though when it again occurred to him he would carry on without any realization of the fact that there had been a break in the continuity of his endeavor.

Tarzan was of course entirely aware of this inherent weakness in his little friend, but he knew too from experience that however many lapses might occur Nkima would never entirely abandon any design upon which his mind had been fixed, and having himself none of civilized man's slavish subservience to time, he was prone to overlook Nkima's erratic performance of a duty as a fault of almost negligible consequence. Some day Nkima would arrive at his destination. Perhaps it would be too late. If such a thought occurred at all to the ape-man, doubtless he passed it off with a shrug. . . .

But time is of the essence of many things to civilized man. He fumes and frets and reduces his mental and physical efficiency if he is not accomplishing something concrete during the passage of every minute of that medium which seems to him like a flowing river, the waters of which are utterly wasted if they are not utilized as they pass by.

Imbued by some such insane conception of time, Wayne Colt sweated and stumbled through the jungle, seeking his companions as though the very fate of the universe hung upon the slender chance that he should reach them without the loss of a second.

The futility of his purpose would have been entirely apparent to him could he have known that he was seeking in the wrong direction for his companions. Wayne Colt was lost. Fortunately for him he did not know it—at least not yet; that stupefying conviction was to come later.

Days passed; still his wanderings revealed no camp. He was hard put to it to find food and his fare was meager and often revolting, consisting of such fruits as he had already learned to know and of rodents, which he managed to bag only with the greatest difficulty and an appalling waste of that precious time which he still prized above all things. He had cut himself a stout stick and would lie in wait along some tiny runway where observation had taught him he might expect to find his prey, until some unwary little creature came within striking distance. He had learned that dawn and dusk were the best hunting hours for the only animals that he could hope to bag—and he learned other things as he moved through the grim jungle, all of which pertained to his struggle for existence. He had learned, for instance, that it was wiser for him to take to the trees whenever he heard a strange noise. Usually the animals got out of his way as he approached, but once a rhinoceros charged him and again he almost stumbled upon a lion at his kill. Providence intervened in each instance and he escaped unharmed, but thus he learned caution.

About noon one day he came to a river that effectually blocked his further progress in the direction that he had been traveling. By this time the conviction was strong upon him that he was utterly lost, and not knowing which direction he should take, he decided to follow the line of least resistance and travel downstream with the river, upon the shore of which he was positive that sooner or later he must discover a native village.

He had proceeded no great distance in the new direction, following a hard-packed trail, worn deep by the countless feet of many beasts, when his attention was arrested by a sound that reached his ears dimly from a distance. It came from somewhere ahead of him and his hearing, now far more acute than it ever had been before, told him that something was approaching. Following the practice that he had found most conducive to longevity since he had been wandering alone and ill-armed against the dangers of the jungle, he flung himself quickly into a tree and sought a point of vantage from where he could see the trail below him. He could not see it for any distance ahead, so tortuously did it wind through the jungle. Whatever was coming would not be visible until it was almost directly beneath him but that now was of no importance. This experience of the jungle had taught him patience, and perchance he was learning also a little of the valuelessness of time, for he settled himself comfortably to wait at his ease.

The noise that he heard was little more than an imperceptible rustling, but presently it assumed a new volume and a new significance, so that now he was sure it was some one running rapidly along the trail, and not one but two—he distinctly heard the footfalls of the heavier creature mingling with those he had first heard.

Then he heard a man's voice cry "Stop!" Now the sounds were very close to him, just around the first bend ahead. The sound of running feet stopped, to be followed by that of a scuffle and strange oaths in a man's voice.

And then a woman's voice spoke. "Let me go! You will never get me where you are taking me alive."

"Then I'll take you for myself now," said the man.

Colt had heard enough. There had been something familiar in the tones of the woman's voice. Silently he dropped to the trail, drawing his dagger, and stepped quickly toward the sounds of the altercation. As he rounded the bend in the trail he saw just before him only a man's back—by thôb and thorib evidently an Aarab—but beyond the man and in his clutches Colt knew the woman was hidden by the flowing robes of her assailant.

Leaping forward he seized the fellow by the shoulder and jerked him suddenly about; as the man faced him Colt saw that it was Abu Batu and now he knew too why the voice of the woman had seemed familiar—she was Zora Drinov.

Abu Batu grew purple with rage at this interruption, but great as was his anger, so too was his surprise great, as he recognized the American. Just for an instant he thought that possibly this was the advance guard of a party of searchers and avengers from Zveri's camp, but as he observed the unkempt, disheveled, unarmed condition of Colt he realized that the man was alone and doubtless lost.

"Dog of a Nasrâny!" he cried, jerking away from Colt's grasp. "Lay not your filthy hand upon a true believer!" At the same time he moved to draw his pistol. In that instant Colt was upon him again, and the two men went down in the narrow trail, the American on top.

What happened then, happened very quickly. Abu Batu drew his pistol; in doing so he caught the hammer in the folds of his thôb and the weapon was discharged. The bullet went harmlessly into the ground, but the report warned Colt of his imminent danger and in self-defense he ran his blade through the Sheik's throat.

As he rose slowly from the body of the Aarab, Zora Drinov grasped him by the arm. "Quick!" she said. "That shot will bring the others. They must not find us."

He did not wait to question her, but, stooping, quickly salvaged Abu Batu's weapons and ammunition, including a long musket that lay in the trail beside him; then with Zora in the lead they ran swiftly up the trail, down which he had just come.

Presently, hearing no indication of pursuit, Colt halted the girl.

"Can you climb?" he asked.

"Yes," she replied. "Why?"

"We are going to take to the trees," he said. "We can go into the jungle a short distance and throw them off the trail."

"Good!" she said, and with his assistance clambered into the branches of a tree beneath which they stood.

Fortunately for them, several large trees grew close together so that they were able to make their way with comparative ease for a full hundred feet from the trail, where, climbing high into the branches of a great tree, they were effectually hidden from sight in all directions.

When at last they were seated side by side in a great crotch, Zora turned toward Colt. "Comrade Colt!" she said. "What has happened? What are you doing here alone? Were you looking for me?"

The man grinned. "I was looking for the whole party," he said. "I have seen no one since we entered Opar. Where is the camp and why was Abu Batu pursuing you?"

"We are a long way from the camp," replied Zora. "I do not know how far, though I could return to it if it were not for the Aarabs." And then briefly she told the story of Abu Batu's treachery and of her captivity. "The Sheik made a temporary camp shortly after noon today. The men were very tired and for the first time in days they relaxed their vigilance over me. I realized that at last the moment I had been awaiting so anxiously had arrived and while they slept I escaped into the jungle. My absence must have been discovered shortly after I left and Abu Batu overtook me. The rest you witnessed."

"Fate has functioned deviously and altogether wonderfully," he said. "To think that your only chance of rescue hinged upon the contingency of my capture at Opar!"

She smiled. "Fate reaches back farther than that," she said. "Suppose you had not been born?"

"Then Abu Batu would have carried you off to the harem of some black sultan, or perhaps another man would have been captured at Opar."

"I am glad that you were born," said Zora.

While listening for signs of pursuit, they conversed in low tones, Colt narrating in detail the events leading up to his capture, though some of the details of his escape he omitted through a sense of loyalty to the unknown girl who had aided him. Neither did he stress Zveri's lack of control over his men, or what Colt considered the leader's inexcusable cowardice in leaving the American and Romero to their fate within the walls of Opar without attempting to succor them, for Colt believed that the girl was Zveri's sweetheart.

"What became of Comrade Romero?" she asked.

"I do not know," he said. "The last I saw of him he was fighting off those crooked little demons."

"Alone?" she asked.

"I was pretty well occupied myself," he said.

"I do not mean that," she replied. "Of course, I know you were there with Romero, but who else?"

"The others had not arrived," said Colt evasively.

"You mean you two went in alone?" she asked.

Colt hesitated. "You see," he said, "the blacks refused to enter the city, so the rest of us had to go in or abandon the attempt to get the treasure."

"But only you and Miguel did go in. Is that not true?"

"I passed out so soon, you see," he said with a laugh, "that really I do not know exactly what did happen."

The girl's eyes narrowed. "It was beastly!" she said quietly.

As they talked, Colt's eyes were often upon the girl's face. How lovely she was, even beneath the rags and the dirt that were the outward symbols of her captivity among the Aarabs. She was thinner than when he had last seen her and her eyes were tired and her face drawn from privation and worry. But, perhaps by very contrast, her beauty was the more startling. It seemed incredible that she could love the coarse, loud-mouthed Zveri.

Presently she broke a short silence. "We must try to get back to the base camp," she said. "It is vital that I be there. So much must be done; so much that no one can do but me."

"You think only of the cause," he said, "never of yourself. You are very loyal."

"Yes," she said in a low voice. "I am loyal to the thing I have sworn to accomplish."

"I am afraid," he said, "that for the past few days I have been thinking more of my own welfare than of that of the proletariat."

"I am afraid that at heart you are still bourgeois," she said, "and that you cannot yet help but look upon the proletariat with contempt."

"What makes you say that?"

"Often a slight unconscious inflection in the use of a word alters the significance of a whole statement, revealing a speaker's secret thoughts."

Colt laughed good-naturedly. "You are a dangerous person to talk to," he said. "Am I to be shot at sunrise?"

She looked at him seriously. "You are different from the others," she said. "I think you could never imagine how suspicious they are. What I have said is only in the way of warning you to watch your every word when you are talking with them. Some of them are narrow and ignorant and they are already suspicious of you because of your antecedents. They are sensitively jealous of a new importance which they believe their class has attained."

"*Their* class?" he asked. "I thought you told me once that *you* were of the proletariat?"

If he had thought that he had surprised her and that she would show embarrassment, he was mistaken. She met his eyes squarely and without wavering. "I am," she said; "but I can still see the weaknesses of my class."

"Kill!" said La. The lion crouched and charged—while Hajellan stood paralyzed with fright.

He looked at her steadily for a long moment, the shadow of a smile touching his lips. "I do not believe—"

"Why do you stop?" she asked. "What is it that you do not believe?"

"Forgive me," he said. "I was starting to think aloud."

"Be careful, Comrade Colt," she warned him. "Thinking aloud is sometimes fatal."

Further conversation was interrupted by the sound of the voices of men. "They are coming," said the girl.

Colt nodded, and the two remained silent, listening to the sounds of approaching voices and footsteps. The men came abreast of them and halted and Zora, who understood the Aarab tongue, heard one of them say, "The trail stops here. They have gone into the jungle."

"Who can the man be who is with her?" asked another.

"It is a Nasrâny. I can tell by the imprint of his feet."

"They would go toward the river," said a third. "That is the way that I would go if I were trying to escape."

"*Wullah!* You speak words of wisdom," said the first speaker. "We will spread out here and search toward the river. But look out for the Nasrâny—he has the pistol and the musket of the Sheik."

The two fugitives heard the sound of pursuit diminishing in the distance as the Aarabs forced their way into the jungle toward the river. "I think we had better get out of this," said Colt, "and while it may be pretty hard going I believe that we had better stick to the brush for awhile and keep on away from the river."

"Yes," replied Zora, "for that is the general direction in which the camp lies." And so they commenced their long and weary march in search of their comrades.

They were still pushing through dense jungle when night overtook them. Their clothes were in rags and their bodies scratched and torn, painful reminders of the thorny way.

Hungry and thirsty, they made a dry camp among the branches of a tree, where Colt built a rude platform for the girl, while he prepared to sleep upon the ground at the foot of the great bole. But to this Zora would not listen.

"That will not do at all," she said. "We are in no position to permit ourselves to be victims of every silly convention that would ordinarily order our lives in civilized surroundings. I appreciate your thoughtful consideration, but I would rather have you up here in the tree with me than down there where the first hunting lion that passed might get you." And so with the girl's help, Colt built another platform close to the one that he had built for her and as darkness fell, they stretched their tired bodies on the rude couches and sought to sleep.

Presently Colt dozed and in his dream he saw the slender figure of a star-eyed goddess, whose cheeks were wet with tears; but as he took her in his arms and kissed her he saw that she was Zora Drinov. Then a hideous sound from the jungle below awakened him with a start, so that he sat up, seizing the musket of the Sheik in readiness.

"A hunting lion," said the girl in a low voice.

"Phew!" exclaimed Colt. "I must have been asleep, for that certainly gave me a start."

"Yes, you were asleep," said the girl. "I heard you talking"—and he felt that he detected laughter in her voice.

"Was I, really?"

"Yes. I wonder who you were talking to?"

"I wonder," said Colt, recalling that in his dream the figure of one girl had merged into that of another.

The lion, hearing their voices, moved away, growling. He was not hunting the hated man-things.

CHAPTER XII

DOWN TRAILS OF TERROR

SLOW days dragged by for the man and woman searching for their comrades. Days filled with fatiguing effort, most of which was directed toward the procuring of food and water for their sustenance. Increasingly was Colt impressed by the character and personality of his companion. With apprehension he noticed that she was gradually weakening beneath the strain of fatigue and the scant and inadequate food he had been able to procure for her. But still she kept a brave front and tried to hide her fatigue from him. Never once had she complained. Never by word or look had she reproached him for his inability to procure sufficient food, a failure which he looked upon as indicative of inefficiency. She did not know that he himself often went hungry that she might eat, telling her when he returned with food that he had eaten his share where he had found it, a deception that was made possible by the fact that when he hunted he often

"Have you seen a Tarmangani she?" demanded Tar-zan. "No," replied Nkima, "there were no shes among the Tarmangani—only bulls."

left Zora to rest in some place of comparative security.

He had left her thus one day, safe in a great tree beside a winding stream. She was very tired. It seemed to her that now she was always tired. The thought of continuing the march appalled her, yet she knew that it must be undertaken. She wondered how much longer she could go on before she sank exhausted for the last time. It was not, however, for herself that she was most concerned, but for this man—this scion of wealth and capitalism and power, whose constant consideration and cheerfulness and tenderness had been a revelation to her. She knew that when she could go no farther, Colt would not leave her—and that thus his chances of escape from the grim jungle would be jeopardized and perhaps lost forever. But from thought of death she shrank, not because of the fear of death—as well might have been the case—but for an entirely new reason, the sudden realization of which gave her a distinct shock. The tragedy of this sudden self-awakening left her numb with terror. It was a thought that must be put from her, one that she must not entertain; yet it persisted.

Colt had gone farther afield than usual that morning in his search for food, for he had sighted an antelope and, thrilled by the contemplation of so much meat in a single kill, and what it would mean for Zora, he had clung doggedly to the trail, lured on by an occasional glimpse of his quarry in the distance.

The antelope was only vaguely aware of an enemy, for he was upwind from Colt and had not caught his scent, while the occasional glimpses he had had of the man had served mostly to arouse his curiosity, so that though he moved away he stopped often and turned back in an effort to satisfy his wonder. Presently he waited a moment too long and Colt chanced a long shot. As the animal dropped, the man gave a loud cry of exultation. . . .

As time, that she had no means of measuring, dragged on, Zora grew increasingly apprehensive on Colt's account. Never before had he left her for so long a time and she began to construct all sorts of imaginary calamities which might have overtaken him. She wished now that she had gone with him. If she had thought it possible to track him, she would have followed him, but she knew that that was impossible. However, her forced inactivity made her restless. Her cramped position in the tree became unendurable and assailed by thirst, she lowered herself to the ground and walked toward the river.

She had drunk and was about to return to the tree when she heard the sound of something approaching from the direction in which Colt had gone. Instantly her heart leaped with gladness; her depression and even much of her fatigue seemed to vanish and she realized suddenly how very lonely she had been without him. How dependent we are upon the society of our fellow-men we seldom realize until we become the victims of enforced solitude, and there now were tears of happiness in Zora Drinov's eyes as she advanced to meet Colt. Then the bushes before her parted and there stepped into view before her horrified gaze, a monstrous hairy ape!

To-yat, the king ape, was as much surprised as the girl, but his reactions were almost opposite. It was with no horror that he viewed this soft white she Man-

"Go—taking the heart of Nao with you!" she said. "I shall never see you again, but I shall have the memory of this hour."

gani. To the girl there was naught but ferocity in his mien, though in his breast was an entirely different emotion.

He lumbered toward her and as though released from a momentary paralysis, Zora turned to flee—but how futilely she realized an instant later, as a hairy paw gripped her roughly by the shoulder.

For an instant she had forgotten the Sheik's pistol that Colt always left with her for self-protection. Jerking it from its holster she turned upon the beast, but To-yat, seeing in the weapon a club with which she intended to attack him, wrenched it from her grasp and hurled it aside. Then, though she struggled and fought to regain her freedom, he lifted her lightly to his hip and lumbered off into the jungle in the direction he had been going.

COLT tarried at his kill only long enough to remove the feet, head and viscera, by that much reducing the weight of the burden he must carry back to camp, for he was aware that privation had greatly reduced his strength. Lifting the carcass to his shoulder he started back toward camp, exulting in the thought that for once he was returning with an ample quantity of strength-giving meat.

As he staggered along beneath the weight of the small antelope, he made plans that imparted a rosy hue to the future. They would rest now until their strength returned and while they were resting they would smoke all of the meat of his kill that they did not eat at once; thus they would have a reserve supply of food which he felt would carry them a great distance. Two days' rest with plenty of food would fill them with renewed vitality.

As he started laboriously along the back trail, he began to realize that he had come much farther than he had thought, but it had been well worth while even though he reached Zora in a state of utter exhaustion. He did not fear but that he would reach her, so confident was he of his own powers of endurance and the strength of his will.

As he staggered at last to his goal he looked up into the tree and called her by name. There was no reply and in that first brief instant of silence, a dull- and sickening premonition of disaster crept over him. He dropped the carcass of the deer and looked hurriedly about.

"Zora! Zora!" he cried, but only the silence of the jungle was his answer. Then his searching eyes found the pistol of Abu Batu where To-yat had dropped it and his worst fears were substantiated, for he knew that if Zora had gone away of her own volition she would have taken the weapon with her. She had been attacked by something and carried off, of that he was positive, and presently as he examined the ground closely he discovered the imprints of a great man-like foot.

A sudden madness seized Wayne Colt. The cruelty of the jungle, the injustice of Nature, aroused within his breast a red rage. He wanted to kill the thing that had stolen Zora Drinov. He wanted to tear it with his hands and rend it with his teeth. All the savage instincts of primitive man were reborn within him, as, forgetting the meat that the moment before had meant so much to him, he plunged headlong into the jungle upon the faint spoor of To-yat the king ape. . . .

La of Opar made her way slowly through the jungle after she had escaped from Ibn Dammuk and his companions. Her native city called to her, though she knew that she might not enter it in safety. But where else was there in all the world that she might go? Some-thing of a conception of the im-mensity of the great world had been im-pressed upon her during her wandering since she had left Opar and the futility of searching any farther for Tarzan had been indelibly impressed upon her mind. So she would go back to the vicinity of Opar and maybe some day again Tarzan would come there. That great dangers beset her way she did not care, for La of Opar was indif-ferent to a life that had never brought her much of happi-ness. She lived be-cause she lived and it is true that she would strive to prolong life because such is the law of Nature, which imbues the most miserable unfortunates with as powerful an urge to prolong their misery as it gives to the fortunate few, who are happy and contented, a similar desire to live.

Presently she became aware of pursuit, so she increased her speed and kept ahead of those who were following her. Finding a trail, she followed it, but if it permitted her to increase her speed, she knew that it would permit her pursuers also to increase theirs and now she could not hear them as plainly as she

Ibn Dammuk moved to draw his pistol. In that instant Colt was upon him again.

had before when they were pushing their way through the jungle. Still she was confident that they could not overtake her and she was moving swiftly on when a turn in the trail brought her to a sudden stop, for there, blocking her retreat, stood a great maned lion. This time La remembered the animal, not as Jad-bal-ja, the hunting mate of Tarzan, but as the lion that had rescued her from the leopard, after Tarzan had deserted her.

Lions were familiar creatures to La of Opar, where they were often captured by the priests while cubs and where it was not unusual to raise some of them occasionally as pets, until their growing ferocity made them unsafe. Therefore, La knew that lions could associate with people without devouring them and, having had experience of this lion's disposition and having as little sense of fear as Tarzan himself, she quickly made her choice between the lion and the Aarabs pursuing her and advanced directly toward the great beast, in whose attitude she saw there was no immediate menace. She was a sufficient child of nature to know that death came quickly and painlessly in the embrace of a lion and so she had no fear but only a great curiosity.

Jad-bal-ja had long had the scent-spoor of La in his nostrils as she moved with the wind along the jungle trails and so he had awaited her, his curiosity aroused by the fainter scent-spoor of the men who trailed her, and now as she came toward him along the trail he stepped to one side that she might pass and, like a great cat, rubbed his maned neck against her legs.

La paused and laid a hand upon his head and

spoke to him in low tones in the language of the first man—the language of the great apes that was the common language of her people, as it was Tarzan's language. . . .

Hajellan, leading his men in pursuit of La, rounded a bend in the trail and stopped aghast. He saw a great lion facing him, a lion that bared its fangs now in an angry snarl, and beside the lion, one hand tangled in its thick black mane, stood the white woman.

The woman spoke a single word to the lion in a language that Hajellan did not understand. "Kill!" said La in the language of the great apes.

So accustomed was the high priestess of the Flaming God to command that it did not occur to her that the beast might do other than obey and so, although she did not know that it was thus that Tarzan had been accustomed to command Jad-bal-ja, she was not surprised when the lion crouched and charged.

Fodil and Dareyem had pushed close behind their companion as he halted and great was their horror when they saw the lion leap forward. They turned and fled, colliding with the blacks behind them, but Hajellan only stood paralyzed with fright as Jad-bal-ja reared upon his hind feet and seized him, his great jaws crunching through the man's head and shoulders, cracking his skull like an eggshell. He gave the body a vicious shake and dropped it. Then he turned and looked inquiringly at La.

In the woman's heart was no more sympathy for an enemy than in the heart of Jad-bal-ja—she only wished to be rid of them. She did not care whether

The two remained silent listening to the approaching voices. Zora heard one of them say: "The trail stops here."

they lived or died and so she did not urge Jad-bal-ja after those who had escaped. She wondered what the lion would do now that he had made his kill and knowing that the vicinity of a feeding lion was no safe place, she turned and moved on along the trail. But Jad-bal-ja was no eater of men, because he was young and active and had no difficulty in killing prey which he relished far more than he did the salty flesh of man. Therefore, he left Hajellan lying where he had fallen and followed after La along the shadowy jungle trails.

A black man, naked but for a gee-string, bearing a message from the Coast for Zveri, paused where two trails crossed. From his left the wind was blowing and to his sensitive nostrils it bore the faint odor that announced the presence of a lion. Without a moment's hesitation, the man vanished into the foliage of a tree that overhung the trail.

Perhaps Simba was not hungry, perhaps Simba was not hunting; but the black messenger was taking no chances. He was sure that the lion was approaching and he would wait here where he could see both trails until he discovered which one Simba took.

Watching with more or less indifference because of the safety of his sanctuary, the negro was ill-prepared for the shock which the sight which presently broke upon his vision induced. Never in the lowest steps of his superstition had he conceived such a scene as he now witnessed and he blinked his eyes repeatedly to make sure that he was awake. But no there could be no mistake. It was indeed a white woman—almost naked but for golden ornaments and a soft strip of leopard-skin beneath her narrow stomacher—a white woman who walked with the fingers of one hand tangled in the black mane of a great golden lion.

Along the trail they came and at the crossing they turned to the left into the trail that he had been following. As they disappeared from his view the black man fingered the fetish that was suspended from a cord about his neck and prayed to Mulungo, the god of his people—and when he again set out toward his destination he took another and a more circuitous route.

OFTEN, after darkness had fallen, Tarzan had come to the camp of the conspirators and perching a tree above them listened to Zveri outlining his plans to his companions, so that the ape-man was now entirely familiar with what they intended.

Now, knowing that they would not be prepared

to strike for some time, he was roaming the jungle far away from the presence of man, enjoying to the full the peace and freedom that were his life. He knew that Nkima should have reached his destination by this time and delivered the message that Tarzan had dispatched by him. He was still puzzled by the strange disappearance of La and piqued by his inability to pick up her trail. He was genuinely grieved by her disappearance, for already he had plans well formulated to restore her to her throne and punish her enemies, but he gave himself over to no futile regrets as he swung through the trees in sheer joy of living, or when hunger overtook him, stalked his prey in the grim and terrible silence of the hunting beast.

Sometimes he thought of the good-looking young American to whom he had taken a fancy in spite of the fact that he considered him an enemy and had he known of Colt's now almost hopeless plight it is possible that he would have come to his rescue. But he knew nothing of it and so, alone and friendless, sunk to the uttermost depths of despair, Wayne Colt stumbled through the jungle in search of Zora Drinov and her abductor. Already he had lost the faint trail and To-yat, far to his right, lumbered along with his captive, safe from pursuit.

WEAK from exhaustion and shock, thoroughly terrified now by the hopelessness of her hideous position, Zora had lost consciousness. To-yat feared that she was dead, but he carried her on nevertheless that he might at least have the satisfaction of exhibiting her to his tribe as evidence of his prowess and, perhaps, to furnish an excuse for another Dum-Dum. Secure in his might, conscious of few enemies that might with safety to themselves molest him, To-yat did not take the precaution of silence, but wandered on through the jungle heedless of all dangers.

Many were the keen ears and sensitive nostrils which carried the message of his passing to their owners, but to only one did the strange mingling of the scent-spoor of the bull ape with that of a she Mangani suggest a condition worthy of investigation. As To-yat pursued his careless way another creature of the jungle, moving silently on swift feet,

Though she fought to regain her freedom, To-yat lifted her lightly to his hip and lumbered off into the jungle.

"Kill!" said La. The lion crouched and charged—while Hajellan stood paralyzed with fright.

bore down upon him, and when from a point of vantage keen eyes beheld the shaggy bull and the slender, delicate girl, a lip curled in a silent snarl and a moment later To-yat the king ape was brought to a snarling, bristling halt as the giant figure of a bronzed Tarmangani dropped lightly into the trail before him.

The wicked eyes of the bull shot fire and hate. "Go away," he said. "I am To-yat. Go away or I kill."

"Put down the she," Tarzan demanded.

"No!" bellowed To-yat. "She is mine."

"Put down the she," repeated Tarzan, "and go your way, or I kill. I am Tarzan of the Apes."

Tarzan drew the hunting-knife of his father and crouched as he advanced toward the bull.

To-yat snarled and seeing that the other meant to give battle, he cast the body of the girl aside that he might not be handicapped.

As they circled, each looking for an advantage,

there came a sudden, terrific crashing sound in the jungle down-wind from them.

Tantor the elephant, asleep in the security of the depth of the forest, had been suddenly awakened by the growling of the two beasts. Instantly his nostrils caught a familiar scent-spoor—the scent-spoor of his beloved Tarzan—and his ears told him that Tarzan was facing in battle the great Mangani, whose scent was also in the nostrils of Tantor.

To the snapping and bending of trees, the great bull elephant rushed through the forest and as he emerged suddenly, towering above them, To-yat the king ape, seeing death in those angry eyes and gleaming tusks, turned and fled into the jungle.

CHAPTER XIII

THE LION-MAN

PETER ZVERI was in a measure regaining some of the confidence that he had lost in the ultimate success of his plan, for his agents were succeeding at last in getting to him some of his much-needed supplies, together with contingents of disaffected blacks wherewith he might recruit his forces to sufficient numbers to insure the success of his contemplated invasion of Italian Somaliland. It was his plan to make a swift and sudden incursion, destroying native villages and capturing an outpost or two, then—retreating quickly across the border—pack away the French uniforms for possible future use and undertake the overthrow of Ras Tafari in Abyssinia, where his agents had told him conditions were ripe for a revolution. With Abyssinia under his control to serve as a rallying point, his agents assured him that the native tribes of all Northern Africa would flock to his standards.

In distant Bokhara a fleet of some two hundred

planes—bombers, scouts and fighting-planes—made available through the greed of American capitalists, were being mobilized for a sudden dash across Persia and Arabia to his base in Abyssinia. With these to support his great native army, he felt that his position would be secure. The malcontents of Egypt would join forces with him and, with Europe embroiled in a war that would prevent any concerted action against him, his dream of empire might be assured and his position made impregnable for all time.

Perhaps it was a mad dream; perhaps Peter Zveri was mad, but then what great world-conqueror has not been a little mad? He saw in his mind his frontiers then pushed toward the south as little by little, he extended his dominion until at last he should rule a great continent—Peter I, Emperor of Africa!

"You seem happy, Comrade Zveri," said Antonio Mori one day.

"Why should I not be, Tony?" demanded the dreamer. "I see success just before us. We should all be happy, but we are going to be very much happier later on."

"Yes," said Tony, "when the Philippines are free, I shall be very happy. Do you not think that then I should be a very big man back there, Comrade Zveri?"

"Yes," said the Russian, "but you can be a bigger man if you stay here and work for me. How would you like to be a Grand Duke, Tony?"

"A Grand Duke!" exclaimed the Filipino. "I thought there were no more Grand Dukes."

"But perhaps there may be again."

The varying threads of this skillfully woven tale begin to draw together in a vivid pattern of intriguing adventure.

"They were wicked men who ground down the working-classes," said Tony.

"To be a Grand Duke who ground down the rich and took their money from them might not be so bad," said Peter. "Grand Dukes are very rich and powerful. Would you not like to be rich and powerful, Tony?"

"Well, of course—who would not?"

"Then always do as I tell you, Tony, and some day I shall make you a Grand Duke," said Zveri.

The camp was filled with activity now at all times, for Zveri had conceived the plan of whipping his native recruits into some semblance of military order and discipline. Romero, Dorsky and Ivitch had had military experience, and the camp was filled with marching men, deploying, charging and assembling, practicing the manual of arms and being

He indicated that she was free to go to the camp.

instructed in the rudiments of fire discipline.

The day following his conversation with Zveri, Tony was assisting the Mexican, who was sweating over a company of black recruits.

During a period of rest, the Mexican and Filipino were enjoying a smoke when Tony turned to his companion. "You have traveled much, comrade," said the Filipino. "Perhaps you can tell me what sort of a uniform a Grand Duke wears."

"I have heard," said Romero, "that in Hollywood and New York many of them wear aprons."

Tony grimaced. "I do not think," he said, "that I want to be a Grand Duke."

The blacks in the camp, kept sufficiently interested and busy in drills to keep them out of mischief, with plenty of food and with the prospects of fighting and marching still in the future, were a contented and happy lot. Those who had undergone the harrowing experiences of Opar and those other untoward incidents that had upset their equanimity had now regained their self-confidence, a condition for which Zveri took all the credit to himself, assuming that it was due to his remarkable gift for leadership. And then a runner arrived in camp with a message for him and with a wild story of having seen a white woman hunting in the jungle with a black-maned golden lion.

This was sufficient to recall to the blacks the other weird occurrences and to remind them that there were supernatural agencies at work in this territory, that it was peopled by ghosts and demons, and that at any moment some dire calamity might befall them.

But if this story upset the equanimity of the blacks, the message that the runner brought to Zveri precipitated an emotional outbreak in the Russian that bordered closely upon the frenzy of insanity. Blaspheming in a loud voice, he strode back and forth before his tent—nor would he explain to any of his lieutenants the cause of his anger.

And while Zveri fumed, other forces were gathering against him. Through the jungle moved a hundred ebon warriors, their smooth, sleek skin, their rolling muscles and elastic step bespeaking physical fitness. They were quite naked but for narrow loincloths of leopard- or lion-skin, and a few of those ornaments that are dear to the hearts of savages—anklets and armbands of copper, and necklaces of the claws of lions or leopards—while above the head of each floated a white plume. But here the primitiveness of their equipment ceased, for their weapons were the weapons of modern fighting-men—high-powered service rifles, revolvers and bandoleers of cartridges. It was, indeed, a formidable-appearing company that swung steadily and silently through the jungle, and upon the shoulder of the black chief who led them rode a little monkey. . . .

Tarzan was relieved when Tantor's sudden and unexpected charge drove To-yat into the jungle, for

"Always do as I tell you, Tony, and some day I shall make you a Grand Duke," said Zveri.

Tarzan of the Apes found no pleasure in quarreling with the Mangani, which he considered above all other creatures his brothers. He never forgot that he had been nursed at the breast of Kala the she ape, nor that he had grown to manhood in the tribe of

Kerchak the king. From infancy to manhood he had thought of himself only as an ape and even now it was often easier for him to understand and appreciate the motives of the great Mangani than those of man.

At a signal from Tarzan, Tantor stopped and assuming again his customary composure, though still alert against any danger that might threaten his friend, he watched while the ape-man turned and knelt beside the prostrate girl. Tarzan had at first thought her dead, but he soon discovered that she was only in a swoon. Lifting her in his arms, he spoke a half-dozen words to the great pachyderm, who turned about and putting down his head started off straight into the dense jungle, making a pathway along which Tarzan bore the unconscious girl.

Straight as an arrow moved Tantor the elephant to halt at last upon the bank of a considerable river, beyond which was a spot that Tarzan had in mind to which he wished to convey To-yat's unfortunate captive, whom he had recognized immediately as the young woman he had seen in the base camp of the conspirators. A cursory examination of her convinced him she was upon the verge of death from starvation, shock and exposure.

Once again he spoke to Tantor and the great pachyderm, twining his trunk around their bodies, lifted the two gently to his broad back. Then he waded into the river and set out for the opposite shore.

The channel in the center was deep and swift and Tantor was swept off his feet and carried downstream for a considerable distance before he found

Tarzan discovered she was only in a swoon. Lifting her in his arms, he spoke to the great pachyderm, who started into the jungle, making a pathway.

footing again, but eventually he won to the opposite bank and here again he went ahead, making trail until at last he broke into a broad, well-marked game trail.

Now Tarzan took the lead and Tantor followed, and while they moved thus silently toward their destination, Zora Drinov opened her eyes. Instantly recollection of her plight came to her consciousness; then almost simultaneously she realized that her cheek, resting upon the shoulder of her captor, was not pressing against a shaggy coat but against the smooth skin of a human body—and she turned her head and looked at the profile of the creature that was carrying her.

She thought at first that she was the victim of some strange hallucination of terror, for, of course, she could not measure the time that she had been unconscious, nor recall any of the incidents that had occurred during that period.

The last thing she remembered was that she had been in the arms of a great ape, who was carrying her off to the jungle. She had closed her eyes and when she opened them again the ape had been transformed into a handsome demigod of the forest.

She closed her eyes and turned her head so that she faced back over the man's shoulder. She thought that she would keep her eyes tightly closed for a moment, then open them and turn them stealthily once more toward the face of the creature who was carrying her so lightly along the jungle trail. Perhaps this time he would be an ape again, and then she would know that she was indeed mad, or dreaming. When she did open her eyes the sight that met them convinced her that she was experiencing a nightmare, for plodding along the trail directly behind her was a giant bull elephant.

Tarzan, apprised of her returning consciousness by the movement of her head upon his shoulder, turned his own to look at her and saw her gazing at Tantor in wide-eyed astonishment. Then she turned toward him and their eyes met.

"Who are you?" she asked in a whisper. "Am I dreaming?" But the ape-man only turned his eyes to the front and made no reply.

Zora thought of struggling to free herself, but she realized that she was very weak and helpless and at last she resigned herself to her fate and let her cheek fall again to the bronzed shoulder of the ape-man.

When Tarzan finally stopped and laid his burden upon the ground, it was in a little clearing through which ran a tiny stream of clear water. Great trees arched almost overhead and through their foliage the great sun dappled the grass beneath them.

As Zora Drinov lay stretched upon the soft turf she realized for the first time how weak she was, for she attempted to rise and found that she could not. As her eyes took in the scene about her, it seemed more than ever like a dream—the great bull elephant standing almost above her and the bronzed figure of an almost naked giant squatting upon his haunches beside the little stream. She saw him fold a great leaf into the shape of a cornucopia and, after filling it with water, rise and come toward her. Without a word he stooped and putting an arm beneath her shoulders, he raised her to a sitting position and offered her the water from his improvised cup.

She drank deeply for she was very thirsty; then, looking up into the handsome f ace above her, she voiced her thanks, but the man did not reply and naturally she thought that he did not understand her.

When she had satisfied her thirst, he lowered her gently to the ground again, after which he swung lightly into a tree and disappeared into the forest. But above her the great elephant stood as though on guard, his huge body swaying gently to and fro. The quiet and peace of her surroundings tended to soothe her nerves, but in her mind was a conviction that her situation was most precarious.

The man was a mystery to her and while she knew, of course, that the ape which had stolen her had not been transformed miraculously into a handsome forest god, yet she could not account in any way for his presence or for the disappearance of the ape, except upon the rather extravagant hypothesis that the two had worked together, the great ape having stolen her for this man who was its master.

There had been nothing in the man's attitude to suggest that he intended to harm her and yet so accustomed was she to gauge all men by the standards of civilized society that she could not conceive that he had other than sinister designs.

To her analytical mind the man presented a paradox that intrigued her imagination, seeming, as he did, so utterly out of place in this savage African jungle, while at the same time he harmonized perfectly with his surroundings, in which he seemed absolutely at home and assured of himself—a fact that was still further impressed upon her by the presence of the wild bull elephant, to which the man paid no more attention than one would to a lap-dog. Had he been unkempt, filthy and of a degraded appearance, she would have catalogued him immediately as one of those social outcasts, usually half demented, who are occasionally found far from the haunts of men, living the life of wild beasts—whose high standards of decency and cleanliness, however, they uniformly fail to observe. But this creature had suggested more the trained athlete in whom cleanliness was a fetish, nor did his well-shaped head and intelligent eyes even remotely suggest mental or moral degradation.

And as she pondered him, the man returned, bearing a great load of straight branches from which the twigs and leaves had been removed. With a celerity and adeptness that bespoke long years of practice, he constructed a shelter upon the bank of the rivulet. He gathered broad leaves to thatch its roof and leafy branches enclosed it upon three sides, so that it formed a protection against the prevailing winds. Then he floored it with leaves and small twigs and dry grasses, after which he came and, lifting the girl in his arms, bore her to the rustic bower he had fabricated.

Once again he left her and when he returned he brought a little fruit, which he fed to her sparingly, for he guessed that she had been long without food and knew that he must not overtax her stomach. Always he worked in silence and though no word had passed between them, Zora Drinov felt growing within her a conviction of his trustworthiness.

The next time that he left her he was gone a considerable time, but still the elephant stood in the clearing, like some titanic sentinel upon guard.

When next the man returned he brought the car-

Tantor lifted the two gently to his broad back, waded into the river and set out for the opposite shore.

cass of a deer and then Zora saw him make fire, after the manner of primitive men, and as the meat
roasted above it the fragrant aroma came to her nostrils, bringing consciousness of a ravening hunger.
When the meat was cooked the man came and
squatted beside her, cutting small pieces with his
keen hunting-knife and feeding her as though she
had been a helpless child. He gave her only a little at
a time, making her rest often, and while she ate he
spoke for the first time, but not to her, nor in any
language that she had ever heard. He spoke to the
great elephant, and the huge pachyderm wheeled
slowly about and entered the jungle, where she
could hear the diminishing noise of his passage until
it was lost in the distance.

Before the meal was over it was quite dark, and
she finished it in the fitful light of the fire that shone
redly on the bronzed skin of her companion, and
shot back from mysterious gray eyes which gave the
impression of seeing everything, even her inmost
thoughts.

Then he brought her a drink of water, after which
he squatted down outside her shelter and proceeded
to satisfy his own hunger.

Gradually the girl had been lulled to a feeling of
security by the seeming solicitude of her strange
protector, but now distinct misgivings assailed her
and suddenly she felt a strange new fear of the silent
giant in whose power she was, for when he ate she
saw that he ate his meat raw, tearing the flesh like a
wild beast; and when there came the sound of something moving in the jungle just beyond the firelight
and he raised his head and looked, and there came a

low and savage growl of warning from his lips, the girl closed her eyes and buried her face in her arms in sudden terror and revulsion.

From the darkness of the jungle there came an answering growl, but the sound moved on and presently all was silent again.

It was some time before Zora dared open her eyes again and when she did she saw that the man had finished his meal and was stretched out on the grass between her and the fire. She was afraid of him, of that she was quite certain; yet, at the same time, she could not deny that his presence there imparted to her a feeling of safety that she had never before felt in the jungle, and as she tried to fathom this she dozed and presently was asleep.

The young sun was already bringing renewed warmth to the jungle when she awoke. The man had replenished the fire and was sitting before it, grilling small fragments of meat. Beside him were some fruits, which he must have gathered since he awakened. As she watched him she was still further impressed by his great physical beauty, as well as by a certain marked nobility of bearing that harmonized well with the dignity of his poise and the intelligence of his keen gray eyes. She wished that she had not seen him devour his meat like a—ah, that was it— like a lion! How much like a lion he was, in his strength and dignity and majesty and with all the quiet suggestion of ferocity that pervaded his every act. And so it was that she came to think of him as her lion-man, and though trying to trust him, always fearing him not a little.

Again he fed her and brought her water before he

satisfied his own hunger.

Before he started to eat he arose and voiced a long low call and then once more he squatted upon his haunches and devoured his food, but while he held it in his strong brown hands and ate the flesh raw, she saw now that he ate slowly and with the same quiet dignity that marked his every act, so that presently she found him less revolting. Once again she tried to talk with him, addressing him in various languages and several African dialects, but as for any sign he gave that he understood her she might as well have been addressing a dumb brute. Doubtless her disappointment would have been replaced by anger could she have known that she was addressing an English Lord, who perfectly understood every word that she uttered, but who, for reasons which he himself best knew, preferred to remain the dumb brute to this woman whom he looked upon as an enemy.

However, it was well for Zora Drinov that he was what he was, for it was the prompting of the English Lord and not that of the savage carnivore which had moved him to succor her because she was alone and helpless and a woman. The beast in Tarzan would not have attacked her but would merely have ignored her, letting the law of the jungle take its course as it must with all creatures.

Shortly after Tarzan had finished his meal, a crashing in the jungle announced the return of Tantor and when he appeared in the little clearing the girl realized that the great brute had come in response to the call of the man, and again she marveled.

And so the days wore on and slowly Zora Drinov regained her strength, guarded at night by the silent forest god and during the day by the great bull elephant. Her only apprehension now was for the safety of Wayne Colt, who was seldom from her thoughts.

Nor was her apprehension groundless, for the young American had fallen upon bad days. . . . Almost frantic with concern for the safety of Zora, he had exhausted his strength in futile search for her and her abductor, forgetful of himself until hunger and fatigue had taken their toll of his strength and he had awakened at last to the realization that his condition was dangerous; and now when he needed food most the game he had formerly found reasonably plentiful seemed to have deserted the country. Even the smaller rodents that had once sufficed to keep him alive were either too wary for him or were not present at all. Occasionally he found fruits that he could eat, but they seemed to impart little or no strength to him, and at last he was forced to the conviction that he had reached the end of his endurance and his strength and that nothing short of a miracle could preserve him from death.

He was so weak that he could stagger only a few steps at a time and then, sinking to the ground, he was forced to lie there for a long time before he could arise again, and always there was the knowledge that eventually he would not arise. Yet he would not give up. Something more than the urge to live drove him on. He could not die—he must not die—while Zora Drinov was in danger! He had found a well-beaten trail at last where he was sure that sooner or later he must meet a native hunter, or perhaps find his way to the camp of his fellows. He could only crawl now, for he had not the strength to rise, and then suddenly the moment came that he had striven so long to avert—the moment that seemed to mark the end, though it came in a form he had only vaguely anticipated as one of several which might ring the curtain upon his earthly existence.

As he lay in the trail resting before he dragged himself on again, he was suddenly conscious that he was not alone. He had heard no sound, for doubtless his hearing had been dulled by exhaustion, but he was aware through the medium of that strange sense, the possession of which each of us has felt at some time in his existence, that told him eyes were upon him.

With an effort he raised his head to look and there before him in the trail, stood a great lion, his lips drawn back in an angry snarl, his yellow-green eyes glaring balefully.

CHAPTER XIV

SHOT DOWN

TARZAN went almost daily to watch the camp of his enemy, moving swiftly through the jungle by trails unknown to man. He saw that preparations for the first bold stroke were almost completed and finally he saw uniforms being issued to all the members of the party—uniforms which he recognized as those of French Colonial troops and he realized that the time had come when he must move. He hoped little Nkima had carried his message safely, but if not, Tarzan would find some other way.

Zora Drinov's strength was slowly returning. Today she had arisen and taken a few steps out into the sunlit clearing. The great elephant regarded her. She had long since ceased to fear him, as she had ceased to fear the strange white man who had befriended her. Slowly the girl approached the great bull and Tantor regarded her steadily out of his little eyes as he weaved his trunk to and fro.

He had been so docile and harmless all the days he had guarded her that it had grown difficult for Zora to conceive him capable of inflicting injury upon her—but as she looked into his little eyes now there was an expression there which brought her to a sudden halt and as she realized that after all he was only a wild bull elephant, she suddenly appreciated the rashness of her act. She was already so close to him that she could have reached out and touched him, as had been her intention, with the thought that she would thus make friends with him.

It was in her mind to fall back with dignity, when the weaving trunk shot suddenly out and encircled her body. Zora Drinov did not scream. She only closed her eyes and waited. She felt herself lifted from the ground and a moment later the elephant

The vision of a beautiful girl running toward the savage beast almost overwhelmed Wayne Colt.

had crossed the little clearing and deposited her in her shelter. Then he backed off slowly and resumed his post of duty. He had not hurt her; a mother could not have lifted her baby more gently, but he had impressed upon Zora Drinov that she was a prisoner and that he was her keeper.

As a matter of fact, Tantor was only carrying out Tarzan's instructions, which had nothing to do with forcible restraint of the girl, but were only a measure of precaution to prevent her wandering into the jungle where other dangers might overtake her.

Zora had not fully regained her strength and the experience left her trembling, though she now realized that her sudden fears for her safety had been groundless. She decided that she would take no more liberties with her mighty warden.

It was not long after that Tarzan returned, much earlier in the day than was his custom. He spoke only to Tantor, and the great beast, touching him

Though Colt lay but a few yards from a feeding lion, yet it seemed an eternity since he had felt such contentment and security.

almost caressingly with his trunk, turned and lumbered off into the forest.

Then Tarzan advanced to where Zora sat in the opening of her shelter. Lightly he lifted her from the ground and tossed her to his shoulder and then, to her infinite surprise at his strength and agility, he swung into a tree and was off through the jungle.

At the edge of the river that they had crossed before, Tantor was awaiting them and once more he carried Zora and Tarzan safely to the other bank.

Tarzan himself had crossed the river twice a day since he had made the camp for Zora, but when he went alone he needed no help from Tantor or any other, for he swam the swift stream, his eye alert and his keen knife ready should Gimla the crocodile attack him. But for the crossing of the woman, he had enlisted the services of Tantor that she might not be subjected to the danger and hardship of the only other means of crossing that was possible.

Tantor clambered up the muddy bank and Tarzan dismissed him with a word, as with the girl in his arms he leaped into a near-by tree.

That flight through the jungle was an experience which would long stand vividly in the memory of Zora Drinov. That a human being could possess the strength and agility of the creature who carried her seemed unbelievable and she might easily have attributed a supernatural origin to him had she not felt the life in the warm flesh that was pressed against hers. Leaping from branch to branch, swinging across breathless voids, she was borne swiftly through the middle terrace of the forest. At first she was terrified, but gradually fear left her, to be replaced by that utter confidence which Tarzan of the Apes has inspired in many a breast.

At last he stopped and, lowering her to the branch upon which he stood, pointed through the surrounding foliage ahead of them. Zora looked, and to her astonishment saw the camp of her companions lying ahead and below her.

Once more the ape-man took her in his arms and dropped lightly to the ground into a wide trail that swept past the base of the tree in which he had halted. With a wave of his hand he indicated that she was free to go to the camp.

"Oh, how can I thank you?" exclaimed the girl. "How can I ever make you understand how splendid you have been and how I appreciate all that you have done for me?" But his only reply was to turn and swing lightly into the tree above them.

With a rueful shake of her head, Zora Drinov started along the trail toward camp, while above her Tarzan followed through the trees to make certain that she arrived in safety.

Paul Ivitch had been hunting and was just returning to camp when he saw something move in a tree at the edge of the clearing. He saw the spots of a leopard and raising his rifle, he fired. At the moment that Zora entered the camp the body of Tarzan of the Apes lunged from a tree almost at her side, blood trickling from a bullet-wound in his head as the sunshine played upon the leopard-spots of his loin-cloth. . . .

The sight of the lion growling above him might well have shaken the nerves of a man in far better physical condition than was Wayne Colt, but the vision of a beautiful girl running quickly toward the savage beast from the rear was the final stroke that almost overwhelmed him.

Through his brain ran a medley of recollection and conjecture. In a brief instant he recalled the fact that men had said they had felt no pain while being mauled by a lion—neither pain nor fear—and he also recalled that men went mad from thirst and hunger. If he was to die now it would not be painful, and of that he was glad; but if he did not die, then surely he was mad, for the lion and the girl must be the hallucination of a crazed mind.

Fascination held his eyes fixed upon the two. How real they were! He heard the girl speak to the lion and then he saw her brush past the great savage beast and come and bend over him where he lay helpless in the trail. She touched him and then he knew that she was real.

"You have killed him!" Zora cried. "You beast! He was worth more than a dozen such as you!"

"Who are you?" she asked, in limping English that was beautiful with a strange accent. "What has happened to you?"

"I have been lost," he said, "and I am about done up. I have not eaten for a long while." Then he fainted. . . .

Jad-bal-ja the golden lion had conceived a strange affection for La of Opar. Perhaps it was the call of one kindred savage spirit to another; perhaps it was merely the recollection that she was Tarzan's friend. But be that as it may, he seemed to find the same pleasure in her company that a faithful dog finds in the company of his master. He had protected her with fierce loyalty and when he made his kill he shared the flesh with her, though after she had cut off a portion that she wanted she had always gone away a little distance to build her primitive fire and cook the flesh, nor ever had she ventured back to the kill after Jad-bal-ja had commenced to feed, for a lion is yet a lion and the grim and ferocious growls that accompanied his feeding warned the girl against presuming too far upon the new-found generosity of the carnivore.

They had been feeding when the approach of Colt had attracted the lion's attention and brought him into the trail from his kill.

For a moment La had feared that she might not be able to keep the lion from the man and she had wanted to do so, for something in the stranger's appearance reminded her of Tarzan, whom he more nearly resembled than he did the grotesque priests of Opar. Because of this fact she thought that possibly the stranger might be from Tarzan's country.

Perhaps he was one of Tarzan's friends and if so, she must protect him. To her relief, the lion had obeyed her when she had called upon him to halt, and now he evinced no further desire to attack.

La tried to raise Colt to his feet and with considerable difficulty and some slight assistance from the man she succeeded in doing so. She put one of his arms across her shoulders and supporting him thus, guided him back along the trail, while Jad-bal-ja followed at their heels. She had some trouble in getting him through the brush to the hidden glen where Jad-bal-ja's kill lay and her little fire was burning a short distance away. But at last she succeeded and when they had come close to her fire, she lowered the man to the ground, while Jad-bal-ja turned once more to his feeding and his growling.

La fed Colt tiny pieces of the meat that she had cooked and he ate ravenously all that she would give him. A short distance away ran the river, where La and the lion would have gone to drink after they had fed, but she doubted that she could get the man so great a distance through the jungle, and so when he had eaten all that she dared to feed him, she left him there with the lion and went down to the river, but first she told Jad-bal-ja to guard him.

Near the river La found what she sought—a fruit with a hard rind. With her knife she cut an end from one of these fruits and scooped out the pulpy interior, producing a primitive but entirely practical cup, which she filled with water from the river.

The water, as much as the food, refreshed and strengthened Colt and though he lay but a few yards from a feeding lion, yet it seemed an eternity since he had experienced such feeling of contentment and security.

"You are a friend of Tarzan of the Apes?" asked La.

He shook his head. "No," he said. "I have heard of him, but I do not know him."

When Tarzan released the shaft it buried itself in the sentry's leg.

La frowned. "You are his enemy then?" she demanded.

"Of course not," replied Colt. "I do not even know him. I am an American; my name is Wayne Colt."

A sudden light flashed in La's eyes. "Do you know Zora?" she asked.

Colt came to his elbow with a sudden start. "Zora Drinov?" he demanded. "What do you know of her?"

"She is in trouble," La asserted.

"Yes, I know it; but how did you know?"

"I was with her when she was taken prisoner by the men of the desert. They took me also, but I escaped."

"How long ago was that?"

"The Flaming God has gone to rest many times since I saw Zora," replied the girl.

"Then I have seen her since."

"Where is she?"

"I do not know. She was with the Aarabs when I found her. We escaped from them and then, while I was hunting in the jungle, something came and carried her away. I do not know whether it was a man or a gorilla for though I saw its footprints, I could not be sure. I have been searching for her for a long time, but I could not find food and it has been some time since I have had water; so I lost my strength and you found me as I am."

"You shall not want for food nor water now," said La, "for Numa the lion will hunt for us and if we can find the camp of Zora's friends, they will go out and search for her."

"You know where the camp is?" he asked. "Is it near?"

"I do not know where it is. I have been searching for it to lead her friends after the men of the desert."

Colt had been studying the girl as they talked. He had noted her strange, barbaric apparel and the staggering beauty of her face and figure.

"You have not told me who you are," he said.

"I am La of Opar," she replied, "high priestess of the Flaming God."

Opar! Now indeed Colt knew that she was not of his world. Opar, the city of mystery, the city of fabulous treasures. Could it be that the same city that housed the grotesque warriors with whom he and Romero had fought produced also such beautiful creatures as Nao and La, and only these? He wondered why he had not connected her with Opar at once, for now he saw that her stomacher was similar to that of Nao's and of the priestess that he had seen upon the throne in the great chamber of the ruined temple. Recalling his attempt to enter Opar and loot it of its treasures, he deemed it expedient to make no mention of any familiarity with the city of the girl's birth.

The lion and the girl and the man lay up for the night beside Jad-bal-ja's kill and in the morning Colt found that his strength had partially returned. During the night Numa the lion had finished his kill and after the sun had risen, La found fruits which she and Colt ate.

"Numa will not kill again until tomorrow," she said, "so we shall have no meat until then, unless we are fortunate enough to kill something ourselves."

Colt had long since abandoned the heavy rifle of the Aarabs, to the burden of which his growing weakness had left his muscles inadequate, so he had nothing but his bare hands and La only a knife with which they might make a kill.

"Then I guess we will eat fruit until the lion kills again," he said. "In the meantime we might as well be trying to find the camp."

She shook her head. "No," she said, "you must rest. You were very weak when I found you and it is not well that you should exert yourself until you are strong again. Numa will sleep all day. You and I will cut some sticks and lie beside a little trail, where the small things go."

WHEN Zora Drinov saw her lion-man lying lifeless on the ground she ran quickly to him and knelt at his side. She had heard the shot; now seeing blood running from the wound upon his head, she thought some one had killed him intentionally and as Ivitch came out, rifle in hand, she turned upon him like a tigress.

"You have killed him," she cried. "You beast! He was worth more than a dozen such as you!"

The sound of the shot and the crashing of the body to the ground had brought men running from all parts of the camp, so that Tarzan and the girl were soon surrounded by a curious and excited throng of blacks, among which the remaining whites were pushing their way.

Ivitch was stunned, not only by the sight of the giant white man lying apparently dead before him, but also by the presence of Zora Drinov, whom all within the camp had given up as irretrievably lost.

"I had no idea, Comrade Drinov," he explained,

"that I was shooting at a man. I see now what caused my mistake. I saw something moving in a tree and I thought that it was a leopard—but instead it was the leopard-skin that he wears about his loins."

By this time Zveri had elbowed his way to the center of the group. "Zora!" he cried in astonishment as he saw the girl. "Where did you come from? What has happened? What is the meaning of this?"

"It means that this fool, Ivitch, has killed the man who saved my life," cried Zora.

"Who is he?" asked Zveri.

"I do not know," replied Zora. "He has never spoken to me. I think that he does not understand any language with which I am familiar."

"He is not dead," cried Ivitch. "See, he moved."

Romero knelt and examined the wound in Tarzan's head. "He is only stunned," he said. "The bullet struck him a glancing blow. There are no indications of a fracture of the skull. I have seen men hit thus before. He may be unconscious for a long time, or he may not, but I am sure that he will not die."

"Who the devil do you suppose he is?" asked Zveri.

Zora shook her head. "I have no idea," she said. "I only know that he is as splendid as he is mysterious."

"I know who he is," said a black, who had pushed forward to where he could see the figure of the prostrate man. "And if he is not already dead, you had better kill him, for he will be your worst enemy."

"What do you mean?" Zveri demanded. "Who is he?"

"He is Tarzan of the Apes," replied the black.

"You are certain?" snapped Zveri.

"Yes, Bwana," replied the black. "I saw him once before, and one never forgets Tarzan of the Apes."

"Yours was a lucky shot, Ivitch," said the leader, "and now you may as well finish what you started."

"Kill him, you mean?" demanded Ivitch.

"Our cause is lost and our lives with it, if he lives," replied Zveri. "I thought that he was dead or I should never have come here, and now that Fate has thrown him into our hands we would be fools to let him escape, for we could not have a worse enemy than he."

"I cannot kill him in cold blood," said Ivitch.

"You always were a weak-minded fool," said Zveri, "but I am not. Stand aside, Zora!" As he spoke he drew his revolver and advanced toward Tarzan.

The girl threw herself across the ape-man, shielding his body with hers.

"You cannot kill him," she cried. "You must not!"

"DON'T be a fool, Zora," snapped Zveri.

"He saved my life and brought me back here to camp. Do you think I am going to let you murder him?" she demanded.

"I am afraid you can't help yourself, Zora," replied the man. "I do not like to do it, but it is his life or the Cause. If he lives, we fail."

The girl leaped to her feet and faced Zveri. "If you kill him, Peter, I shall kill you—I swear it by everything that I hold most dear! Hold him prisoner if you will, but as you value your life, do not kill him."

Zveri went pale with anger. "Your words are treason," he said. "Traitors to the Cause have died for less than what you have said."

Zora Drinov realized that the situation was extremely dangerous. She had little reason to believe that Zveri would make good his threat toward her, but she saw that if she would save Tarzan she must act quickly. "Send the others away," she said to Zveri. "I have something to tell you before you kill this man."

For a moment the leader hesitated. Then he turned to Dorsky who stood at his side. "Have the fellow securely bound and taken to one of the tents," he said. "We shall give him a fair trial after he has regained consciousness, and then place him before a firing-squad." And then to the girl: "Come with me, Zora, and I will listen to what you have to say."

In silence the two walked to Zveri's tent. "Well?" inquired Zveri, as the girl halted before the entrance, "what have you to say to me that you think will change my plans relative to your lover?"

Zora looked at him for a long minute, a faint sneer of contempt curling her lips. "You *would* think such a thing," she said. "You are wrong. But however you may think, you shall not kill him."

"And why not?" demanded Zveri.

"Because if you do I shall tell them all what your plans are, that you yourself are a traitor to the Cause and that you have been using them all to advance your own selfish ambition to make yourself Emperor of Africa."

"You would not dare," cried Zveri "nor would I let you—for as much as I love you I shall kill you here on the spot, unless you promise not to interfere in any way with my plans."

"You do not dare kill me," the girl taunted. "You have antagonized every man in the camp, Peter, and they all like me. Some of them, perhaps, love me a little. Do you think that I should not be avenged within five minutes after you had killed me? You will have to think of something else, my friend, and the best thing that you can do is to take my advice. Keep Tarzan of the Apes a prisoner if you will, but on your life do not kill him or permit anyone else to do so."

Zveri sank into a camp-chair. "Everyone is against me," he said. "Even you, the woman I love, turn against me!"

"I have not changed toward you in any respect, Peter," said the girl.

"You mean that?" he asked, looking up.

"Absolutely," she replied.

"How long were you alone in the jungle with that man?" he demanded.

Zora shrugged.

"Don't start that, Peter," she said. "He could not have treated me differently if he had been my own brother and certainly, all other considerations aside, you should know me well enough to know that I have no such weakness in the direction your tone implied."

"You have never loved me, that is the reason," he said. "But I would not trust you or any other woman with a man she loves or with whom she was temporarily infatuated."

"That," she said, "has nothing to do with what we are discussing. Are you going to kill Tarzan of the

Apes, or are you not?"

"For your sake, I shall let him live," replied the man. "Even though I do not trust you," he added. "I trust no one. How can I? Look at this,"—and he took a code message from his pocket and handed it to her. "This came a few days ago. The damn' traitor—I wish I could get my hands on him! I should like to have killed him myself; but I suppose I shall have no such luck, as he is probably already dead."

Zora took the paper. Below the message, in Zveri's scrawling hand, it had been decoded in Russian script. As she read it her eyes grew large with astonishment.

"It is incredible," she said.

"It is the truth, though," said Zveri. "I always suspected the dirty hound!" With an oath, he added, "I think that damn' Mexican is just as bad."

"At least," said Zora, "his plan has been thwarted, for I take it that his message did not get through."

"No," said Zveri. "By error it was delivered to our agents instead of his."

"Then no harm has been done."

"Fortunately, no; but it has made me suspicious of everyone and I am going to push the expedition through at once before anything further can occur to interfere with my plans."

"Everything is ready, then?" she asked.

Zveri nodded.

"Everything is ready," he replied. "We march to-morrow morning. And now tell me what happened while I was at Opar. Why did the Aarabs desert and why did you go with them?"

"Abu Batu was angry and resentful because you

left him to guard the camp. The Aarabs felt that it was a reflection upon their courage and I think they would have deserted you anyway, regardless of me. Then, the day after you left, a strange woman wandered into camp. She was a very beautiful white woman from Opar and Abu Batu conceived the idea of profiting through the chance that Fate had sent him and so he took us with him with the intention of selling us into captivity on his return march to his own country."

"Are there no honest men in the world?" demanded Zveri.

"I am afraid not," replied the girl—but as Zveri was staring moodily at the ground he did not see the slightly contemptuous curl of her lip that accompanied her evasive reply.

She told him of the luring of La from Abu Batu's camp and of the Sheik's anger at the treachery of Ibn Dammuk; then she told of her own escape, though she did not men tion Wayne Colt's connection with it, but led Zveri to believe she had wandered alone in the jungle until the great ape captured her. She dwelt at length upon Tarzan's kindness and consideration and told of the great elephant who had guarded her by day.

"Sounds like a fairy story," said Zveri, "but I have heard enough about this ape-man to believe almost anything concerning him, which is one reason why I believe we shall never be safe while he lives."

"He cannot harm us while he is our prisoner and certainly, if you love me as you say you do, the man who saved my life deserves better from you than ignominious death."

"Speak no more of it," said Zveri. "I have already told you that I would not kill him." But in his treacherous mind he was formulating a plan whereby Tarzan might be destroyed, while still Zveri adhered to

The three friends stood in silent communion as the shadows lengthened.

the letter of his promise to Zora—that he would not kill Tarzan.

Early on the following morning the expedition filed out of camp, the savage black warriors arrayed in the uniforms of French Colonial troops while Zveri, Romero, Ivitch and Mori wore the uniforms of French officers.

Zora Drinov accompanied the marching column, for though she had asked to be permitted to remain and nurse Tarzan, Zveri would not permit her to do so, saying that he would not again let her out of his sight. Dorsky and a handful of blacks were left behind to guard the prisoner and watch over the store of provisions and equipment that were left in the base camp.

As the column had been preparing to march, Zveri gave his final instructions to Dorsky.

"I leave this matter entirely in your hands," he said. "It must appear that he escaped, or, at worst, that he met an accidental death."

"You need give the matter no further thought, Comrade Zveri," replied Dorsky. "Long before you return this stranger will have been removed."

A long and difficult march lay before the invaders, their route lying across southeastern Abyssinia into Italian Somaliland, five hundred miles of rough and savage country.

It was Zveri's intention to make no more than a demonstration in the Italian colony, merely sufficient to arouse the anger of the Italians still further against the French and to give the fascist dictator the excuse which Zveri believed was all that he awaited to carry a dream of Italian conquest across Europe.

Perhaps Zveri was a little mad, but then he was a disciple of mad men whose greed for power wrought distorted images in their minds, so that they could not differentiate between the rational and the bizarre.

Too, Zveri had for so long dreamed his dream of empire that he saw now only his goal and none of the insurmountable obstacles that beset his path. He saw a new Roman emperor ruling Europe and he saw himself as Emperor of Africa making an alliance with this new European power against all the balance of the world. He pictured two splendid golden thrones; upon one of them sat the Emperor Peter I, and upon the other the Empress Zora—and so he dreamed through the long hard marches toward the east. . . .

It was not until the morning of the day following that upon which he had been shot, that Tarzan regained consciousness. He felt very weak and sick and his head ached horribly. When he tried to move he discovered that his wrists and ankles were securely bound. He did not know what had happened and at first he could not imagine where he was, but, as recollection slowly returned and he recognized about him the canvas walls of a tent, he understood that in some way his enemies had captured him. He tried to wrench his wrists free from the cords that held them, but they resisted his every effort.

He listened intently and sniffed the air, but he could detect no evidence of the teeming camp that he had seen when he had brought the girl back. He knew that at least one night had passed, for the shadows that he could see through the tent opening indicated that the sun was high in the heavens, whereas it had been low in the west when last he saw it. He heard voices and knew that he was not alone, though he was confident there must be comparatively few men in camp.

Deep in the jungle he heard an elephant trumpeting, and once, from far off, came faintly the roar of a lion.

Tarzan strove again to snap the bonds that held him, but they would not yield. Then he turned his head so that he faced the opening in the tent and from his lips burst a long low cry.

Dorsky, who was lolling in a chair before his own tent, leaped to his feet. The blacks, before their own shelters, who had been talking animatedly, grew suddenly quiet and seized their weapons.

"What was that?" Dorsky demanded of his black boy.

The fellow, wide-eyed and trembling, shook his head. "I do not know, Bwana," he said. "Perhaps the man in the tent has died, for such a noise may well have come from the throat of a ghost."

"Nonsense," said Dorsky. "Come, we'll have a look at him." But the black held back and the white man went on alone.

The sound, which had come apparently from the tent in which the captive lay, had had a peculiar effect upon Dorsky, causing the flesh of his scalp to creep and a strange foreboding to fill him; so as he neared the tent he went more slowly and held his revolver ready in his hand.

When he entered the tent he saw the man lying where he had been left, but now his eyes were open and when they met those of the Russian, the latter had a sensation similar to that which one feels when he comes eye to eye with a wild beast that has been caught in a trap.

"Well," said Dorsky, "so you have come to, have you? What do you want?"

The captive made no reply, but his eyes never left the other's face. So steady was the unblinking gaze that Dorsky became uneasy. "You had better learn to talk," he said gruffly, "if you know what is good for you!"

Then it occurred to him that perhaps the man did not understand him, so he turned in the entrance and called to some of the blacks, who had advanced, half in curiosity, half in fear, toward the tent of the prisoner.

"One of you fellows come here," he said.

At first no one seemed inclined to obey, but presently a stalwart warrior advanced. "See if this fellow can understand your language. Come in and tell him that I have a proposition to make to him, and that he had better listen to it."

"If this is indeed Tarzan of the Apes," said the black, "he can understand me." And he came warily to the entrance of the tent.

The black repeated the message in his own dialect, but by no sign did the ape-man indicate that he understood.

Dorsky lost his patience. "You damned ape!" he said. "You needn't try to make a fool of me. I know perfectly well that you understand this fellow's gibberish and I know too that you are an Englishman and that you understand English. I'll give you just five minutes to think this thing over and then I am coming back. If you have not made up your mind to talk by that time, you can take the consequences."

Then he turned on his heel and left the tent.

CHAPTER XV

"KILL, TANTOR, KILL!"

LITTLE NKIMA had traveled far. Around his neck was a stout thong, supporting a small leather bag, in which reposed a message. This eventually he had brought to Muviro, war chief of the Waziri, and when the Waziri had started out upon their long march, Nkima had ridden proudly upon the shoulder of Muviro. For some time he had remained with the black warriors, but then, moved perhaps by some caprice of his erratic mind, or by a great urge that he could not resist, he had left them and, facing alone all the dangers that he feared most, had set out by himself upon business of his own.

Many and narrow were the escapes of Nkima as he swung through the giants of the forest. Could he have resisted temptation, he might have passed with reasonable safety, but that he could not do and so he was forever getting himself into trouble by playing pranks upon strangers, who, if they possessed any sense of humor themselves, certainly failed to appreciate little Nkima.

Nkima could not forget that he was the friend and confidant of Tarzan, Lord of the Jungle, though he seemed often to forget that Tarzan was not there to protect him when he hurled taunts and insults at other monkeys less favored. That he came through alive speaks more eloquently for his speed than for his intelligence or courage, so much of the time was he fleeing in terror, emitting shrill screams of mental anguish. Yet he never seemed to learn from experience, and having barely eluded one pursuer intent upon murdering him he would be quite prepared to insult or annoy the next creature he met, especially selecting, it would seem, those who were larger and stronger than himself.

Sometimes he fled in one direction, sometimes in another, so that he occupied much more time than was necessary in making his journey. Other-

*"Think well, ape," said the Russian, "and remember that when
I slip this between your ribs there will be no sound."*

The sinuous trunk twined around the Russian and the great elephant trumpeted shrilly as he raised Dorsky high above his head.

wise he would have reached his master in time to be of service to him at a moment that Tarzan needed a friend as badly, perhaps, as ever he had needed one before in his life.

And now, while far away in the forest Nkima fled from an old dog baboon, whom he had hit with a well-aimed stick, Michael Dorsky approached the tent where Nkima's master lay bound and helpless. The five minutes were up and Dorsky had come to demand Tarzan's answer. He came alone and as he entered the tent his simple plan of action was well formulated in his mind.

The expression upon the prisoner's face had changed. He seemed to be listening intently. Dorsky listened then too but could hear nothing, for by comparison with the hearing of Tarzan of the Apes Michael Dorsky was deaf, and what Tarzan heard filled him with quiet satisfaction.

"Now," said Dorsky, "I have come to give you your last chance. Comrade Zveri has led two expeditions to Opar in search of the gold that we know is stored there. Both expeditions failed. It is well known that you know the location of the treasure vaults of Opar and can lead us to them. Agree that you will do this when Comrade Zveri returns and not only will you not be harmed, but you will be released as quickly as Comrade Zveri feels that it would be safe to have you at liberty. Refuse, and you

Nkima was gnawing frantically at the bonds when Dango charged again, evidently convinced by this time that the great Tarmangani was helpless.

die!" He drew a knife from its sheath at his belt. "If you refuse to answer, I shall accept that as evidence that you have not accepted my proposition."

As the ape-man maintained his stony silence, the Russian held the sharp blade low before his eyes. "Think well, ape," he said, "and remember that when I slip this between your ribs there will be no sound. It will pierce your heart and I shall leave it there until the blood has ceased to flow. Then I shall remove it and close the wound and later in the day you will be found dead and I shall tell the blacks that you died from the accidental gun-shot. Thus your friends will never learn the truth. You will not be avenged and you will have died uselessly."

The dagger was very near Tarzan's face now. Of a sudden, like a wild beast, he raised his body and his jaws closed like a steel trap upon the wrist of the Russian.

With a scream of pain, Dorsky drew back. The dagger dropped from his nerveless fingers and at the same instant Tarzan swung his legs around the feet of the would-be assassin and as Dorsky rolled over on his back, he dragged Tarzan of the Apes on top of him.

The ape-man knew from the snapping of Dorsky's wrist-bones between his teeth that the man's right hand was useless and so he released it. Then to the Russian's horror, the ape-man's jaws sought his jugular vein, while from the giant's throat there rumbled the growl of a savage beast at bay.

Screaming for his men to come to his assistance, Dorsky tried to reach the revolver at his right hip with his left hand, but he soon saw that unless he could rid himself of Tarzan's body he would be unable to do so.

Already he heard his men running toward the tent, shouting among themselves; then he heard exclamations of surprise and screams of terror, and the next instant the tent vanished from above them and Dorsky saw a huge bull elephant towering above him and his savage antagonist.

Instantly Tarzan ceased his efforts to close his teeth on Dorsky's throat and at the same time rolled quickly from the body of the Russian. As he did so, Dorsky's hand found his revolver.

"Kill, Tantor!" shouted the ape-man. "Kill!"

The sinuous trunk of the pachyderm twined around the Russian. The little eyes of the elephant flamed red with hate and he trumpeted shrilly as he raised Dorsky high above his head and wheeling about hurled him out into the camp, while the terrified blacks, casting affrighted glances over their shoulders, fled into the jungle. Then Tantor charged his victim. With his great tusks he gored him; then, in a frenzy of rage, trumpeting and squealing, he trampled him—until nothing remained of Michael Dorsky but a bloody pulp.

From the moment Tantor seized the Russian, Tarzan had sought ineffectually to stay the great brute's fury, but Tantor was deaf to commands until he had wreaked his vengeance upon this creature that had dared attack his friend. But when his rage had spent its force and nothing remained against which to vent it, he came quietly to Tarzan's side and at a word from the ape-man, lifted the big brown body gently in his powerful trunk and bore him away into the forest.

Deep into the jungle to a hidden glade, Tantor carried his helpless friend; there he placed him gently on soft grasses beneath the shade of a tree. Little more could the great bull do other than to stand guard. As a result of the excitement attending the killing of Dorsky and Tantor's concern for Tarzan, the elephant was nervous and irritable. He stood with upraised ears, alert for any menacing sound, waving his sensitive trunk to and fro, searching each vagrant air-current for the scent of danger.

The pain of his wound annoyed Tarzan far less than the pangs of thirst.

To little monkeys watching him from the trees he called: "Come, Manu, and untie the thongs that bind my wrists."

"We are afraid," said an old monkey.

"I am Tarzan of the Apes," said the man reassuringly. "Tarzan has been your friend always. He will not harm you."

"We are afraid," repeated the old monkey. "Tarzan deserted us. For many moons the jungle has not known Tarzan, but other Tarmangani and strange Gomangani came and with thundersticks they hunted little Manu and killed him. If Tarzan had still been our friend, he would have driven these strange men away."

"If I had been here the strange men-things would not have harmed you," said Tarzan. "Still would Tarzan have protected you. Now I am back, but I cannot destroy the strangers or drive them away until the thongs are taken from my wrists."

"Who put them there?" asked the monkey.

"The strange Tarmangani," replied Tarzan.

"Then they must be more powerful than Tarzan," said Manu. "So what good would it do to set you free? If the strange Tarmangani found out that we had done it, they would be angry and come and kill us. Let Tarzan, who for many rains has been Lord of the Jungle, free himself!"

Seeing that it was futile to appeal to Manu, Tarzan, as a forlorn hope, voiced the long, plaintive, uncanny help-call of the great apes. With slowly increasing crescendo it rose to a piercing shriek that drove far and wide through the silent jungle.

In all directions, beasts, great and small, paused as the weird note broke upon their sensitive eardrums.

None was afraid, for the call told them that a great bull was in trouble and, therefore, doubtless harmless, but the jackals interpreted the sound to mean the possibility of flesh and trotted off through the jungle in the direction from which it had come, and Dango the hyena heard and slunk nearer on soft pads, hoping he would find a helpless animal that would prove easy prey.

Far away, and faintly, a little monkey heard the call, and recognized the voice of the caller.

Swiftly, then, he flew through the jungle, impelled as he was upon rare occasions by a directness of thought and a tenacity of purpose that brooked no interruption.

Tarzan had sent Tantor to the river to fetch water in his trunk. From a distance he caught the scent of the jackals and the horrid scent of Dango and he hoped that Tantor would return before they came creeping upon him.

He felt no fear, only an instinctive urge toward self-preservation. The jackals he held in contempt, for he knew that though bound hand and foot he still could keep the timid creatures away—but Dango was different; if the filthy brute realized Tarzan's helplessness, those powerful jaws would make quick work of him.

The jackals came first, standing at the edge of the little glade and watching him. Then they circled slowly, coming nearer, but when he raised himself to a sitting position they ran yelping away.

Three times they crept closer, trying to force their courage to the point of actual attack; then a horrid slinking form appeared upon the edge of the glade, and the jackals withdrew to a safe distance— Dango the hyena had come!

Tarzan was still sitting up and the beast stood eying him, filled with curiosity and with fear. He growled and the man-thing facing him growled back and then from above them came a great chattering and Tarzan, looking up, saw little Nkima dancing upon the limb of a tree above him.

"Come down, Nkima," he cried, "and untie the thongs that bind my wrists."

Nkima hesitated, trembling.

"Dango! Dango!" he shouted. "Little Nkima is afraid of Dango."

"If you come now," said Tarzan, "it will be safe— but if you wait too long Dango will kill Tarzan and then to whom may little Nkima go for protection?"

"Nkima comes," shouted the little monkey, and dropping quickly through the trees he leaped to Tarzan's shoulder.

The hyena bared his fangs and laughed his horrid laugh.

"Quick, the thongs, Nkima," urged Tarzan; and the little monkey, his fingers trembling with terror, went to work upon the leather thongs at Tarzan's wrists.

Dango, his ugly head lowered, made a sudden rush, and from the deep lungs of the ape-man came a thunderous roar that might have done credit to Numa himself.

With a yelp of terror the cowardly Dango turned and fled to the extremity of the glade, where he stood bristling and growling.

"Hurry, Nkima," said Tarzan. "Dango will come again. Maybe once, maybe twice, maybe many times before he closes on me—but in the end he will realize that I am helpless and then he will not stop or turn back."

"Nkima's fingers are sick," said the little Manu. "They are weak and they tremble so that they will not untie the knot."

"Nkima has sharp teeth," Tarzan reminded him. "Why waste your time with sick fingers over knots that they cannot untie? Let your sharp teeth do the work."

Instantly Nkima commenced to gnaw upon the strands. Silent perforce because his mouth was otherwise occupied, Nkima strove diligently and without interruption.

Dango, in the meantime, made two short rushes, each time coming a little closer, but each time turning back before the menace of the ape-man's roars and savage growls, which by now had aroused the jungle.

Above them, in the tree-tops, the monkeys chattered, scolded and screamed and in the distance the voice of Numa rolled like far thunder, while from the river came the squealing and trumpeting of Tantor.

Little Nkima was gnawing frantically at the bonds when Dango charged again, evidently convinced by this time that the great Tarmangani was helpless—for now, with a growl, he rushed in and closed upon the man.

With a sudden surge of the great muscles of his arms that sent little Nkima sprawling, Tarzan sought to tear his hands free that he might defend himself against the savage death that menaced him in those slavering jaws, and the thongs, almost parted by Nkima's sharp teeth, gave at the terrific strain of the ape-man's efforts.

As Dango leaped for the bronzed throat, Tarzan's hand shot forward and seized the beast by the neck, though the impact of the heavy body carried him backward to the ground.

Dango twisted, struggled and clawed in a vain effort to free himself from the death-grip of the ape-man; but those steel fingers closed relentlessly upon his throat until, gasping for breath, the great brute sank helplessly upon the body of its intended victim.

Until death was assured, Tarzan did not relinquish his grasp, but when at last there could be no doubt, he hurled the carcass from him and, sitting up, fell quickly to the thongs that secured his ankles.

During the brief battle, Nkima had taken refuge among the topmost branches of a lofty tree, where he leaped about, screaming frantically at the battling beasts beneath him.

Not until he was quite sure the fearsome Dango was dead did he descend. Warily he approached the body, lest perchance he had been mistaken, but again convinced by closer scrutiny, he leaped upon it and struck it viciously, again and again; then he stood upon it shrieking his defiance at the world with all the assurance and bravado of one who has overcome a dangerous enemy.

Tantor, startled by the help-cry of his friend, had turned back from the river without taking water. Trees bent beneath his mad rush as, ignoring winding trails, he struck straight through the jungle toward the little glade in answer to the call of the ape-man, and now, infuriated by the sounds of battle, he came charging into view, a titanic engine of rage and vengeance.

Tantor's eyesight is none too good and it seemed that in his mad charge he must trample the ape-man who lay directly in his path. But Tarzan spoke to him and the great beast came to a sudden stop at his side and pivoting, wheeled about in his tracks, his ears forward, his trunk raised, trumpeting a savage warning as he searched for the creature that had been menacing his friend.

"Quiet, Tantor! It was Dango. He is dead," said the ape-man, and as the eyes of the elephant finally located the carcass of the hyena he charged and trampled it, as he had trampled Dorsky.

His ankles freed of their bonds, Tarzan was upon his feet and, when Tantor had vented his rage upon the body of Dango, he called the elephant to him.

Tantor came then quietly to his side and stood with his trunk touching the ape-man's body, his rage quieted and his tingling nerves soothed by the reassuring calm of the ape-man.

And now Nkima came, making an agile leap from a swaying bough to the back of Tantor and then to the shoulder of Tarzan, where, with his little arms about the ape-man's neck, he pressed his cheek close against the bronzed cheek of the great Tarmangani who was his master and his god.

Thus the three friends stood in the silent communion that only beasts know, as the shadows lengthened and the sun set behind the forest.

CHAPTER XVI

"TURN BACK!"

THE privations that Wayne Colt had endured had weakened him far more than he had realized and before his returning strength could bring renewed powers of resistance, he was stricken with fever.

The high priestess of the Flaming God, versed in the lore of ancient Opar, was conversant with the medicinal properties of many roots and herbs and, as well, with the mystic powers of incantation that drove demons from the bodies of the sick.

By day she gathered and brewed and at night she sat at the feet of her patient, intoning weird prayers, the origin of which reached back through countless ages to vanished temples, above which now rolled the waters of a mighty sea. While she wrought with every artifice at her command to drive out the demon of sickness that had possessed this man of an alien world, Jad-bal-ja the golden lion hunted for all three, and though at times he made his kill at a dis-

When La, upon her knees, prayed to the sun, Colt was sure that the fever was worse and that he had become delirious again.

tance he never failed to carry the carcass of his prey back to the hidden lair where the woman nursed the man.

Days of burning fever, days of delirium, shot with periods of rationality, dragged their slow length. Often Colt's mind was confused by a jumble of bizarre impressions, in which La might one moment be Zora Drinov, a ministering angel from heaven the next, and then a Red Cross nurse; but in whatever guise he found her it seemed always a pleasant one and when she was absent from his side, as she was sometimes forced to be, he was depressed and unhappy.

When, upon her knees at his feet, she prayed to the rising sun, or to the sun at zenith, or to the setting sun, as was her wont, or when she chanted strange, weird songs in an unknown tongue, accompanying them with the mysterious gestures that were a part of the ritual, he was sure that the fever was worse and that he had become delirious again.

And so the days dragged on and while Colt lay helpless, Zveri marched toward Italian Somaliland, and Tarzan, recovered from the shock of his wound, followed the plain trail of the expedition, and from his shoulder little Nkima scolded and chattered through the day.

Behind him he had left a handful of terrified blacks in the camp of the conspirators.

They had been lazing in the shade, following their breakfast, one morning a week after the killing of Dorsky and the escape of his captive.

Fear of the ape-man at liberty, that had so terrified them at first, no longer concerned them greatly. Psychologically akin to the brutes of the forest, they happily soon forgot their terrors, nor did they harass their minds by anticipating those which might assail them in the future, as it is the silly custom of civilized man to do.

And so it was this morning that a sight which

burst suddenly upon their astonished eyes found them entirely unprepared.

They heard no noise, so silently go the beasts of the jungle, however large or heavy they may be, yet suddenly in the clearing at the edge of the camp there appeared a great elephant and upon his head sat the recent captive, whom they had been told was Tarzan of the Apes, and upon the man's shoulder perched a little monkey.

With exclamations of terror, the blacks leaped to their feet and dashed into the jungle upon the opposite side of camp.

Tarzan leaped lightly to the ground and entered Dorsky's tent. He had returned for a definite purpose and his effort was crowned with success, for in the tent of the Russian he found his rope and his knife that had been taken away from him at the time of his capture.

For bow and arrows and a spear he had only to look to the shelters of the blacks and, having found what he wanted, he departed as silently as he had come.

Now the time had arrived when Tarzan must set out rapidly upon the trail of his enemy, leaving Tantor to the peaceful paths that he loved best.

"I go, Tantor," he said. "Search out the forest where the young trees have the tenderest bark and watch well against the men-things, for they alone in all the world are the enemies of all living creatures."

He was off through the forest then, with little Nkima clinging tightly to his bronzed neck.

Plain lay the winding trail of Zveri's army before the eyes of the ape-man, but he had no need to follow any trail. Long weeks before, as he had kept vigil above their camp, he had heard the principals discussing their plans and so he knew their objectives. He knew too how rapidly they could march and therefore about where he might hope to overtake them.

Unhampered by files of porters sweating under heavy loads, earthbound to no winding trails, Tarzan was able to travel many times faster than the expedition.

He saw their trail only when his own chanced to cross it as he lay a straight course for a point far in advance of the sweating column.

When he overtook the expedition night had fallen and the tired men were in camp. They had eaten and were happy and many of the men were singing.

To one who did not know the truth it might have appeared to be a military camp of French Colonial troops, for there was a military precision about the arranging of the fires and the temporary shelters and of the placing of the officers' tents that would not have been undertaken by a hunting or scientific expedition, and in addition there were the uniformed sentries pacing their beats.

All this was the work of Miguel Romero, to whose superior knowledge of military matters Zveri had been forced to defer in all matter of this nature, though there had been no diminution of the hatred which each felt for the other.

From his tree Tarzan watched the scene below, attempting to estimate as closely as possible the number of armed men that formed the fighting force of the expedition, while Nkima, bent upon some mysterious mission, swung nimbly through the trees toward the east.

Tarzan realized that Zveri had recruited a force that might constitute a definite menace to the peace of Africa, since among its numbers were represented many large and war-like tribes who might easily be persuaded to follow this leader, if success were to crown his initial engagement.

It was, however, to prevent this very thing that Tarzan of the Apes had interested himself in the activities of Peter Zveri, and here before him was another opportunity to undermine the Russian's dream of empire while it was still only a dream and might be effectively dissipated by trivial means.

Tarzan fitted an arrow to his bow. Slowly his right hand drew back the feathered end of the shaft until the point rested almost upon his left thumb. His manner was marked by easy, effortless grace. He did not appear to be taking conscious aim and yet when he released the shaft it buried itself in the fleshy part of a sentry's leg precisely as Tarzan of the Apes had intended that it should.

With a yell of surprise and pain the black collapsed upon the ground, more frightened however than hurt, and as his fellows gathered around him, Tarzan of the Apes melted away into the shadows of the jungle night.

Attracted by the cry of the wounded man, Zveri, Romero and the other leaders of the expedition hastened from their tents and joined the throng of excited chattering blacks who surrounded the victim of Tarzan's new campaign of terrorism.

Tarzan touched her shoulder in a half-caress. "La the immutable!" he murmured.

"Who shot you?" demanded Zveri, when he saw the arrow protruding from the sentry's leg.

"I do not know," replied the man.

"Have you an enemy in camp who might want to kill you?" demanded Zveri.

"Even if he had," said Romero, "he couldn't have shot him with an arrow—because no bows or arrows were brought with the expedition."

"I hadn't thought of that," said Zveri.

"So it must have been some one outside camp," said Romero.

With difficulty and to the accompaniment of the screams of their victim, Ivitch and Romero cut the arrow from the sentry's leg, while Zveri and Kitembo discussed various conjectures as to the exact portent of the affair.

"We have evidently run into a group of hostile natives," said Zveri.

"Cut that!" snapped Romero. "I have you covered and if it wasn't for Senorita Drinov I would kill you on the spot!"

Kitembo shrugged noncommittally. "Let me see the arrow," he said to Romero. "Perhaps that will tell us something."

As the Mexican handed the missile to the black chief, the latter carried it close to a camp fire and examined it closely while the white men gathered about him waiting for his findings.

At last Kitembo straightened up. The expression upon his face was serious and when he spoke his voice trembled slightly.

"This is bad," he said.

"What do you mean?" demanded Zveri.

"This arrow bears the mark of a warrior who was left behind in our base camp," replied the chief.

"That is impossible," cried Zveri.

Kitembo shrugged. "I know it," he said. "But it is true."

"With an arrow out of the air the Hindu was slain," said a black headman, standing near Kitembo.

"Shut up, you fool," snapped Romero, "or you'll have the whole camp in a blue funk."

"That's right," said Zveri. "We must hush this thing up." He turned to the headman. "You and Kitembo," he said, "must not repeat this to your men. Let us keep it to ourselves."

Both Kitembo and the headman agreed to guard the secret, but within half an hour every man in camp knew that the sentry had been shot with an arrow that had been left behind in the base camp and immediately their minds were prepared for other things that lay ahead of them upon the long trail.

The effect of the incident upon the minds of the black soldiers was apparent during the following day's march. They were quieter and more thoughtful and there was much low-voiced conversation among them; but if they had given signs of nervousness during the day, it was nothing as compared

"Look!" said the black scout to
Kitembo. "It is a warning!"

with their state of mind after darkness fell upon their camp that night.

The sentries evidenced their terror plainly by their listening attitudes and nervous attention to the sounds that came out of the blackness surrounding the camp. Most of them were brave men who would have faced a visible enemy with courage, but to a man they were convinced that they were confronted by the supernatural, against which they knew neither rifle nor bravery might avail. They felt the ghostly eyes were watching them and the result was as demoralizing as would an actual attack have been.

Yet they need not have concerned themselves so greatly, for the cause of all their superstitious apprehension was moving rapidly through the jungle, miles away from them; every instant the distance between him and them was increasing.

Another force, that might have caused them much greater anxiety had they been aware of it, lay even further away upon the trail they still must traverse to reach their destination.

Around tiny cooking fires squatted a hundred black warriors, whose white plumes nodded and trembled as they moved. Sentries guarded these stalwart warriors—sentries who scorned to be timorous or afraid, since these men had little fear of ghosts or demons. They wore their amulets in leather pouches that swung from cords about their necks and they prayed to strange gods, but deep in their hearts lay a growing contempt for both. They had learned from experience and from the advice of a wise leader to look more to themselves and their weapons for victory than to their god.

They were a cheerful, happy company, veterans of many an expedition. Like all veterans, they took advantage of every opportunity for rest and relaxation, the value of both of which is enhanced by the maintenance of a cheerful frame of mind, and so there was much laughing and joking among them, and of ten both the cause and butt of this was a little monkey, now teasing, now caressing, and in return being himself teased or caressed. That there was a bond of deep affection between him and these clean-limbed black giants was constantly apparent.

When they pulled his tail they never pulled it very hard, and when he turned upon them in apparent fury, his sharp teeth closing upon their fingers or arms, it was noticeable that he never drew blood. Their play was rough, for they were all rough and primitive creatures; nevertheless it was all playing and it was based upon a foundation of mutual affection.

THESE men had just finished their evening meal when a figure, materializing as though out of thin air, dropped silently into their midst from the branches of a tree which overhung their camp.

Instantly a hundred warriors sprang to arms and then as quickly they relaxed, as with shouts of "Bwana! Bwana!" they ran toward the bronzed giant standing silently in their midst.

As to an emperor or a god they went upon their knees before him and those who were nearest him touched his hands and his feet in reverence, for to the Waziri Tarzan of the Apes, who was their king, was yet something more and of their own volition they worshiped him as their living god.

But if the warriors were glad to see him, little Nkima was fairly frantic with joy. He scrambled quickly over the bodies of the kneeling blacks and leaped thence to Tarzan's shoulder, where he clung about the bronzed neck, jabbering excitedly.

"You have done well, my children," said the ape-man, "and little Nkima has done well. He bore my message to you and I find you ready where I had planned that you should be."

"We have kept always a day's march ahead of the strangers, Bwana," said Muviro, "camping well off the trail that they might not discover our fresh camp sites and become suspicious."

"They do not suspect your presence," said Tarzan. "I listened above their camp last night, and they said nothing that would indicate they dreamed that another party was preceding them along the trail."

"Where the dirt of the trail was soft a warrior who marched at the rear of the column, brushed away the freshness of our spoor with a leafy bough," explained Muviro.

"Tomorrow we shall wait here for them," said the ape-man, "and tonight you shall listen to Tarzan while he explains the plans that you will follow."

AS Zveri's column took up the march upon the following morning, after a night of rest that had passed without incident, the spirits of all had risen to an appreciable degree. The blacks had not forgotten the grim warning that had sped out of the night surrounding their previous camp, but they were of a race whose spirits soon rebound from depression.

The leaders of the expedition now were encouraged, for over a third of the distance to their goal had been covered.

For various reasons they were anxious to complete this phase of the plan. Zveri believed that upon its successful conclusion hinged his whole dream of empire. Ivitch, a natural-born trouble-maker, was happy in the thought that the success of the expedition would cause untold annoyance to millions of people and perhaps, also, by the dream of his return to Russia as a hero.

Romero and Mori wanted to have it over for entirely different reasons. They were thoroughly disgusted with the Russian. They had lost all confidence in the sincerity of Zveri, who, filled as he was with his own importance and his delusions of future grandeur, talked too much, with the result that he had convinced Romero that he and all his kind were frauds, bent upon accomplishing their selfish ends with the assistance of their silly dupes and at the expense of the peace and prosperity of the world.

It had not been difficult for Romero to convince Mori of the truth of his deductions and now, thoroughly disillusioned, the two men continued on with the expedition because they believed that they could not successfully accomplish their intended desertion until the party was once more settled in the base camp.

The march had continued uninterruptedly for about an hour after camp had been broken when one of Kitembo's black scouts, leading the column, halted suddenly in his tracks.

"Look!" he said to Kitembo, who was just behind

him.

The chief stepped to the warrior's side and there, before him in the trail, sticking upright in the earth, was an arrow.

"It is a warning!" said the warrior.

Gingerly, Kitembo plucked the arrow from the earth and examined it. He would have been very glad to keep the knowledge of his discovery to himself, although not a little shaken by what he had seen, but the warrior at his side had seen, too. "It is the same," he said. "It is another of the arrows that were left behind in the base camp."

When Zveri came abreast of them, Kitembo handed him the arrow. "It is the same," he said to the Russian, "and it is a warning for us to turn back."

"Pooh!" exclaimed Zveri contemptuously. "It is only an arrow sticking in the dirt and cannot stop a column of armed men. I did not think that you were a coward, too, Kitembo."

The black scowled. "Nor do men with safety call me a coward," he snapped; "but neither am I a fool and better than you do I know the danger signals of the forest. We shall go on because we are brave men, but many will never come back. Also, your plans will fail."

At this Zveri flew into one of his frequent rages and though the men continued the march, they were in a sullen mood and many were the ugly glances that were cast at Zveri and his lieutenants.

Shortly after noon the expedition halted for the noon-day rest. They had been passing through a dense woods, gloomy and depressing, and there was neither song nor laughter, nor a great deal of conversation as the men squatted together in little knots while they devoured the cold food that constituted their midday meal.

Suddenly, from somewhere far above, a voice floated down to them. Weird and uncanny, it spoke to them in a Bantu dialect that most of them could understand. "Turn back, children of Mulungu," it cried. "Turn back before you die! Desert the white men before it is too late."

That was all. The men crouched fearfully, looking up into the trees. It was Zveri who broke the silence. "What the hell was that?" he demanded. "What did it say?"

"It warned us to turn back," said Kitembo.

"There will be no turning back," snapped Zveri.

"I do not know about that," replied Kitembo.

"I thought you wanted to be a king," cried Zveri. "You'd make a hell of a king."

For the moment Kitembo had forgotten the dazzling prize that Zveri had held before his eyes for months—to be king of Kenya. That was worth risking much for. "We will go on," he said.

"You may have to use force," said Zveri, "but stop at nothing. We must go on, no matter what happens." Then he turned to his other lieutenants. "Romero, you and Mori go to the rear of the column and shoot every man who refuses to advance."

The men had not as yet refused to go on and when the order to march was given, they sullenly took their places in the column.

For an hour they marched thus and then, far ahead, came the weird cry that many of them had heard before at Opar and a few minutes later a voice out of the distance called to them. "Desert the white men," it said.

The blacks whispered among themselves and it was evident that trouble was brewing, but Kitembo managed to persuade them to continue the march, a thing that Zveri never could have accomplished.

"I wish we could get that trouble-maker," said Zveri to Zora Drinov, as the two walked together near the head of the column.

"It is some one familiar with the workings of the native mind," said the girl. "Probably a medicine-man of some tribe through whose territory we are marching."

"I hope that it is nothing more than that," replied Zveri. "I have no doubt but that the man is a native, but I may be afraid that he is acting on instructions from either the British or the Italians, who hope thus to disorganize and delay us until they can mobilize a force with which to attack us."

"It has certainly shaken the morale of the men," said Zora, "for I believe that they attribute all of the weird happenings, from the mysterious death of Jafar to the present time, to the same agency, to which their superstitious minds naturally attribute a supernatural origin."

"So much the worse for them then," said Zveri, "for they are going on whether they wish to or not and when they find that attempted desertion means death, they will wake up to the fact that it is not safe to trifle with Peter Zveri."

"They are many, Peter," the girl reminded him, "and we are few, in addition to which they are, thanks to you, well armed. It seems to me that you may have created a Frankenstein's monster that in the end will destroy us all."

"You are as bad as the blacks," growled Zveri, "making a mountain out of a molehill. Why, if I—"

Behind the rear of the column and again apparently from the air above them sounded the warning voice: "Desert the whites." Silence fell again upon the marching column, but the men moved on, exhorted by Kitembo and threatened by the revolvers of their white officers.

Presently the forest broke at the edge of a small plain, across which the trail led through buffalo grass that grew high above the heads of the marching men. They were well into this when, ahead of them, a rifle spoke, and then another and another, seemingly in a long line across their front.

Zveri ordered one of the blacks to rush Zora to the rear of the column into a position of safety, while he followed close behind her, ostensibly searching for Romero and shouting words of encouragement to the men. As yet no one had been hit, but the column had stopped and the men were rapidly losing all semblance of formation.

"Quick, Romero," shouted Zveri, "take command up in front. I will cover the rear with Mori and prevent desertions."

The Mexican sprang past him and with the aid of Ivitch and some of the black chiefs he deployed one company in a long skirmish line with which he advanced slowly, while Kitembo followed with half the balance of the expedition acting as a support, leaving Ivitch, Mori and Zveri to organize a reserve from the remainder.

After the first widely scattered shots, the firing had ceased, to be followed by a silence even more ominous to the overwrought nerves of the black soldiers.

The utter silence of the enemy, the lack of any sign of movement in the grasses ahead of them, coupled with the mysterious warnings which still rang in their ears, convinced the blacks that they faced no mortal foe.

"Turn back!" came mournfully from the grasses ahead. "This is the last warning. Death will follow disobedience."

The line wavered, and to steady it Romero gave the command to fire. In response came a rattle of musketry out of the grasses ahead of them and this time a dozen men went down, killed or wounded.

"Charge!" cried Romero, but instead the men wheeled about and broke for the rear and safety.

At sight of the advance line bearing down upon them, throwing away their rifles as they ran, the support turned and fled, carrying the reserve with it, and the whites were carried along in the mad rout.

In disgust, Miguel Romero fell back alone. He saw no enemy, for none pursued him and this fact induced within him an uneasiness that the singing bullets had been unable to arouse. As he plodded on alone far in the rear of his companions he began to share to some extent the feeling of unreasoning terror that had seized his black companions, or at least, if not to share it, to sympathize with them.

It is one thing to face a foe that you can see and quite another to be beset by an invisible enemy, of whose very appearance, even, one is ignorant.

Shortly after Romero reëntered the forest he saw some one walking along the trail ahead of him and presently, when he had an unobstructed view, he saw that it was Zora Drinov.

He called to her then and she turned and waited for him.

"I was afraid that you had been killed, Comrade," she said.

"I was born under a lucky star," he replied, smiling. "Men were shot down on either side of me and behind me. Where is Zveri?"

Zora shrugged. "I do not know," she said.

"Perhaps he is trying to reorganize the reserve," suggested Romero.

"Doubtless," said the girl shortly.

"I hope he is fleet of foot then," said the Mexican.

"Evidently he is," replied Zora.

"You should not have been left alone like this," said the man.

"I can take care of myself," replied Zora.

"Perhaps," he said, "but if you belonged to me—"

"I belong to no one, Comrade Romero," she replied icily.

"Forgive me, señorita," he said. "I know that. I merely chose an unfortunate way of trying to say that if the girl I loved were here she would not have been left alone in the forest, especially when I believe, as Zveri must believe, that we are being pursued by an enemy."

"You do not like Comrade Zveri, do you, Romero?"

"Even to you, señorita," he replied, "I must admit, since you ask me, that I do not."

"I know that he has antagonized many."

"He has antagonized all—except you, señorita."

"Why should I be excepted?" she asked. "How do you know that he has not antagonized me also?"

"Not deeply, I am sure," he said, "or else you would not have consented to become his wife."

"And how do you know that I have?" she asked.

"Comrade Zveri boasts of it often," replied Romero.

"Oh, he does!" Nor did she make any other comment.

CHAPTER XVII

A GULF THAT WAS BRIDGED

THE general rout of Zveri's forces ended only when their last camp had been reached and even then only for part of the command, for as night fell it was discovered that fully twenty-five per cent of the men were missing and among the absentees were Zora and Romero.

As the stragglers came in Zveri questioned each about the girl, but no one had seen her. He tried to organize an expedition to go back in search of her, but no one would accompany him. He threatened and pleaded, only to discover that he had lost all control of his men.

Perhaps he would have gone back alone as he insisted that he intended doing, but he was relieved of this necessity when, well after dark, the two walked into camp together.

At sight of them Zveri was both relieved and angry. "Why didn't you remain with me?" he snapped at Zora.

"Because I cannot run so fast as you," she replied, and Zveri said no more.

From the darkness of the trees above the camp came the now familiar warning: "Desert the whites!" A long silence followed this, broken only by the nervous whisperings of the blacks, and then the voice spoke again. "The trails to your own countries are free from danger, but death walks always with the white men. Throw away your uniforms and leave the white men to the jungle and to me."

A black warrior leaped to his feet and stripped the French uniform from his body, throwing it upon a cooking fire that burned near him. Instantly others followed his example.

"Stop that!" cried Zveri.

"Silence, white man!" growled Kitembo.

"Kill the whites!" shouted a naked Basembo warrior.

Instantly there was a rush toward the whites, who were gathered near Zveri, and then from above them came a warning cry. "The whites are mine!" it cried. "Leave them to me."

For an instant the advancing warriors halted and then he, who had constituted himself their leader, maddened perhaps by his hatred and his blood lust, advanced again, grasping his rifle menacingly.

From above a bow-string twanged. The black, dropping his rifle, screamed as he tore at an arrow protruding from his chest and, as he fell forward upon his face, the other blacks fell back, and the whites were left alone, while the negroes huddled by themselves in a far corner of the camp.

Many of them would have deserted that night,

but they feared the darkness of the jungle and the menace of the thing hovering above them.

Zveri strode angrily to and fro, cursing his luck, cursing the blacks, cursing everyone. "If I had had any help, if I had had any cooperation," he grumbled, "this would not have happened, but I cannot do everything alone."

"You have done this pretty much alone," said Romero.

"What do you mean?" demanded Zveri.

"I mean that you have made such an over-bearing ass of yourself that you have antagonized everyone in the expedition, but even so they might have carried on if they had had any confidence in your courage —no man likes to follow a coward."

"You call me that, you yellow greaser?" shouted Zveri, reaching for his revolver.

"Cut that," snapped Romero. "I have you covered. And let me tell you now that if it wasn't for Señorita Drinov I would kill you on the spot and rid the world of at least one crazy mad dog that is threatening the entire world with the hydrophobia of hate and suspicion. Señorita Drinov saved my life once. I have not forgotten that and because, perhaps, she loves you, you are safe, unless I am forced to kill you in self-defense."

"This is utter insanity," cried Zora. "There are

"Come!" said the black chief—but as he uttered the word something hummed above their heads, and Kitembo clutched at an arrow in his chest.

five of us here alone with a band of unruly blacks who fear and hate us. Tomorrow, doubtless, we shall be deserted by them. If we hope ever to get out of Africa alive, we must stick together. Forget your quarrels, both of you, and let us work together in harmony hereafter for our mutual salvation."

"For your sake, señorita, yes," said Romero.

"Comrade Drinov is right," said Ivitch.

Zveri dropped his hand from his gun and turned

"I thought that a hideous gulf separated us, one that I could never span."

sulkily away, and for the balance of the night peace, if not happiness, held sway in the disorganized camp of the conspirators.

When morning came the whites saw that the blacks had all discarded their French uniforms, and from the concealing foliage of a near-by tree other eyes had noted this same fact—gray eyes that were touched by the shadow of a grim smile.

There were no black boys now to serve the whites, for even their personal servants had deserted them to for-gather with the men of their own blood, and so the five prepared their own breakfast, after Zveri's attempt to command the services of some of their boys had met with surly refusal.

While they were eating, Kitembo approached them, accompanied by the headmen of the different tribes that were represented in the personnel of the expedition. "We are leaving with our people for our own countries," said the Basembo chief. "We leave food for your journey to your own camp. Many of our warriors wish to kill you and that we cannot prevent if you attempt to accompany us, for they fear the vengeance of the ghosts that have followed you for many moons. Remain here until tomorrow. After that you are free to go where you will."

"But," expostulated Zveri, "you can't leave us like this, without porters or askaris."

"No longer can you tell us what we can do, white man," said Kitembo, "for you are few and we are many and your power over us is broken. In everything you have failed. We do not follow such a leader."

"You can't do it," growled Zveri. "You will all be

punished for this, Kitembo."

"Who will punish us?" demanded the black. "The English? The French? The Italians? You do not dare go to them. They would punish you, not us. Perhaps you will go to Ras Tafari. He would have your heart cut out and your body thrown to the dogs, if he knew what you were planning."

"But you can't leave this white woman alone here in the jungle without servants or porters or adequate protection," insisted Zveri.

"I do not intend to leave the white woman," said Kitembo. "She is going with me." And then it was that for the first time, the whites realized that the headmen had surrounded them and that they were covered by many rifles.

As he had talked, Kitembo had come closer to Zveri, at whose side stood Zora Drinov, and now the black chief reached out quickly and grasped her by

She turned fiercely upon Zveri. "I could have killed you any one of a dozen times in the last few years—but I wanted more than your life!"

the wrist. "Come!" he said, and as he uttered the word something hummed above their heads and Kitembo, chief of the Basembos, clutched at an arrow in his chest.

"Do not look up," cried a voice from above. "Keep your eyes upon the ground, for whosoever looks up dies. Listen well to what I have to say, black men. Go your way to your own countries, leaving behind you all of the white people. Do not harm them. They belong to me. I have spoken."

Wide-eyed and trembling, the black headmen fell back from the whites, leaving Kitembo writhing upon the ground. They hastened to cross the camp to their fellows, all of whom were now thoroughly terrified, and before the chief of the Basembos ceased his death-struggle, the black tribesmen had seized the loads which they had previously divided amongst them and were pushing and elbowing for precedence along the game trail that led out of camp toward the west.

Watching them depart, the whites sat in stupefied silence, which was not broken until after the last black had gone and they were alone.

"What do you suppose that thing meant by saying we belong to him?" asked Ivitch in a slightly thickened voice.

"How could I know?" growled Zveri.

"Perhaps it is a man-eating ghost," suggested Romero with a smile.

"It has done about all the harm it can do now," said Zveri. "It ought to leave us alone for awhile."

"It is not such a malign spirit," said Zora. "It can't be, for it certainly saved me from Kitembo."

"Saved you for itself," said Ivitch.

"Nonsense!" said Romero. "The purpose of that mysterious voice from the air is just as obvious as is the fact that it is the voice of a man. It is the voice of some one who wanted to defeat the purposes of this expedition and I imagine Zveri guessed pretty close to the truth yesterday when he attributed it to English or Italian sources that were endeavoring to delay us until they could mobilize a sufficient force against us."

"Which proves," said Zveri, "what I have suspected for a long time: that there is more than one traitor among us!" And he looked meaningly at Romero.

"What it means," said Romero, "is that crazy, harebrained theories always fail when they are put to the test. You thought that all the blacks in Africa would rush to your standard and drive all the foreigners into the ocean. In theory, perhaps, you were right, but in practice one man, with a knowledge of native psychology which you did not have, burst your entire dream like a bubble, and for every other harebrained theory in the world there is always a stumblingblock of fact."

"You talk like a traitor to the cause," said Ivitch threateningly.

"And what are you going to do about it?" demanded the Mexican. "I am fed up with all of you and your whole rotten, selfish plan. There isn't an honest hair in your head nor in Zveri's. I can accord Tony and Señorita Drinov the benefit of a doubt, for I cannot conceive either of them as knaves. As I was deluded, so may they have been deluded, as you and your kind have striven for years to delude countless millions of others."

"You are not the first traitor to the cause," said Zveri, "nor will you be the first traitor to pay the penalty of his treason."

"That is not a good way to talk now," said Mori. "We are not already too many. If we fight and kill one another, perhaps none of us will come out of Africa alive. But if you kill Miguel, you will have to kill me, too, and perhaps you will not be successful. Perhaps it is you who will be killed."

"Tony is right," said the girl. "Let us call a truce until we reach civilization." And so it was that under something of the nature of an armed truce, the five set forth the following morning on the back trail toward their base camp, while upon another trail, a full day ahead of them, Tarzan and his Waziri warriors took a short-cut for Opar.

"LA may not be there," Tarzan exclaimed to Muviro, "but I intend to punish Oah and Dooth for their treachery and thus make it possible for the high priestess to return in safety, if she still lives."

"But how about the white enemies in the jungle back of us, Bwana?" asked Muviro.

"They shall not escape us," said Tarzan. "They are weak and inexperienced to the jungle. They move slowly. We may always overtake them when we will. It is La who concerns me most, for she is a friend, while they are only enemies."

Many miles away, the object of his friendly solicitude approached a clearing in the jungle, a man-made clearing that was evidently intended for a camp site for a large body of men, though now only a few rude shelters were occupied by a handful of blacks.

At the woman's side walked Wayne Colt, his strength now fully regained, and at their heels paced Jad-bal-ja the golden lion.

"We have found it at last," said the man.

"Yes, but it is deserted," replied La. "They have all left."

"No," said Colt, "I see some blacks over by those shelters at the right."

"It is well," said La. "And now I must leave you."

"I hate to say good-by," said the man, "but I know where your heart is and that all your kindness to me has only delayed your return to Opar. It is futile for me to attempt to express my gratitude, but I think that you know what is in my heart."

"Yes," said the woman, "and it is enough for me to know that I have made a friend, I who have so few loyal friends."

"I wish that you would let me come with you to Opar," he said. "You are going back to face enemies and you may need whatever little help I should be able to give you."

She shook her head. "No, that cannot be," she replied. "All the suspicion and hatred of me that was engendered in the hearts of some of my people was caused by my friendship for a man of another world. Were you to return with me and assist me in regaining my throne, it would but arouse their suspicions still further. If Jad-bal-ja and I cannot suc-ceed alone, three of us could accomplish no more."

"Won't you at least be my guest for the balance of the day?" he asked. "I can't offer you much hospitality," he added with a rueful smile.

"No, my friend," she said. "I cannot take the chance of losing Jad-bal-ja; nor could you take the chance of losing your blacks, and I fear that they would not remain together in the same camp. Goodby, Wayne Colt. But do not say that I go alone, at whose side walks Jad-bal-ja."

From the base camp La knew the trail back to Opar and as Colt watched her depart, he felt a lump rise in his throat, for the beautiful girl and the great lion seemed personifications of loveliness and strength and loneliness.

With a sigh he turned into the camp and crossed to where the blacks lay sleeping through the midday heat.

He awoke them and at sight of him they were all very much excited, for they had been members of his own safari from the Coast and recognized him immediately.

Having long given him up for lost, they were at firstinclined to be a little bit frightened until they had convinced themselves that he was, indeed, flesh and blood.

Since the killing of Dorsky they had had no master and they confessed to him that they had been seriously considering deserting the camp and returning to their own countries, for they had been unable to rid their minds of the weird and terrifying occurrences that the expedition had witnessed in this strange country, in which they felt very much alone and helpless without the guidance and protection of a white master.

ACROSS the plain of Opar, toward the ruined city, walked a girl and a lion, and behind them, at the summit of the escarpment which she had just scaled, a man halted, looking out across the plain, and saw them in the distance.

Behind him a hundred warriors swarmed up the rocky cliff. As they gathered about the tall, bronzed, gray-eyed figure that had preceded them, the man pointed.

"La!" he said.

"And Numa!" said Muviro. "He is stalking her. It is strange, Bwana, that he does not charge."

"He will not charge," said Tarzan. "Why, I do not know, but I know he will not—because it is Jad-bal-ja."

"The eyes of Tarzan are like eyes of the eagle," said Muviro.

"Muviro sees only a woman and a lion, but Tarzan sees La and Jad-bal-ja."

"I do not need my eyes for those two," said the ape-man. "I have a nose."

"I, too, have a nose," said Muviro, "but it is only a piece of flesh that sticks out from my face."

Tarzan smiled. "As a little child you did not have to depend upon your nose for your life and your food," he said, "as I have always done, then and since. Come, my children, La and Jad-bal-ja will be glad to see us."

It was the keen ears of Jad-bal-ja that caught the first faint warning noises from the rear. He halted and turned, his great head raised majestically, his ears forward, the skin of his nose wrinkling to stimulate his sense of smell.

Then he voiced a low growl and La stopped and turned back to discover the cause of his displeasure.

As her eyes noted the approaching column, her heart sank. Even Jad-bal-ja could not protect her against so many. She thought then to attempt to outdistance them to the city, but when she glanced again at the ruined walls at the far side of the valley she knew that that plan was quite hopeless, as she would not have the strength to maintain a fast pace for so great a distance, while among those black warriors there must be many trained runners who could easily outdistance her.

And so, resigned to her fate, she stood and waited, while Jad-bal-ja, with flattened head and twitching tail, advanced slowly to meet the oncoming men and as he advanced his savage growls rose to the tumult of tremendous roars that shook the earth as he sought to frighten away this menace to his loved mistress.

But the men came and then, of a sudden, La saw that one who came in advance of the others was lighter in color and her heart leaped in her breast. Then she recognized him and tears came to the eyes of the savage high priestess of Opar.

"It is Tarzan! Jad-bal-ja, it is Tarzan!" she cried.

Perhaps at the same instant the lion recognized his master, for the roaring ceased, the eyes no longer glared, no longer was the great head flattened as he trotted forward to meet the ape-man.

Like a great dog, he reared up before Tarzan, and with a scream of terror little Nkima leaped from the ape-man's shoulder and scampered, screaming, back to Muviro, since bred in the fiber of Nkima was the knowledge that Numa was always Numa.

With his great paws on Tarzan's shoulder Jad-bal-ja licked the bronzed cheek, and then Tarzan pushed him aside and walked rapidly toward La, while Nkima, his terror gone, jumped frantically up and down on Muviro's shoulder, calling the lion many jungle names for having frightened him.

"At last!" exclaimed Tarzan, as he stood face to face with La.

"At last," repeated the girl, "you have come back from your hunt."

"I came back immediately," replied the man, "but you had gone."

"You came back?" she asked.

"Yes, La," replied Tarzan. "I traveled far before I made a kill, but at last I found meat and brought it to you, and you were gone and the rain had obliterated your spoor and though I searched for days I could not find you."

"Had I thought that you intended to return," she said, "I would have remained there forever."

"You should have known that I would not have left you thus," replied Tarzan.

"La is sorry," she said.

"And you have not been back to Opar since?" he asked.

"Jad-bal-ja and I are on our way to Opar now," she said. "I was lost for a long time. Only recently did I find the trail to Opar and then, too, there was the white man who was lost and sick with fever. I remained with him until the fever left him and his strength came back, because I thought that he might be a friend of Tarzan's."

"What was this man's name?" asked the ape-man.

"Wayne Colt," she replied.

The ape-man smiled. "Did he appreciate what you did for him?" he asked.

"Yes, he wanted to come to Opar with me and help me regain my throne."

"You liked him then, La?" he asked.

"I liked him very much," she said, "but not in the same way that I like Tarzan."

He touched her shoulder in a half-caress. "La, the immutable!" he murmured, and then, with a sudden toss of his head as though he would clear his mind of sad thoughts, he turned once more toward Opar. "Come," he said, "the Queen is returning to her throne."

The unseen eyes of Opar watched the advancing column. They recognized La and Tarzan and the Waziri and some there were who guessed the identity of Jad-bal-ja, and Oah was frightened and Dooth trembled and little Nao, who hated Oah, was almost happy, as happy as one may be who carries a broken heart in one's bosom.

Oah had ruled with a tyrant hand, and Dooth had been a weak fool, whom no one longer trusted, and there were whisperings now among the ruins, whisperings that would have frightened Oah and Dooth had they heard them, and the whisperings spread among the priestesses and the warrior priests, with the result that when Tarzan and Jad-bal-ja led the Waziri into the courtyard of the outer temple there was no one there to resist them, but instead voices

called down to them from the dark arches of surrounding corridors pleading for mercy and voicing
earnest assurance of their future loyalty to La.

As they made their way into the city they heard
far in the interior of the temple a sudden burst of
noise. High voices were punctuated by loud screams,
and then came silence, and when they came to the
throne-room the cause of it was apparent to them,
for lying in a welter of blood were the bodies of Oah
and Dooth, with those of a half-dozen priests and
priestesses who had remained loyal to them—and,
but for these, the great throne-room was empty.

Once again did La, the high priestess of the Flaming God, resume her throne as Queen of Opar.

That night Tarzan, Lord of the Jungle, ate again
from the golden platters of Opar, while young girls
soon to become priestesses of the Flaming God
served meats and fruits and wines so old that no living man knew their vintage, nor in what forgotten
vineyard grew the grapes that went into their making.

But in such things Tarzan found little interest and
he was glad when the new day found him at the
head of his Waziri crossing the plain of Opar toward
the barrier cliffs. Upon his bronzed shoulder sat
Nkima, and at the ape-man's side paced the golden
lion, while in column behind him marched his hundred Waziri warriors.I

IT was a tired and disheartened company of whites
that approached their base camp after a long, mo-
notonous and uneventful journey.

Zveri and Ivitch were in the lead, followed by

Zora Drinov, while a considerable distance to the rear Romero and Mori walked side by side, and such had been the order in which they had marched all these long days.

Wayne Colt was sitting in the shade of one of the shelters and the blacks were lolling in front of another, a short distance away as Zveri and Ivitch came into sight.

Colt rose and came forward, and it was then that Zveri spied him.

"You damned traitor!" Zveri cried. "I'll get you if it's the last thing I do on earth!" And even as he spoke he drew his revolver and fired point blank at the unarmed American.

His first shot grazed Colt's side without breaking the skin, but Zveri fired no second shot, for almost simultaneously with the report of his own shot another rang out behind him and Peter Zveri, dropping his pistol and clutching at his back, staggered drunkenly upon his feet.

Ivitch wheeled about. "My God, Zora, what have you done?" he cried.

"What I have been waiting to do for twelve years," replied the girl. "What I have been waiting to do ever since I was little more than a child."

Wayne Colt had run forward and seized Zveri's gun from the ground where it had fallen, and Romero and Mori now came up at a run.

Zveri had sunk to the ground and was glaring savagely about him.

"Who shot me?" he screamed. "I know—it was that damned greaser."

"It was I," said Zora Drinov.

"You!" gasped Zveri.

Suddenly she turned to Wayne Colt. "You might as well know the truth," she said. "I am not a Red and never have been. This man killed my father and my mother and an older brother and sister. My father was—well, never mind who he was. He is avenged now." She turned fiercely upon Zveri. "I could have killed you any one of a dozen times in the last few years," she said, "but I waited because I wanted more than your life. I wanted to help kill the hideous schemes with which you and your kind are seeking to wreck the happiness of a world."

Peter Zveri sat on the ground, staring at her incredulously, his wide eyes slowly glazing. Suddenly he coughed and a torrent of blood gushed from his mouth. Then he sank back dead.

Romero had moved close to Ivitch. Suddenly he poked the muzzle of a revolver into the Russian's ribs. "Drop your gun," he said. "I'm taking no

"I do not know who he is," said Zora, "other than that he is the man who saved my life."

chances on you either."

Ivitch, paling, did as he was bid.

Across the clearing a figure stood at the edge of the jungle. It had not been there a scant instant before; it had appeared silently as though out of thin air. Zora Drinov was the first to perceive it. She voiced a cry of surprised recognition and as the others turned to follow the direction of her eyes, they saw a bronzed white man, naked but for a loin-cloth of leopard skin, coming toward them. He moved with the easy, majestic grace of a lion and there was much about him that suggested the king of beasts.

"Who is that?" asked Colt.

"I do not know who he is," replied Zora, "other than that he is the man who saved my life when I was lost in the jungle."

The man halted before them.

"Who are you?" demanded Wayne Colt.

"I am Tarzan of the Apes," replied the other. "I

have seen and heard all that has occurred here. The plan that was fostered by this man," he nodded at the body of Zveri, "has failed and he is dead. This girl has avowed herself. She is not one of you. My people are camped a short distance away. I shall take her to them and see that she reaches civilization in safety. For the rest of you I have no sympathy. You may get out of the jungle as best you may. I have spoken."

"They are not all what you think them, my friend," said Zora.

"What do you mean?" demanded Tarzan.

"Romero and Mori have learned their lesson. They avowed themselves openly during a quarrel when our blacks deserted us."

"I heard them," said Tarzan.

She looked at him in surprise. "You heard them?" she asked.

"I have heard much that has gone on in many of your camps," replied the ape-man, "but I do not know that I may believe all that I hear."

"I think you may believe what you heard them say," Zora assured him. "I am quite confident that they are sincere."

"Very well," said Tarzan. "if they wish they may come with me also, but these other two will have to shift for themselves."

"Not the American," said Zora.

"No? And why not?" demanded the ape-man.

"Because he is a special agent in the employ of the United States Government," replied the girl.

The entire party, including Colt, looked at her in astonishment.

"How did you learn that?" demanded Colt.

"The message that you sent when you first came to camp and we were here alone was intercepted by one of Zveri's agents. Now do you understand how I know?"

"Yes," said Colt. "It is quite plain."

"That is why Zveri called you a traitor and tried to kill you," Zora explained.

"And how about this other?" demanded Tarzan, indicating the surly Ivitch. "Is he also merely a sheep in wolf's clothing?"

"He is one of those paradoxes who are so numerous," replied Zora scornfully. "He is one of those Reds who is all yellow."

Tarzan turned to the blacks who had come forward and were standing, listening questioningly to a conversation they could not understand.

"I know your country," he said to them in their own dialect. "It lies near the end of the railroad that runs to the Coast."

"Yes, master," said one of the blacks.

"You will take this white man with you as far as the railroad. See that he has enough to eat and is not harmed, and then tell him to get out of the country. Start now." Then he turned back to the whites. "The rest of you will follow me to my camp." And with that he turned and swung away toward the trail by which he had entered the camp.

Behind him followed the four who owed to his humanity more than they could ever know, nor had they known could they have guessed that his great tolerance, courage, resourcefulness and the protective instinct that had often safeguarded them sprang not from his human progenitors, but from his life-long association with the natural beasts of the forest and the jungle, who have these instinctive qualities far more strongly developed than do the unnatural beasts of civilization, in whom the greed and lust of competition have dimmed the luster of these noble qualities where they have not eradicated them entirely.

Behind the others walked Zora Drinov and Wayne Colt, side by side.

"I thought you were dead," she said.

"And I thought that you were dead," he replied.

"And worse than that," she continued, "I thought that, whether dead or alive, I might never tell you what was in my heart."

"And I thought that a hideous gulf separated us, one that I could never span to ask you the question I wanted to ask you," he answered in a low tone.

She turned toward him, her eyes filled with tears, her lips trembling.

"And I thought, Wayne, that, whether alive or dead, I could never say yes to that question, if you did ask me," she replied.

A curve in the trail hid them from the sight of the others as he took her in his arms and drew her lips to his.

THE END